She paused with her hand on the door handle.

Again she reprimanded her pounding heart, this time silently. But the rebellious organ just didn't seem to believe her reimbursement/research reasoning. She took a deep breath and slowly blew it out. She took another one, and managed to get her skeptical heart calmed down.

That was, until she pulled open the door.

Nate stood on the back stoop, looking—wonderful. He had on a black wool dress coat, beige scarf, and tailored black trousers. His shaggy hair was tamed slightly, although wayward locks still fell over his forehead in rebellious waves. His lips were quirked into that crooked half smile that looked both sweet and sexy at the same time.

"Hi," he said.

BOOK YOUR PLACE ON OUR WEBSITE AND MAKE THE READING CONNECTION!

We've created a customized website just for our very special readers, where you can get the inside scoop on everything that's going on with Zebra, Pinnacle and Kensington books.

When you come online, you'll have the exciting opportunity to:

- View covers of upcoming books

- Read sample chapters

- Learn about our future publishing schedule (listed by publication month *and author*)

- Find out when your favorite authors will be visiting a city near you

- Search for and order backlist books from our online catalog

- Check out author bios and background information

- Send e-mail to your favorite authors

- Meet the Kensington staff online

- Join us in weekly chats with authors, readers and other guests

- Get writing guidelines

- AND MUCH MORE!

**Visit our website at
http://www.kensingtonbooks.com**

Wanting Something More

Kathy Love

ZEBRA BOOKS
Kensington Publishing Corp.
www.kensingtonbooks.com

ZEBRA BOOKS are published by

Kensington Publishing Corp.
850 Third Avenue
New York, NY 10022

All Kensington titles, imprints, and distributed lines are available at special quantity discounts for bulk purchases for sales
promotion, premiums, fund-raising, educational, or institu-
tional use.

Special book excerpts or customized printings can also be
created to fit specific needs. For details, write or phone the
office of the Kensington Special Sales Manager: Attn. Special
Sales Department. Kensington Publishing Corp., 850 Third
Avenue, New York, NY 10022. Phone: 1-800-221-2647.

Zebra and the Z logo Reg. U.S. Pat. & TM Off.

ISBN 0-8217-7614-2

First Printing: July 2005
10 9 8 7 6 5 4 3 2 1

Printed in the United States of America

For Darrell, Gerry, Teresa and Cindy.

ACKNOWLEDGEMENTS

As always, thank you to the Tarts.
With a special thanks to Lisa for the perfect suggestion.

Thank you to the babysitting squad,
Mom and Dad,
Bill and Mary Ellen,
Teresa, Gary and Megan.
Emily and I really, really appreciate your help.

Thank you Julie, Treena and David.
Everyone needs friends, and I got the best.

Thank you to the gals of the Underground, especially
Starr, Joanne, Steph, Lois, Kari, Viv, Judy, Diane, Deb, Lee,
TK, Stephanie, Cindy, and Anne.
You are the best and you have excellent taste!

Thank you Rog—you were the perfect muse.

And finally thank you to Todd and Em.
I love you.

Prologue

"I don't know how you ever convinced me to do this," Abby muttered.

Marty ignored her sister, mesmerized by the magical scene before her. The swaying shadows, the flashes of colored lights, the laughter and excited voices mingling over the flood of pulsating melodies. It was more than magical, it was thrilling.

Still, the laughter and music couldn't drown out Abby's exasperated sigh.

Marty glanced at her oldest sister.

Abby stood with her arms crossed tightly over her chest. Unrestrained disdain narrowed her eyes as she peered into the room. She obviously didn't see one ounce of enchantment. But then again, Abby wouldn't. She was far too serious to enjoy something as silly as a school dance.

But Marty knew it wasn't silly. Not this dance. Not this night. This was a place where fantasies could come true. A place where her fantasies were *going* to come true. She knew it.

"You should have made Ellie come with you." Abby stepped away from the cafeteria's double doors as if she planned to walk back down the school hallway to the exit.

Abby knew full well that Marty had begged Ellie to come with her. Their shy middle sister had been Marty's first choice because she believed in love at first sight and fairy tales. But Ellie had adamantly refused. She was much happier at home, lost in her romance novels, than in the real world.

Marty glanced back at the crowd swaying slowly around and around in tight circles and debated letting Abby leave. She couldn't. She couldn't do this alone. She was too nervous—too scared. Who knew facing happily ever after could be so frightening?

"Just stay for a few minutes," she pleaded. "If it's really that terrible, then we can go."

Abby hesitated and nodded. "Okay, but I have no idea why this is so important to you."

And Marty had no intention of telling her, either. Abby was just here for support. She didn't need to know the details. She wouldn't approve of Marty coming to meet a boy. But Nathaniel Peck was more than just a boy. Nathaniel was perfect. He was kind. He was a junior *and* he liked her.

Marty turned back to the school-cafeteria-turned-disco, took a deep breath, and stepped through the double doors.

She tried to appear confident as she strode across the room. She didn't even slouch like she normally did to try and disguise her height. Since she was almost six feet tall, it was futile anyway. But tonight, she didn't feel embarrassed about her unusual stature. Nathaniel didn't seem to mind, and he was the only one who really mattered.

She searched the room and easily located him. At

6' 4", he stood out strikingly. Of course his good looks didn't hurt, either.

She watched him as he talked animatedly with a group of his friends. Someone must have said something amusing, because his beautiful, full lips parted into a wide smile.

Then, as though he could feel someone watching him, his eyes scanned the room until he found her. Their eyes locked for a moment, then he inclined his head just slightly in acknowledgment.

Marty's heart raced, but she felt a twinge of disappointment. Why didn't he come over? Was he as nervous as she was? Was he worried about what his friends would think about the two of them?

Marty continued to watch him, and as the minutes seemed to turn to hours, she wondered if he'd changed his mind. How could he? He was the one who'd been pursuing her. He'd been the one to strike up a conversation and had continued to do so every Tuesday and Thursday, fifth period, in the back of Mr. Malia's notoriously lax study hall.

But if that hadn't been enough, Nathaniel also kept showing up everywhere that she was. He always appeared in the library when she was there doing her computer assignments. He'd come to her art class to do extra work on the project he was doing in his regular art class. And one day, he'd even shown up outside her house when she'd been taking Old Miss Strout's ancient and stinky poodle for a walk.

He'd shown her far too much interest to be uninterested now. Hadn't he?

"Ack, I can't stand him," Abby said with such a sudden adamancy that Marty actually startled, thinking she was talking about Nathaniel.

"Who?" Marty asked, her eyes wide.

"Lionel Ritchie. He is so sappy." Abby shuddered.

"Oh," Marty said, still a little unnerved. If she was this worried about her sister's reaction to Nathaniel, then maybe he had a right to be nervous, too.

"I'm going to go get a drink of water. You going to stay here?" Abby asked.

Marty nodded, relieved Abby was leaving her alone. Maybe she *should* have come here by herself.

After Abby left, she turned back to Nathaniel, just in time to see him crossing the dance floor, straight toward her.

"Hi there," he said, stopping directly in front of her.

It was a strange sensation to have to tilt her head up to make eye contact.

"Hi," she breathed, amazed as always by the beauty of his eyes: pale amber like honey in sunlight.

"I'm glad you decided to come." Although he sounded a little stiff. He *was* nervous.

She smiled, putting all her feelings for him into that smile. "Me, too."

"Do you want to dance?"

Marty hesitated. "I don't really know how to."

"Ah, it's easy." His hand captured hers, and she was amazed at how large his hand was.

He tugged her out into the middle of the dance floor, and again, she was struck by how impersonal he seemed. Not at all the guy who'd joked with her, flattered her.

He released her fingers, only to pull her firmly against him, and they began moving in an awkward circle to the pitchy voice of Cyndi Lauper.

After a couple of rotations, she chanced not concentrating on her feet and glanced up at him. He wasn't looking at her, but focusing off the dance floor toward where all his friends stood.

"Is everything okay?"

He blinked down at her as if he were surprised to see her. "Sure. Just . . . thinking."

"Are you worried about your friends? I mean, that they will think it's weird we're hanging out?"

Nathaniel glanced back over at his friends. "No. They understand the deal."

Marty found his wording odd, as odd as his behavior. But when she peeked over at his group of friends, they all seemed to be watching them with pleased expressions on their faces.

"I am going to kiss you now." His statement was so sudden, so unexpected that she halted to a standstill and gaped up at him.

"You are?" she finally managed.

"Yes," Nathaniel said with flat determination. He leaned down, and Marty, even as shocked as she was, lifted her face toward him.

This wasn't how she had pictured their first kiss. She'd thought they'd be alone, and it would just happen naturally as they sat talking and laughing. This seemed too quick, too public. But she wanted it. No matter where or how, she wanted to kiss Nathaniel Peck.

As soon as their lips met, Marty expected fireworks or bells, even a whistle—something. But instead, she only noticed that Nathaniel's lips felt nothing like she'd imagined. They weren't supple and warm, but taut and cool. And he was almost rough.

She moaned, uncomfortable with his aggressiveness, and pulled away.

"Nathaniel," she breathed, regarding him with wide eyes.

He stared down at her, his eyes as hard and cold as his mouth. That mouth was now turned up in a mocking smile.

She frowned, totally baffled by his behavior. "Nathaniel?"

He didn't speak, that almost cruel grin frozen on his face.

Then suddenly she heard them. The roars of laughter. The hoots. The hateful comments.

When she looked around, she realized that they were now surrounded by Nathaniel's friends.

"Oh, God," Nathaniel's best friend, Jared Nye, groaned. "I can't believe you actually did it. That is just gross, man." He thumped Nathaniel on the back with a look of disgusted admiration.

"That is beyond gross," another Nye brother declared. "Shit, you win, Nathaniel. There is no way in hell we'll be able to top that dare. Nasty, man."

Marty shook her head, looking from the swarming crowd to Nate. "What are they talking about?"

Lynette Prue, a petite, busty blonde who was known around school as being more than a little easy, moved to stand beside Nate. She twined her arm through his and grinned evilly at Marty. "We are talking about Nathaniel pulling off the most repulsive dare ever. Kissing the freakiest of the ugly Stepp sisters."

Lynette then turned to Nathaniel, her smile changing from evil to simply wicked. She stroked purple-tipped fingers up his chest. "I should make you brush and gargle before I even think about kissing you. But I really can't wait." She reached up and tugged Nathaniel down to her, kissing him long and hard.

Marty stepped away from them, feeling ill. She didn't even know this person in front of her. This person who'd spent weeks talking and laughing and seeking her out—just to pull off a dare.

She bumped into someone as she continued to move back, trying to escape.

She steadied herself and continued backward. Her eyes clouded with tears and further distorted the already leering faces that surrounded her.

Then Nathaniel stopped kissing Lynette to look back at Marty. She saw something there that was worse than all the hateful, mocking looks of the others. She saw pity.

Something snapped inside Marty, and she rushed forward and raised a hand to slap him. But he caught her wrist before her palm could make contact.

The pity was replaced by a cool, fixed stare. "I wouldn't do that if I were you."

Marty yanked her hand away and glared up at him. "You can go to hell."

"Oh, I plan on it," he said with a smug grin, and his buddies chuckled.

Marty didn't wait to hear any more. This time, she turned and fled.

Chapter 1

"You're doing the right thing," Marty told herself for at least the fiftieth time since she'd gotten into her small sports car and simply decided to drive away. Away from New York City, away from her modeling career, and away from Rod.

This was all a long time coming. It was what she wanted. It was what she needed. *And you don't have to decide anything definite right this minute.* Another thing she'd told herself fifty times. She wasn't running away. She was taking a break. A little time to think.

Right now, however, you need to think about your driving, she thought as her car fishtailed again. When she finally decided to flee her life, it would be to head straight into a nor'easter. Somehow, it seemed oddly appropriate.

The snow had begun to fall heavily once she'd crossed the Maine state line. Now, the white flakes were so blinding that the road seemed only to exist as far ahead as the yellowy beams of her headlights could reach, then it dropped off into a swirling white oblivion.

She sat forward, clutched the steering wheel, and concentrated on the vanishing road.

Just a few more miles and she would be home. Despite the terrible traveling, she fought the urge to press down harder on the accelerator. She'd been patient this long. It wouldn't do to go careening off the road now.

She looked into her rearview mirror and noticed the car that had been tailing her for the last several miles was still there.

What kind of nut would be out on a night like this? Besides herself, that is.

She glanced at the twin lights again, then back to the road just in time to see another curve materializing in front of her. She touched her brakes too abruptly, and again, the car skidded, but she managed to keep control.

Argh! She would be happy to get to her grandmother's house, even though the house was empty now. Grammy had passed away years ago, and Ellie, her middle sister who inherited the house and still owned it, didn't live there any longer. She had a home with her husband now. And Marty's oldest sister, Abby, who had been living across the street from her grandmother's, had just moved, too.

Marty checked the clock on her dash. It was well after midnight. She couldn't show up at either of her sisters' places this late. They'd be in bed and probably not all that pleased to have their baby sister arrive unannounced in the dead of night. She should have called them to say she was coming. But that would have been the act of a person with a plan. There was no planning here.

Although she wouldn't have wanted to keep either Ellie or Abby up, waiting and worrying. Ellie and her husband, Mason, had an eighteen-month-old daughter who kept them on the run. Abby was three months pregnant, and at this point was more green than glowing. It was better to let them sleep tonight and see them tomorrow, if they all could dig out. The snow was really falling.

Marty leaned farther over her steering wheel, peering at the road. Besides, she really wanted to go to her childhood home tonight. She wanted to sleep in her old bed under the quilt her grandmother made her. She wanted to drink a cup of tea in the huge country kitchen. She wanted to feel . . . safe.

Ellie had told her that they were keeping the heat on at Grandmother's house for the winter so that the pipes wouldn't freeze. So that meant the old place would be warm. And that also meant that Ellie kept the electricity on. She knew all three sisters would be too sad to see the old house standing dark, cold, and empty.

Yeah, she'd go home tonight.

Out of habit, she turned off Route 1 to take the Gory Boar Road, a shortcut, into Millbrook. As soon as she did, she realized her mistake. The old back road was caked with snow so thick that she couldn't see the center line and she could barely make out the soft shoulder.

"Darn it," she muttered, now gripping the steering wheel so tight her fingers were numb. The snow scraped the bottom of her car, making a nerve-wracking whooshing noise. She should turn around and head back to Route 1.

She checked her mirrors, prepared to turn around right in the road, when she saw that the car that had been following her was still there.

Why had this person turned too? Presumably this person actually wanted to be on this treacherous road.

But Marty didn't, and the other car was making it a little difficult for her to pull a U-ee. Gritting her teeth, Marty decided she was going to have to continue on, at least until she found a proper place to turn around.

About a half mile farther, a faint glow in the distance caught her attention.

"What is that?" She frowned, narrowing her eyes, trying to focus through the eddying snowflakes.

Then she remembered a new gas station that had been in the process of being built last summer. That had to be what it was.

She could turn around there and head back to the better-traveled Route 1.

As she got closer, she realized the station was open and there was also a convenience store attached.

Maybe this was a sign. Maybe she'd better stop and get a few supplies before she headed back in the other direction, just in case the storm stuck around for a while and she was trapped in Grammy's house for a few days.

She pulled up to the front of the building, turned off the engine, and began to rummage through her shoulder bag on the passenger's side seat. Her wallet had to be in there somewhere.

She groped around, making contact with a small rectangular item. Her cell phone. She tossed it back in and tried again. This time she found a granola bar and then a stick of deodorant. Next, she found a tin of mints and a container of hair goo.

Well, she might have no wallet and no life and be stuck in a blizzard, but at least she had a healthy snack, no body odor, fresh breath, and funky hair. And if her phone had a signal, she could call someone and tell them about it.

She rooted through the bag for a moment longer, and just when she decided that she must have lost her wallet back at the gas station in Rhode Island, she noticed the corner of it sticking out from under the seat.

Her sports car wasn't exactly roomy. So rather than struggle to get the wallet while still inside, she took her keys out of the ignition, grabbed her gloves off the dash, and got out of the car.

The frigid winter air bit at her, and she quickly bent back into the car to grab her wallet. Just as she was about to straighten up, wallet in hand, a deep voice close to her said, "That's not exactly the best car for driving in a blizzard."

Marty jumped, bumping her head on the door frame. "Ouch! Damn it! It's not exactly wise to startle a person when . . ." Her voice trailed off as she spun around and stared at—a broad chest. For Marty, six feet tall in flats, that did not happen often. For a moment, she was stunned—again.

A hand came up to touch her arm, and even through the suede and fur lining of her coat, she could feel each long finger.

"I'm sorry. I didn't mean to surprise you."

She blinked up at the man. His back was to the convenience store, making him a giant, broad-shouldered silhouette against the glare of bluish green fluorescent lights and swirling white snow.

"Is your head okay?" the giant asked, and Marty was struck by how his voice seemed to perfectly match his towering build, deep and with a slight husky quality.

Apparently, he thought she had done some damage, because he continued to hold her and leaned forward as if to inspect her head.

Gradually, her eyes adjusted a bit to the light, and

she could make out the man's shaggy hair and a long, straight nose, his nostril flared just slightly.

"Do your sisters know you're coming?" That husky voice sounded even more amazing coming from the sculpted lips she could vaguely make out in the faint light.

Then Marty actually heard the words, rather than the pleasing intonation of them. "How do you . . . Do I know you?"

The giant paused, then those wide, sculpted lips curved into a slight smile. "Well, you used to know me."

All of a sudden, Marty knew exactly who this was standing so close to her. She took a step back, bumping against her car, and she jerked her arm out from underneath his hand.

"And I don't think you were particularly fond of me," he added wryly.

She didn't respond, but she was sure her glare validated his assumption. On a night like this, when most sane people were home, staying out of the storm, she would still run into Millbrook's biggest jerk. *Nathaniel Peck.* Apparently the postal creed was the same for creeps . . . "Neither sleet nor rain nor driving snow" . . . Or however it went.

His smile slipped, replaced by seriousness. "Listen, why don't you leave this car here and let me give you a lift to your sister's. Are you staying with Abby or Ellie?"

Marty stared at him, completely outraged. "You want me to leave my car here—and ride with you? Even in a raging snowstorm, you are still trying to pick up women? Are you totally crazy?"

This guy never gave up. The last time she'd seen him, at her sister's wedding, he'd hit on her the whole night.

And asked rude, suggestive questions about her body parts. Particularly her chest—and the authenticity of it.

Nathaniel didn't react for a moment. But when he did, his voice was calm and even as if Marty hadn't spoken at all, much less questioned his sanity. "I've been following you for the past ten miles, and that car is dangerous in this weather. Not to mention that you are driving too fast for the conditions."

Marty glared at him. How dare this *pig* criticize her driving. And her car! He was such a—jerk!

"You know, I think you should just mind your own business—and go back to ogling Calvin Klein ads," Marty knew the comment was stupid as soon as it was out of her mouth, but she didn't pause. She turned and got back into her car, slamming her door angrily.

It took her a few moments to locate her keys in her coat pocket. But once she did, she shoved the correct one in the ignition and rolled out of the gas station as fast as the accumulating snow would allow. The car only skidded once.

How dare that awful man even approach her! She glanced in the rearview mirror and saw that Nathaniel was still standing in parking lot, watching her drive away. Then she also noticed the police car parked some distance behind him.

"Ah," she groaned. Nathaniel Peck was a cop! She'd forgotten. Now he was probably going to ticket her for reckless driving. Knowing him, he'd probably put out a warrant for her arrest for evading a police officer. Great!

She drove on, imagining herself stuck in a cell with that wretched man. But after a few moments, she realized something presently more worrisome. In her irritation, she hadn't turned back toward Route 1. She was still on the snow-covered Gory Boar Road taking the back way to Millbrook.

Damn that man!

Nate cringed as he watched Marty Stepp spin out onto the back road heading toward Millbrook.

What was she thinking? On a night like this, Route 1 was the safest road to travel. Although from what he'd witnessed following her, she wasn't exactly the most sensible driver.

He shook his head, and after her taillights disappeared around a corner, he headed into the store to pick up a few things, like a toothbrush and something for breakfast.

He'd originally intended to head home after his shift, but there was no way the road leading to his cabin would be passable tonight. A definite drawback to living down a dirt camp road.

When he entered the bright, new convenience store, he saw Greg Tucker working behind the counter. Greg was only sixteen. Nate couldn't imagine letting his kid work the night shift at a place like this, as isolated as it was. Not that there was a lot of crime in this area.

Of course, Nate was living proof there was some crime, some very violent crime.

"Hey, Chief Peck," the boy greeted him. "How's the knee?"

"Not too bad," Nate answered, although in truth, his knee was killing him. The cold weather. But Doc Hall kept assuring him that his knee would heal completely.

"Pretty wild night, huh?"

"Sure is," Nate agreed. Too wild for this kid to be out

on the roads later. "Is your uncle coming to get you at the end of your shift?"

"Yeah. He'll come with his plow."

Nate nodded. Derek Nye, Greg's uncle and Nate's longtime buddy, did a nice little side business plowing out driveways during storms. Normally, he would have gotten Derek to plow out his road, but not now. They hadn't really spoken since his attack.

He limped toward the back wall of glass-fronted refrigerators. A rack lined with colorful, glossy magazines caught his attention. He paused, perusing the covers. Marty Stepp didn't grace any of them—not this month. But she often did. Nate wasn't sure what the actual requirements were to be considered a supermodel, but he suspected Marty met them all. She'd been on the covers of all the major fashion magazines. She'd been the cover model for sports magazines' swimsuit issues. And she had done huge ad campaigns for top designers.

Suddenly, a vague memory started to return to him, lurking at the edge of his mind as if his brain were a sieve and the tidbit of information was just a tad too large to sift through.

Calvin Klein. Marty had made that cryptic comment in the parking lot, and now he seemed to recall that should mean something to him.

Calvin Klein. He'd seen her ads for the designer. Black-and-white photos of Marty entwined with a lean, almost androgynous guy. Beautiful shots of her bare, smooth skin in varying shades of gray.

Smooth skin? Smooth skin? And just like that, the memory shifted and slipped back into his brain. He'd asked Marty about those photos at her oldest sister's wedding. Asked her if she'd been airbrushed or if her skin was really that flawless everywhere. And would she like to go to his place and show him.

He almost groaned. Sometimes he wished the memories would just stay lost, but it didn't seem to work that way. They always came back eventually, with the inevitable embarrassment. And he had a *lot* to be embarrassed by—Nathaniel Peck was an ass. He already knew that, he just wished he didn't have to remember all the details.

He continued toward the refrigerators and grabbed a half gallon of orange juice and some eggs. He started to reach for a package of bacon, the action automatic, then he stopped. He grabbed a half gallon of milk instead. He located the rest of the items he needed and headed to the counter.

"Man, I saw you talking to that woman with the cool car," Greg said as he rang Nate up. "That was a Jag, wasn't it?"

"Yeah."

"Man, that thing is awesome." Greg shook his head, impressed.

Nate nodded absently. He hadn't been awed by the expensive vehicle. He'd been too busy noting that it was fast and terrible in the snow. She'd be lucky if she didn't end up wrapped around a tree out there, if she wasn't already.

He paid and gathered up the bags. He had to follow her. It was more than a feeling of civic duty. In fact, there was a time when he wouldn't have hesitated in letting her go on her way and he'd have gone his. He would have figured it was her own problem if she was a bad driver and foolish enough to be out in weather like this. He would have told himself that he was off duty, and the woman with her inappropriate car was now the next officer's problem. When Nathaniel Peck was done for the day, he was done for the day.

But Nate didn't feel that way anymore. He knew he had an obligation to make sure people were all right, and it had nothing to do with being the chief of police. It had to do with being a human being.

Not for the first time, he found it incredible that he'd had to die to figure out how to live.

Chapter 2

Sheer relief washed over Marty as she finally slid her key into the door and stepped into the old house. Tentatively she reached for the light switch, silently praying that the storm hadn't knocked out the electricity. This place was notorious for losing its power. Again, relief flooded her as the ceiling light in the center of the large kitchen snapped to life.

She stepped farther into the room, looking around. Despite the house's uninhabited state, it still felt the same. Homey. Comforting. Safe. If not a little chilly.

Marty let out a long, grateful breath, then headed into the front hallway to the thermostat. She turned the dial to seventy-four. Then, as if her grandmother were right there, admonishing her for wasting energy, she turned it back to seventy-two. That would be warm enough.

And she'd be even warmer once she got her wet shoes off. The deep snow in the driveway had worked up her pant legs and had encrusted and frozen her cuffs and socks. Her ankles and calves burned from the cold.

She sat down in one of the kitchen's worn ladder-back chairs and tugged off the snow-caked sneakers and icy socks, then rubbed the reddened, painful skin of her feet.

If she was going to stay here any length of time, she'd have to buy some proper winter boots. She glanced over at the two small overnight cases and tote bag, which she'd dropped just inside the doorway. She'd probably have to buy quite a few things. Life in arctic Maine was very different from her life in New York City. And very different was exactly what she wanted.

But right now, she wanted to rest. She grabbed her bags and headed upstairs to her old bedroom. Even her original plan to sit down with a hot cup of tea seemed like too much effort after that harrowing drive. Her car was as ill suited to Maine as her shoes.

She threw her bags onto her bedroom chair with more force than necessary. As childish as it was, she didn't want to agree with Nathaniel Peck about anything. Even something as silly as the bad handling of her car in the snow.

The only positive thing about seeing that wretched man was that it served to remind her why she was going to avoid men for a good long while. Nathaniel. Rod. They were cut from the same loathsome cloth.

Marty unzipped one of her cases and pulled out a pair of pajama bottoms and a sweatshirt. As she changed into the warmer clothes, she considered both men. Even with her intense dislike of Nathaniel, she had to admit it wasn't fair to compare him to Rod. What Nathaniel had done to her was the cruel prank of an immature teenager. Rod was an adult, and there were no excuses for the hurtful things he'd done to her.

She shivered. Would this cold ever leave her? It seemed to have collected in her veins. In her bones.

She crossed back to her packs and dug around for a

pair of socks. The bedsprings squeaked as she sat on the edge to pull on the thick knee-highs. The snow was still falling hard, and she crossed over to the window to watch it for a moment.

She hadn't recognized Nathaniel at all. And it hadn't been just the dark and snow. His hair was longer than she'd ever seen it. He'd always been the type to sport a very short military cut, even in high school. That was how it had been at her sister's wedding. Of course, she hadn't recognized him there either. Not until he opened his rude mouth. God, she disliked that man!

She moved from the window to the bed.

Tossing back the quilt made up of different squares of blue, she started to crawl onto the mattress, then paused. Something clanked downstairs.

She remained perfectly still, the covers clutched in her hand, one knee up on the bed.

The sound repeated, this time closer. Maybe in the hallway? It was hard to tell; the sound seemed to echo through the whole house.

Marty held her breath.

A loud clatter rang out directly behind her. She squealed and spun around to stare at the door. Nothing. But she continued to watch the door, waiting for a shadow to move in the hallway. For a figure to appear.

Clank! Marty jumped. Then she laughed, pressing a hand to her chest.

The radiators.

The ancient radiators had always clanged and banged and made all sorts of noises. How could she have forgotten? She'd spent many nights listening to this old house moan and groan and complain.

Shaking her head and letting out another unsteady laugh, she slid into bed. She'd never been a skittish person, and certainly nothing about this house had ever felt eerie to her. But she did feel a little nervous tonight.

It was just the stress of the day, she decided. And running into Nathaniel Peck. He'd make anyone uneasy. But she didn't ever have to talk to him again. In fact, he was the easiest of her problems to ignore, to forget. Just like he seemed to have forgotten that dance years ago.

She fell back against the pillows and pulled the covers up to her chin. The weight of the quilt felt good as the tension escaped her tired body.

It took her a few moments to get the energy to turn off the light, but after she did, she curled onto her side and watched the snow continue to fall, the flakes reflected against the streetlights. Despite everything, it was so good to be home.

Marty had no idea what woke her. She didn't even remember falling to sleep. But now she was suddenly awake. And she had a weird feeling. A sensation no more substantial than the creep of static electricity over her skin, but it was there nonetheless.

She started to sit up when she heard it—a creak. Just a faint sound. Far less noticeable than the loud knocks of the radiators.

Marty pushed the covers off herself and cautiously stood up, her stocking feet silent on the worn wood floor. She tiptoed toward the door, then she heard it, a sharp squeak like someone stepping on a mouse's tail.

Marty might not have remembered the other noises of the house, but she knew this one. Someone was coming up the staircase.

Pausing, she scanned the room, looking for something to use as a weapon. The room was decorated just as it had been when she was in high school, meaning she'd have to beat the intruder to death with either a stuffed animal or a poster of an eighties pop idol.

She shuffled closer to her bureau and saw a box filled with old odds and ends, including a couple of dust-covered records. She sidled closer and grabbed one.

As far as weapons went, it was a bad one, but better than nothing. She crept back to the door, album raised over her head. Through the crack of the door, she saw the light shift. Her heart hammered in her chest. There *was* someone out there.

She waited a second, trying to stay calm, as the shadow moved past her door and farther down the hall. Then she threw open her door and lunged at the dark figure.

The intruder spun around and disarmed her just as she was about to whack the album against the back of his head.

"Whoa, there," the tall form said.

Marty didn't need the prowler to say anything more. She recognized the voice immediately. She'd already cursed having heard it once tonight.

"I can't believe this," she muttered, stepping back from him. "What the hell are you doing in my house?"

Nathaniel Peck blinked, then squinted at her makeshift weapon. "Apparently about to get brained with . . ." He squinted. "A Quiet Riot album?"

Even in the shadowy light, she could see his smile was so winsome that for a moment she forgot that she hated this man. And that he had broken into her house in the wee hours of the morning. But only for a moment.

"What are you doing here?" she demanded again, crossing her arms over her chest.

"I could ask you the same thing."

"This is *my* house."

"Why aren't you staying with one of your sisters?"

Anger tightened her chest. He was questioning her? This was unbelievable. "Nathaniel, what the hell are you doing here?"

"Nate."

"Excuse me?"

"I prefer to be called Nate now."

Marty gritted her teeth. This man was a lunatic. Absolutely nuts. "Okay, *Nate*, let's forget why you're here and move on to when you're going to leave."

"I have to be in to work at noon."

Marty blinked. Was this a dream? A nightmare? It had to be. "No, you are leaving—" She pretended to think it over. "Now."

Nate crossed his arms over his chest, mimicking her stance almost exactly. "I'd rather not. It's a little too cold to sleep in my cruiser."

The man was apparently both crazy and homeless. "Why don't you just go home?" Marty asked slowly. She was pretty sure he was indeed nutty enough to be Millbrook's vagrant chief of police, but she thought she'd take a chance and give the suggestion a try.

Nate shook his head. "Can't get there from here. At least not tonight."

"So, when you can't get home," she knew she sounded like she was talking to a simpleton, which it appeared she was, "you just break into people's houses?"

"I didn't break in. I have a key."

Marty frowned. "What?"

"A key. I have one."

"Why?"

"To open the door. So I don't have to break in."

Absolutely frustrated, she fought the urge to scream.

***

Nate knew he was being annoyingly obtuse. But he couldn't resist aggravating her a little. He'd been worried about her, and he didn't really care for worrying. That was one of the things he wished had stayed the same as before the attack. Being apathetic had been—well, less worrying.

If she had just agreed to let him drive her to one of her sisters', or here, he'd have been in bed already. Instead, he'd been driving all over Millbrook in a raging snowstorm, looking for her vehicle in a ditch somewhere.

He'd gone to her sisters' houses first. But when he hadn't seen her car, he'd gone back to Gory Boar Road to make sure she wasn't stuck somewhere, and he'd somehow missed her. He should have thought of coming here, but he'd never considered that she'd come here instead of staying with one of her sisters.

He watched Marty. She looked as if she was ready to grab the album from his hand and pummel him to death with it. He supposed he couldn't blame her. And behind her fierce scowl and tightly crossed arms, he got the feeling she was very tense and very wary.

Nate supposed she should be. He was a virtual stranger standing in her house in the dead of night, uninvited. At least by her.

"Listen, Ellie and Mason gave me a key and told me if I was ever working late and need a place to crash, to stay here," he explained.

She studied him for a moment, then tightened her arms around herself a bit more.

Nate could tell she didn't believe him.

"Why would you need a place to stay?" she asked,

suspicion clear in her voice. "Does your girlfriend kick you out or something?"

He smiled. Was she fishing around trying to see if he was single? "No. No girlfriend."

She looked unimpressed and not surprised.

Nope, no fishing there.

"It's nothing so dramatic," he said, shifting his weight slightly. She stepped back as if she expected him to pounce. He remained still. "I live on a dirt road, and when the weather's bad, I sometimes have a problem making it in. Tonight would be impossible."

She regarded him again, her wide, dark eyes scanning his face. Finally she nodded. "Okay."

He smiled again, somehow relieved that she believed him. Again, old Nathaniel wouldn't have cared. Old Nathaniel would already be in bed. With her, if at all possible.

Not that the new Nate wouldn't like that too. Now, he just had enough sense to know she wasn't interested. And likely wasn't going to be anytime soon.

"So you're okay with me staying?"

Marty shrugged, the gesture as indifferent as he'd once been. "I don't really have an option, do I? Like you said, it's too cold to sleep in your car."

"Oh, if it were only a few degrees warmer, huh?" He offered her another smile and received a cold stare in return.

He lost the grin, then sighed. "Okay, well, I'm sorry I woke you. I had intended to sneak in and sneak back out in the morning without disturbing you." He paused, waiting for a response.

She continued to watch him with those distrustful eyes.

"I hope you can get back to sleep all right." He leaned

forward to hand back the album, even though he still wasn't positive she wouldn't hit him with it.

She hesitated, then reached forward and practically snatched the record out of his hand. She stared at him, the album clutched in both hands. Just when he felt like maybe she expected him to say something more, she nodded slightly. "Good night," she said woodenly and half walked, half backed into her room.

Nate frowned as he watched her disappear inside, soundly closing the door behind her. He knew she didn't like him, but he hadn't expected her to actually seem frightened of him. Especially after he explained why he was there.

After all, chauvinist pig or not—and he liked to think he was not, now—he was still the chief of police. That had to be slightly better than the average intruder.

He turned and limped toward the bedroom at the end of the hall when he heard a scraping sound and the doorknob to Marty's room rattle.

She was barring her door.

He shook his head. Was she really that afraid of him, or was Marty Stepp nervous around all men? He actually hoped it was just him; he didn't like to think what would have had to happen to her to make her wary of all men.

He stepped inside the bedroom that he'd always used when he'd stayed here and clicked on the bedside light. The room was cozy, with an antique wrought-iron bed covered with a thick quilt nestled under the eaves. He liked this room.

But even as he stretched out onto the soft mattress and nearly groaned at the weariness in his bones, he knew he wouldn't sleep. Another side effect from his attack. If he could get a couple of hours a night, he was doing well.

He reached over and turned off the light. The wind had really picked up. The tall oak tree outside the window cast eerie shadows on the walls. The chill and dampness in the air still caused his knee to throb.

It should have felt good to have someone else in the house with him on a night like this. Just to know there was another living soul there. Maybe even help him sleep. But it didn't feel better. It just made him realize how alone he really was.

Reaching his hand up to his face, he touched his finger to the scar that started at his temple and curved around his eye to his cheekbone. He knew it was still red and puckered, and there were faint lines where the stitches had been. He touched the mark for a moment longer, then folded his hand behind his head and stared at the ceiling.

It was going to be a long night.

Chapter 3

Marty awoke to singing. A male voice, muffled, distant.

She lifted her head from her pillow and squinted around, disoriented. Pale blue wallpaper with darker blue flowers and a faded picture of Michael J. Fox greeted her. That's right, she was in her room. Home.

Then she saw the chair wedged under the doorknob, and she remembered that she and Michael J. were not alone. Nathaniel Peck was here, and apparently singing.

She let her head fall back onto the pillow and considered cocooning herself in her quilt and trying to sleep until her unwanted guest left.

Then she sighed. This was stupid. She had to go to the bathroom, and she was starving. Plus, this was her house; why was she hiding?

She rose and struggled with the chair, trying to remove it quietly. Now, in the broad daylight, with the sunshine beaming off the snow outside her window, she felt a bit stupid for barricading the door. She really hated it when her nerves got the best of her. And her nerves seemed to be in control a lot lately.

With purposeful calmness, she tugged open the door and stepped out into the hallway. The singing was louder but still distant. Nathaniel wasn't upstairs.

She listened for a moment. He actually had a nice voice. Low and a little raspy. Beneath the soothing sound of his voice, she could tell he was moving around. She heard the occasional scrape of a drawer opening, the swish of metal on metal.

What was he doing? Singing his way off with the family silver? Okay, there was no family silver, but Grammy's Green Stamp flatware was still pretty valuable, to her anyway.

The bathroom forgotten, she headed down the stairs, ready to defend her grandmother's cutlery. But once she got to the kitchen doorway, she didn't charge in. Instead she stopped, motionless, listening and watching.

He stood in front of the stove, waving a fork like a drumstick as he belted out the chorus to "Ready for Love" by Bad Company. The soft material of his faded gray T-shirt stretched against his back and accentuated the muscles of his torso and the cut of his shoulder blades with each drum beat. Marty's gaze drifted lower to the faded denim of the jeans that hugged his firm, tight . . .

Her eyes widened and she forced herself to look away. What was she doing? She was done with men, and she was especially done with this man. She couldn't stand him. So why on earth would she be admiring his . . .

Her eyes strayed back to him and that very nice derriere. Just because she was through with men didn't mean she couldn't recognize nice assets—no pun intended—when she saw them. And she did have to admit he did have some pretty nice assets. Too bad they all disappeared as soon as he opened his mouth.

"Hi."

It took a few moments for Marty to realize that mouth had spoken to her.

Her eyes snapped up to discover Nathaniel was watching her over his shoulder. An irritatingly relaxed smile curved his lips.

Nate fought to keep his smile from widening as Marty's cheeks colored a deep pink. But to her credit, she recovered quickly, crossing her arms across her chest as she leaned against the doorjamb. "What are you doing?"

Again he tried not to grin at her surly tone. Man, she disliked him.

He lifted the frying pan off the stove and tilted it so she could see the yellowy contents sizzling away. "I'm making eggs. Want some?"

She frowned at him.

It was a good thing her smile had been documented on the covers of magazines; otherwise, he wouldn't have believed she ever smiled. Of course, her glower was as attractive as her smile. Not many people looked lovely when they were shooting daggers with their eyes. Marty did.

"They're good," he said cajolingly, waving the pan toward her. "And I made toast."

He could see her hesitation, and although there were no overt signs of nervousness, he still got the feeling she was very wary. Again, he wondered why.

She didn't say anything but, to his shock, she did move to sit down at the large kitchen table.

He returned the frying pan to the stove top and

flipped off the burner. After scooping the eggs onto two plates, he headed toward the table.

Marty stared, watching his approach and the way he walked, the hitch of his gait. Her eyes moved down to his knee, then she seemed to realize she was being rude and looked away. Embarrassment colored her cheeks again.

He didn't take offense at her stare. His limp was hard to ignore. Not to mention that he'd also done too much on it this morning, so the limp was even more pronounced than usual. Doc Hall would give him hell at his next physical-therapy session.

"These were supposed to be omelets," he explained as he set a plate in front of her, feeling the need to ease the awkwardness. "But it's surprisingly harder than you'd think to flip those suckers. So they ended up scrambled." He smiled at her again and was met with a cool glance.

"Thank you," she mumbled and picked up her fork.

He nodded and took the chair across from her.

They both ate in silence for a moment, until he said, "I don't really like eggs. But they are a good source of protein, and if I add enough cheese, they're tolerable."

"There are other sources of protein," she said, the words clipped.

"Did I mention that eggs are easy to cook?"

"Except omelets," she reminded him.

He chuckled. "Exactly." Wow, had that been a joke? Maybe she would loosen up with him yet.

"So you'll be able to get into your house tonight, right?"

Or not. "Yeah, I should be able to get Derek Nye—you remember Derek, don't you?"

She nodded, a slight, indifferent dip of her chin that

clearly stated that if she did remember Derek, she didn't care for him any more than she cared for Nate.

"Well, anyway, he has a plow, so I should able to get him to clear out my road."

She nodded again, never taking her attention off her breakfast.

Nate took advantage of the moment to study at her. Her short, dark hair was tousled, one side sticking out prominently from where she'd slept on it. Her baggy, red sweatshirt completely hid the lithe, willowy body that had graced so many magazines. There was no hint of make-up on her smooth skin. Sitting in the morning sun, she didn't look like a supermodel. She looked like a real woman, her features more striking than beautiful. Although her big, dark eyes and wide, lush lips were pretty darn gorgeous.

But again, he couldn't help noticing that her pale complexion wasn't totally natural. And the sunlight also revealed the purplish smudges under her eyes and the tense set of those full lips.

She was definitely stressed about something. And despite her dislike of him, Nate believed it was something more than his presence. He just wasn't helping her stress level.

He took the last bite of eggs and pushed back from the table, stretching out his long legs. His knee protested. He massaged it, feeling the ridges of scar tissue even through his jeans.

When he looked up, Marty was watching his hand on his knee intently. But she didn't say anything.

"So, are you staying through the holidays?"

She stopped watching his hand, but still didn't look at him. Instead she reached for a piece of toast. "Yes, maybe longer."

"Well, I know your sisters will be thrilled."

She raised an eyebrow, although her attention was still on her eggs. "It seems you know my sisters quite well these days."

"Yeah, well, I've been hanging out with Mason and Chase quite a bit lately."

She nodded, again all her tenseness masked with a look of indifference.

"Okay," he sighed, realizing that she had no intention of warming up in any way. "Well, I guess I'd better get these dishes washed and head to the shower."

"I can do the dishes."

He had no doubt that a sink full of dirty dishes was far more appealing to her than his company.

"Okay, if you want to, have at it." He rose and limped toward the door. Then he turned back to her, his tired muscles reminding him. "Oh, your car is all dug out. And the driveway too, if you want to move it off the street."

"You shoveled the driveway?" she asked, shocked.

"Yeah."

"That had to have taken hours. When did you do that?"

Nate shrugged. "I couldn't sleep, so I figured I might as well be doing something."

"You were out there shoveling in the middle of the night?"

He shrugged. "Nah, more like early morning. Five-ish, maybe."

If he had expected a thank-you or even a look of appreciation, he didn't get it. Instead she frowned again. "That's crazy."

A dry laugh escaped him. "Yeah, I'm getting that a lot lately." In fact, it was one of the things he was getting a little tired of hearing. He ran a hand through his hair.

Marty's eyes widened just slightly as she stared at a point just to the right of his eyes.

She hadn't noticed the scar, he realized. His hair must have hidden it. That probably mixed with the fact that she hadn't really looked at him all morning. Not his face anyway.

The combination of the *crazy* comment and the re-action to his scar suddenly annoyed him. He stood there for a moment until he knew she felt uncomfortable with his stare. Then he said flatly, "A steel-toed boot was the doctor's best guess." He didn't elaborate more, but just left her there with a stunned expression.

Here she had been thinking Nathaniel was the jerk, and she'd been the one who'd acted terribly rude.

Marty finished rinsing the last dish and placed it in the dish drainer. He hadn't made one lewd comment. He hadn't even flirted, really. He'd just made her a good breakfast, saving her from the old, hard granola bar in her purse, and tried to make small talk. She'd been the jerk.

She wiped her hands off on a dish towel, tossed it over the back of a chair, and headed upstairs.

Of course, she did know men, and they could act like perfect gentlemen when it served their purpose. How many times had she fallen for that act before? Hence her wise decision to avoid men. She'd fallen for the charade one too many times.

When she reached the top step, she could hear Nathaniel in the bathroom, the splashing sound of him in the shower. She got a sudden, vivid image of him, naked, the water sluicing over the muscles she had seen outlined by his gray T-shirt.

Okay, who was the lewd one? What the heck was wrong with her? Was swearing off men like dieting? Because she couldn't have any men, she suddenly wanted all men. Even horrible men like Nathaniel Peck? Eek.

She cast a look at the closed bathroom door, then went into her room and shut the door tightly behind her. She grabbed the handles of her tote bag and plopped both herself and the bag on the bed. After much digging, she located her cell phone. She had a signal and no messages. Her initial reaction was relief, then for just a moment, it changed to disappointment. She pushed the feeling aside. It was too early for anyone to even realize she was gone, and she didn't want to deal with anyone anyway.

She put the phone on the nightstand.

A steel-toed boot? Someone had kicked Nathaniel in the face. And then there was his limp. Was it from the same incident? It seemed rather unlikely, and unlucky, that he would have two serious injuries from two unrelated events. But he was a police officer. It could happen, she supposed.

A knock at her door gave her a start. Before she could scramble off the bed, Nathaniel called through the wooden panel. "Marty, I'm leaving. See you around."

By the time she reached the door, she could hear his uneven gait clomping down the stairs. She considered following him and apologizing for her behavior, but decided against it. She shouldn't have been rude to him today, but one day of rudeness was minor compared with the days she'd spent after that school dance. The snickering in the hallways. The teasing. The cruel pranks. He owed *her* the apology and had for a long time.

So instead, she marched to the bathroom. A long, hot shower would get her back to normal.

She shed her clothes and was just about to turn on the shower when the bathroom door opened and Nathaniel walked in.

Marty squealed and jumped into the tub, pulling the blue vinyl curtain in front of her.

"Oh, shit," he said, averting his eyes. "I'm sorry. I didn't realize you were in here." He edged farther into the room, still not looking in her direction, even though she was shielded by the shower curtain.

"Well, I am," she shouted. "So leave!"

"I will. I just left—" He scanned the room, still being careful not to look in her direction. "This." He went to the white wicker hamper in the corner and picked up a brown cowboy-style police hat. "Sorry." He exited, still never looking her way.

Marty waited a minute, then stepped back out of the tub.

She covered her face with her hands, heat burning her cheeks. Well, he'd gotten an eyeful there. Far more than the Calvin Klein ads. She groaned.

The rest of her shower was uneventful, and when she finally was clean and dressed, the house was very empty. But her peace was going to be short-lived. As tempting as it was, she couldn't avoid the outside world for long. If her sisters learned that she was in town and hadn't come directly to see them, they would be very hurt. And now, she didn't even have the excuse of her car being snowbound. Just another reason to be annoyed with Nathaniel Peck.

In truth, she felt guilty that she was tempted to

avoid her siblings for a bit. She *was* excited to see them, she just dreaded the questions. And there would be questions. Why was she here after she said she'd be busy the whole holiday season? Was there something going on with Rod? And what would they think when she told them what she was considering: leaving modeling altogether?

She wandered to the window. It was truly a winter wonderland this morning. Snow glistened. Icicles hung from the eaves of the house across the street. Bundled and rosy-cheeked children played in the whiteness, building snowmen and snow forts.

Marty sighed. It was nice to be home. Nice to feel normal after living in a whirlwind for so long, even if her return had started off a little shaky. Then she noticed her car cleared completely from the snow and the driveway that couldn't have been more snow free even if a commercial snowplow had cleared it.

She shook her head. Out in the dark, shoveling. Maybe that's why Nathaniel hadn't hit on her or made offensive suggestions. He was too exhausted.

And no wonder he was limping so badly. If his leg had been injured in an accident, he probably shouldn't have been shoveling heavy snow in the dead of night. The man obviously had some serious frustrations to work off to be doing such intensive physical labor.

Who knew, maybe he'd sworn off women like she'd sworn off men. Wouldn't that be ironic if they actually had something in common?

Chapter 4

"I can't believe you got into town last night and didn't come right over," Ellie said, setting a cup of tea in front of Marty.

Marty sat with her sisters in the kitchen of Ellie's gorgeous house. The whole room was done in rich, polished oak with huge windows that overlooked the ocean.

Abby probably would have agreed with Ellie, but she was too busy nibbling on a saltine and looking distinctly green.

Ellie placed a cup of peppermint tea in front of Abby. Abby managed a slight nod in thanks.

"Well, like I said, I didn't get into town until late, and I didn't want to wake everyone," Marty explained again. "Plus I really wanted to sleep in my old bed." She paused. "That is, until Nathaniel Peck showed up in the upstairs hallway in the dead of night."

Ellie paused, her own teacup halfway to her lips. She set the cup back down on the kitchen table. She winced. "Oops."

"Yeah," Marty agreed. "It was quite a shock. Why on earth would you let him have a key to our house?"

"The house is just standing empty," Ellie said a tad defensively. "And Nate lives down this twisty, narrow dirt road, and we just figured he might appreciate the offer."

Marty nodded, but she wasn't particularly pleased with Ellie's defense of this person. Ellie was as big-hearted as a person could be, but Marty didn't want her generosity to extend to Nathaniel. He didn't deserve it—even if he did seem different.

"But had we *known* you were going to be in town, we would have warned you," Abby added. Of course her nausea would pass in time to support Ellie's position.

Marty nodded again, deciding she didn't want to discuss Nathaniel Peck anymore, even though the man had been on her mind all day.

"Okay, we are thrilled you are here," Abby said. Her greenness had faded to a mere pasty white, but her practicality seemed to be fine. "But why are you here? You just told me less than a week ago that there was no way you could get up for the holidays."

Marty hesitated. She wasn't ready to tell them that she might be staying here permanently. She wasn't decided. She needed to think.

"I decided I've missed too many holidays." That was certainly the truth. She had missed far too many important moments with her sisters. "And I wanted to see Emily on Christmas morning." One of the most important things she had missed had been the first year of her niece's life.

As if on cue, Mason, Ellie's handsome, blond husband, came in the back door with Emily perched on his shoulders.

"Marty! I thought that was your car outside." He set his daughter on her feet and moved to give Marty a quick hug. Emily stood where Mason put her down, peering at her often-absent aunt from under her red fleece hat.

Marty leaned forward and tweaked Emily's belly through her thick, red woolen coat. "Hey, Emmy, remember me?"

Emily continued to stare at her for a moment, then her face crumpled and she turned to bury her head against Mason's leg.

"She's like her mommy—shy," Mason assured Marty as he picked up the little girl and unzipped her coat and tugged off her hat. "She'll loosen up in a bit."

Emily might or might not have had her mother's personality, but there was no question that she had her mother's looks. The little girl looked like an angel, with a riot of blond curls, blue, blue eyes and plump, rosy cheeks.

"So how did you get away?" Mason asked, as he headed over to Ellie and handed Emily to her. "Ellie said you were doing, like, three fashion shows over the holidays."

"I just decided to pull out of them," Marty said casually. She didn't feel the need to mention that she pulled out without notifying her agent or the shows' organizers. But as soon as they all realized, she was going to have some explaining to do.

"You can do that?" Abby asked. "So close to the show dates?"

Marty nodded. She could do it. People were going to be very, very angry, but she could do it.

"Well, that's great. You're going to stay with us, right?" Mason asked, and Marty knew her brother-in-law's invitation was sincere.

Marty still couldn't believe the way Mason had

changed since he married Ellie. He was happy and friendly, not the hardened guy she'd first met. And Ellie was happier than Marty had ever seen her. They were a wonderful couple.

Mason leaned down and kissed his daughter's head, then his wife's.

And they were crazy in love. Love might happen to some people, but Marty was pretty sure she wasn't one of them. She obviously put out a vibe or pheromone or something that attracted the worst of the opposite sex.

"I actually think I'll stay at the house," Marty said slowly, knowing the idea was going to be met with resistance.

Ellie looked up from murmuring to Emily. "Why?"

Marty couldn't explain that not only did she want time with her family, but she also needed time to herself. They'd ask her why. She wasn't ready for those questions.

"I've been homesick lately, I guess. I just want to stay there. But I'll come see you every day," Marty cooed at Emily.

Emily hid her face in Ellie's shoulder.

"Whether you want me to or not," Marty added wryly.

"She's tired," Ellie said, stroking her daughter's blond curls. "It's past your bedtime, isn't it, sleepyhead?"

Ellie started to rise, but Mason reached for Emily. "I'll put her down. You visit."

Ellie smiled. "Okay." She gave her baby a kiss good night, and daddy and daughter disappeared out of the kitchen.

"I can't believe you drove up here in that storm," Abby said, reaching for another saltine. "You really should have waited a day."

"It was pretty wild," Marty admitted.

"I know you won't appreciate this," Ellie said hesitantly, "but I'm actually glad Nate was with you last night. If the power went out or the furnace, it was probably good he was there."

Marty bristled a little. Did Ellie think she needed a man to rescue her? Although she couldn't really be angry with her sister. Ellie had found her knight in shining armor and, as the acknowledged romantic of the family, she liked the idea that Marty would one day find hers. But Marty knew she wasn't going to find any type of knight, shiny armor or not. Especially not in Nathaniel Peck.

"Yeah, you're right, I don't appreciate that," she said dryly, but tempered the comment with a slight smile. "I think I'd rather freeze to death."

"Nate has changed," Ellie told her. "He—"

A knock sounded at the back door and stopped Ellie.

Chase, Abby's tall, dark, and gorgeous husband, pushed open the door. He kicked the snow from his boots and stepped inside.

"There you are," Abby said. "I was getting worried."

Chase smiled. "Sorry. I ended up running into Nate and going out to his place to try and get the snow cleared out of his road."

Marty frowned. Not again! She was starting to feel like she was in the cult of Nathaniel Peck. People couldn't seem to go more than five minutes without mentioning him.

"Hey, Marty!" Chase said with his usual easygoing, lopsided grin. "I didn't know you were coming for Christmas. You *are* staying for Christmas?"

Marty nodded.

"Good." He went over to Abby and touched her cheek. "Are you feeling okay?"

Abby smiled, and although she still looked wan, she also looked very happy. "Fine."

Chase leaned down and pressed a kiss to her lips, and for a moment, they seemed to forget anyone else was in the room. When they parted, Abby's pale cheeks were tinged with pink.

"Well, there's a way to get her color back," Marty teased.

Abby blushed more.

"Baby girl is out like a light," Mason announced, entering the kitchen. "Hey, Chase, you're here. I was beginning to think you were going to miss the tip-off."

"Yeah, I got hung up trying to help Nate with his road. We got it halfway done, then had to quit. Tommy Leavitt was there with his small plow, but it didn't quite do the trick."

"You should have called me, I could have at least helped shovel," Mason said as he opened the fridge and grabbed a can of diet soda. He held it up. "Want one?"

"Sure," Chase replied, and Mason leaned back in the refrigerator to get another one.

Marty was impressed with not only Mason for his very successful recovery from alcoholism, but also Chase for his support. She knew Chase would normally have a beer when watching the game. And although she didn't think Mason would mind if he did, Chase wouldn't even consider bringing liquor into his friend's house. He had too much respect for Mason's struggle.

"All right, ladies, can you do without our company?" Mason asked, and both men looked at them like eager children.

"I think we'll be fine," Ellie said, her dimples

appearing with her amusement. Mason gave her a quick kiss and the two men disappeared out of the kitchen.

Marty heard Chase say to Mason as they walked down the hall, "Nate is really doing way too much on that knee."

"He is pushing himself too hard," Mason agreed.

Again, Marty wondered what happened to Nathaniel. And why people who had just tolerated him before the "accident" were suddenly rallying around him.

"You should have Chase take the baby swing tonight," Ellie was saying to Abby. "Emily loved it."

Abby laughed. "We have months before we need it."

"Well, you can have it whenever you need it."

"What happened to Nathaniel Peck's knee?"

Both heads snapped toward Marty, her sisters obviously surprised by the sudden question. She was, too. Here she'd been wishing they could talk about something other than Nathaniel, and she was the one reintroducing him back into the conversation.

"He was attacked," Ellie finally said. "In his house while he slept."

Marty had expected her sister to say an accident. A problem while on the job. Not an assault—while he slept.

"Does he know who did it?"

Both Ellie and Abby shook their heads.

"No," Abby said. "There aren't even any suspects, as far as I know. And Nate doesn't remember anything."

Marty thought about that. "He is a police officer, and the truth is, not a very nice person. Both of those things could result in enemies. He must have some suspicions about who might have done it."

"I'm sure if he has any enemies they were checked out," Ellie said, her voice sounding almost indignant.

Marty became annoyed in return. "I don't get what has come over everyone. You all know the kind of guy he is." She turned to Abby. "He crashed your *wedding*, for God's sake. And look at what he did to me in high school. That prank was not just a simple, impulsive joke. He thought that out. He planned it. He worked hard to win my trust. He convinced me that he liked me. Then he embarrassed me in front of the whole school. And forgive me if I seem callous, but I don't find it difficult to believe that he did awful things to other people too. It sounds to me like someone else he hurt decided to fight back."

Abby paled, and this time Marty didn't think it was a result of her pregnancy. Ellie gaped at her.

"He was in a coma for nearly a week. It was a miracle he survived," Ellie said, her usual mild tone downright stern.

Guilt tightened Marty's chest. Marty would bet money he'd hurt lots of other people, but nothing merited that kind of attack. She pictured the angry, red scar that started at his temple and curved onto his cheek. A steel-toed boot, he'd said. Someone kicked him in the face—that was vicious. That was anger.

"Well, I am truly sorry that he was so badly hurt," Marty said sincerely. "But as for this sudden transformation that he has suddenly undergone, I don't buy it. People just do not change that much."

"So are you going ice fishing with us on Saturday?" Sam Peck asked as he reached across the table and speared a large slab of steak from a plate in the middle of the table. Red juices splattered on the speckled Formica as he brought the meat to his own plate.

Nate watched his brother and grimaced slightly. He turned back to his own baked potato. "I don't think so."

Sam set down his fork with a noisy clatter. "Why not? You haven't been out fishing with Dad and me all season."

Nate sighed. "I just don't feel like it."

"Do you hear this?" Sam asked their father as he returned from the kitchen carrying two cans of beer. Wendell Peck, whom everyone called Dell, sat down, handed Sam a beer, and cracked open his own before he said, "Ayuh," in his slow down-eastern drawl.

Nate watched as both men took a swallow of their beers. "Dad, is there more?" He gestured to the can his dad just set on the table.

His father nodded as he stuck his fork into one of the steaks. "I didn't think you drank anymore."

Nate frowned. "Why would you think that?"

"You don't fish and you don't eat meat. It only stands to reason you don't drink beer," Sam said.

"What?" Nate asked, both confused and annoyed. "Because I decided to become a vegetarian, I can't have a beer?"

"Beer and steak. They just sort of go together," his dad said in his very practical Maine drawl. He didn't look up from sawing into his New York strip.

Nate cast a disbelieving look between his father and his brother.

Sam shrugged as if to say that their father did have a point and began to cut into his own steak.

Nate shook his head, then pushed up from the table and went into the kitchen to get his own beer.

This was exactly why he'd been trying to avoid his

family as much as he could. Sam was impossible to avoid, since they worked together at the station, although to Sam's credit, he did manage to keep things pretty professional there.

Of course, Nate was his boss there. Here at home, Nate was just his brother, and Sam didn't feel the need to keep his opinions to himself. And though his father was less vocal, Nate knew that he shared Sam's judgment: Nate had gone mad.

All because, after the attack, he'd decided to go vegetarian and he wasn't interested in hunting and fishing. He wasn't into a lot of stuff the old Nathaniel had been. But the changes hadn't been Nate's conscious choice, they just happened.

He cracked open his beer and took a drink. Now if he told his brother and father that, they'd really think he was a lunatic.

He took another sip, then sighed and headed back into the dining room.

Sam and his father were discussing where his father's friend, Joe Miggs, had caught a huge bass just last week.

They stopped talking when he entered, as if Nate couldn't even bear to hear about fishing.

"Keep talking," he said and began to eat his baked potato.

Sam did, but the conversation was stilted. Finally, he gave up and turned to Nate. "Did you see Dr. Hall today?"

Nate nodded as he finished chewing his bite of green beans. "He thinks I'm doing too much on my knee, but otherwise I'm fine."

Sam nodded, but Nate got the distinct feeling that wasn't the answer he wanted.

There was silence.

"He didn't say anything else?" Sam finally asked. "You know, about your memory loss."

Nate knew Sam was curious about more than the memory loss. He wanted to know if Dr. Hall thought he had brain damage. After all, that was the only reason a person would stop eating meat.

"No. He doesn't think the memory loss is an issue. It's just a mild form of amnesia. The memories are there, I sometimes just need a cue to remember them."

"So try the steak. Maybe you'll remember you like that," his father said matter-of-factly.

Nate set down his fork and turned toward his father. "Dad, why is the vegetarianism such an issue for you?" He glanced at his brother. "Both of you?"

For a moment Nate thought his father was going to simply continue to eat and ignore his question. Then slowly, he set down his fork and knife and pushed his plate away. He looked at Nate.

"It isn't that you don't eat meat." He sighed, the sound weary. "It's that when you were in the hospital, I thought I'd lost you. But then, thank God," he reached over and touched Nate's hand, "thank God, the doctors brought you back to us."

Then he said slowly, "But you aren't the Nathaniel that went into that hospital. You've changed, and in some ways, I feel like I still lost you."

Nate looked at his dad, noticing the deep wrinkles around his eyes. Whiteness peppered his thick hair and bushy eyebrows. His blue eyes, so different than his sons', looked tired. He appeared far older than his fifty-seven years.

It bothered Nate that he had added to his dad's premature aging. Not only as an adolescent but now as an adult. His father had had a tough enough life. He didn't need to be worrying about his adult son.

"Dad, I *have* changed." He squeezed his father's hand, and even that felt old, the skin rough, his fingers gnarled. "But I'd like to think it's for the better. And that doesn't mean I think fishing and hunting and eating meat are bad. It's just not something I'm interested in anymore. I guess, being so close to death, I have a new respect for life."

That explanation was the closest he'd come to telling his father and brother the truth. He wanted to tell them, but if they were having problems understanding him now . . . Well, they'd never accept the full story.

His father stared at him for a moment, then nodded. "Well, I reckon there are worse things."

"Yes," Nate agreed readily.

His father released his hand and pushed away from the table. "Anyone want coffee? The Celts hit the court in about ten minutes."

"That would be great," Nate said.

Dad disappeared into the kitchen.

Nate returned to his dinner, taking a bite of potato before he realized his brother was staring at him.

"What?"

Sam hesitated, his look probing. "You still like girls, though, right? That hasn't changed?"

"Why the hell would you ask that?"

Sam shrugged.

"What out of what I just told Dad would make you think that?" Nate demanded. "What? Do you think being a vegetarian makes a person gay?"

Again Sam hesitated. "You just don't act the same toward women as you did before."

Nate considered his words for a moment, then laughed

humorlessly. "Well, there are plenty of ladies who would say that is a good thing." He sobered. "Yes, Sam, I still like women."

Marty Stepp suddenly popped into his mind.

And if his physical reaction to just picturing her as she'd looked in the bathroom this morning was any indication, his head might be messed up, but other parts of his anatomy were working just fine.

Chapter 5

"Hi, Brandi, is Diana in?"

There was a pause. "Sure, Marty. Hold on, I'll put you through."

New Age music filled Marty's ear as Brandi put her on hold.

She'd dreaded this call. It had taken her a couple days to get up the courage to dial the number to *Flair*, her modeling agency.

Even now, she considered hanging up. But before she could hit the End Call button, she heard Diana snatch up the phone.

"Where the hell are you?" her agent demanded.

Before Marty could answer, she continued. "I've been calling your cell phone. I even called Rod."

Marty could picture Diana shuddering on the other end of the line as she said that name. Diana despised Rod. Marty obviously should have followed her agent's advice on her love life as well as her career.

"I know," Marty said. "I got your messages, and I should have called sooner."

"Well, where are you? Are you all right?"

"Yes," Marty quickly assured her. "Yes, I'm okay. I'm—I'm at home. In Maine."

"What?"

Again, Marty could imagine Diana's shocked expression.

"Marty, you are supposed to be at a fitting appointment with Dara Rhoades as we speak. And you have a show *tomorrow*. Aaron Ashford is paying big bucks for you. But not just that, everyone is saying that Aaron is going to be a heavy hitter in this summer's fashions. We do not want to make an enemy out of him, even if he is a new designer."

"I know," Marty said, guilt heavy in her chest, making it hard for her to breathe. "I am so sorry. But . . . Diana, I had to get away."

There was a pause on the other end. "What happened?"

Marty hesitated; she owed Diana the truth.

When Marty had shown up at Flair with nothing but a few terrible head shots and a dream, Diana had seen beyond the outmoded clothes and ten-dollar haircut. She had transformed Marty into the model who had graced the covers of the most popular magazines, who had headlined the fashion shows of the most prestigious designers, and who had all the top people in the industry clamoring to work with her.

But Diana hadn't just built her career. She had also been a true friend to the naive girl from Millbrook, Maine. Outside of her sisters, Diana was her best friend.

"I often wish you had been able to change my foolish nature as well as you changed my looks," Marty told her.

Diana sighed. "I didn't need to make any changes, Marty. I just had the good sense to see what was already there. As far as your foolishness, you aren't foolish, you're kind. And trusting. Far, far too trusting."

Marty laughed humorlessly. "Actually, I'm not trusting at all. But when I do, it is invariably the wrong person."

"Well, I hope you don't feel that way about me," Diana said. "What's going on?"

Again, Marty hesitated, a combination of shame and fear freezing her tongue.

"Marty? Are you still there?"

"Rod did it again."

Now there was silence on the other end of the phone. Then, "The bastard!"

Marty sighed. "Yeah, well, it wasn't really much of a shock, was it? But I still needed to leave."

"Did you dump his sorry ass?"

Marty paused. "Yeah." She hadn't officially told him so, but she assumed he'd realize it when he couldn't reach her. "That's why I needed to leave for a while." She'd tell Diana the rest of her plans later.

"Yes," Diana readily agreed. She was silent for a moment. "I can handle things here. I'll tell Ashford and Dara Rhoades that you had a family emergency. They will be upset, but what can they do? And they won't burn bridges with me—or you, for that matter."

"I'm so sorry." Marty felt like she was failing Diana not only as a business associate but as a friend as well.

"Don't be sorry. Just take a break. And stay in touch."

"I will," Marty promised.

"Okay, I better make some calls. Keep in touch."

"Okay, bye."

Marty hit the End Call button and simply held the phone for a moment. How had she ended up in such a mess? Why had she ever gotten involved with Rod? No, this was all her own doing. Rod. Her dissatisfaction with her career.

She set down the cell phone just as the avocado telephone on the kitchen wall rang. She jumped up, startled by the ring.

"Hello?" she said.

"Hey. Can I ask you a favor?" It was Ellie.

Marty immediately felt comforted by her sister's voice. "Sure."

"Emily just went down to a nap, and I hate to wake her up to run out to the store. Would you mind picking me up a couple of packages of cream cheese and a bag of powdered sugar? I thought I had enough."

"Ooh, you're making your amazing carrot cake, aren't you?"

"Yes."

"Yay!"

"Yeah, well, you have reason to be happy. You are the only person I know who can eat that cake and not gain an ounce. If you weren't my sister, I'd hate you."

Marty laughed, even as a quick image of Rod scolding her for her sweet tooth flashed through her mind. She ignored it—he was gone now. "You're the one with the super-sexy husband and the gorgeous daughter. All I have is a great metabolism."

"You have far more than that," Ellie said gently. "But I have to admit, my slow metabolism doesn't bother me nearly as much as it once did."

"That is good. Do you need anything else?"

"No, that should do it. Are you sure you don't mind?"

"Of course not. I just need to find something to wear tonight, then I'll be over."

"No rush," Ellie assured her. "Guests don't arrive until seven."

"Okay. See you soon."

Marty hung up the phone, and she was struck with

another wave of guilt, this time for her sisters. Neither Ellie nor Abby had pressured her any further about why she had just shown up out of the blue. Or why she insisted on staying at Grammy's house, alone. Just like with Diana, she owed them an explanation.

At least Diana already knew most of the story about Rod. What a jerk he was. But she didn't even know where to begin with her sisters. Her sisters who had their lives together. Jobs they loved. Wonderful husbands—maybe the only two truly good men out there. How was she supposed tell them that her life was a complete mess?

She sighed. She might not be ready to talk yet. But she did want to be with Ellie. To be surrounded by the smells of the holidays, cookies and spices and pine. She wanted to lick the beaters that Ellie used to make the cream-cheese frosting for the carrot cake. She wanted to feel safe and loved.

She wanted to go back and appreciate the things she had once taken for granted.

She glanced at the clock. It was a little after two. Maybe she'd just get her clothes together and get ready for the party over at Ellie's house.

After looking through her minimal clothing, she finally decided on a green, ribbed turtleneck sweater and black jeans. She suspected other people would be dressed up more, but she was so tired of dressy. After wearing hundreds of evening gowns, crazy fad fashions, and spike-heeled, pointy-toed shoes, she was much happier dressing for comfort.

She had mixed feelings about the party tonight. On one hand, a big crowd would be a welcome distraction, but only if they didn't ask her about her career, her life in New York, or her romantic life. Now, what were the chances of that?

She sighed and looked at the clock. It was 2:30 p.m. She'd have plenty of time to get to the store, grab a quick lunch, and then head over to Ellie's.

That way she could also get a couple of hours to play with Emily before her little niece went off to spend the night with Mason's folks. Emily was still wary of her. But Marty was making headway; she'd gotten a few shy smiles and a few "wasdats?" Emily was already full of questions. At least those questions, Aunt Marty could handle.

She shoved her clothes into her tote bag, along with a pair of chunky-soled, black shoes, and headed back downstairs.

She tugged on a worn parka that she'd found in the front hall closet. The coat was huge and a sort of olive green color, but she really liked it. It was comfy and warm. She guessed it must have belonged to Ellie, although it had to have been enormous on her too. But Marty suspected Ellie had been going for warmth, not fashion. Marty could relate to that. It was darn cold outside. Fashion wasn't worth frostbite.

She put on a pair of bright red earmuffs and a rainbow-colored scarf that had matching mittens, all of which she also found in the front closet. She knew it wasn't a great look, but who was going to be looking at her anyway.

The grocery store parking lot was full, but since it was the Saturday before Christmas, it only made sense.

Marty parked her car next to a beat-up station wagon loaded to the brim with shopping bags, wrapping paper, and bows. It certainly looked like someone was going to have a good Christmas.

She smiled and hummed "It's Beginning to Look a Lot like Christmas." And it did, the fresh snow from a small storm last night, the garland and red bows across the storefronts.

Some of Marty's uneasiness started to subside. She hadn't been fair to Diana, but that was the first time she had ever left her agent in a lurch. Hell, she'd posed for the cover of one fashion magazine with pneumonia. She never shirked her responsibilities—too bad she might be shirking them for good.

Grabbing a shopping cart, she wheeled inside the store. Beckham's was a New England chain of grocery stores, but this one didn't feel like part of a chain. There was an old-fashioned market feel to the place. The floors were polished hardwood and the shelves were also finished wood. But Beckham's had more produce and specialty items than even the store where she shopped in Manhattan. And despite the smaller feel, it was actually a rather large place.

She wove her cart through the produce section, smiling at how fresh and beautiful all the different fruits and vegetables looked heaped in their respective bins and bushel baskets.

She picked up a huge orange and sniffed it, thinking of how the citrus scent seemed Christmasy too. Then she noticed a woman across the aisle watching her, a slight frown creasing her brow.

Marty immediately felt silly. *Smelling fruit.* She started to place it back on top of the others, then thought better of it and put the orange in her cart. Maybe people got weirded out about buying presniffed produce.

She pushed her cart along. What did she want for

lunch? Maybe something light, since she'd be undoubtedly eating tons tonight. She loved Ellie's cooking.

Hmm. She headed over to the deli counter. They had premade sandwiches, several soups, and salads. She considered the choices for a moment, then looked up to get one of the deli staff's attention. But she already had it.

One woman with a net on her head watched her, her expression rather dour. Another younger woman, who looked much more pleasant than the first woman, appeared quite intrigued by Marty. But she looked away when she realized that Marty saw she was staring.

The two men behind the counter didn't look away, however. One smiled. The other looked like he was trying to visualize her naked.

"I'd like one of the turkey wraps, please," Marty said, trying to keep her voice friendly even though she actually felt a bit bothered by the attention. Which wasn't really fair, she knew. She couldn't truly expect people not to recognize her. This was a small town, and the locals did know her.

But she had, probably naively, imagined coming home and just falling back into anonymity. Another fantasy, obviously.

The dour woman snatched up the sandwich from behind the glass counter and moved to another counter to wrap it in foil, all the while looking very put out.

Marty sighed, then decided to ignore the woman.

The young woman offered Marty a tentative smile, which Marty returned readily. That made her feel better, until she noticed the two men speaking quietly and throwing her sidelong glances. One of them made a gesture with his hands in front of his chest—the universal sigh for breasts. Both men laughed. And Marty's temper flared again.

The dour woman slapped the wrapped sandwich down in front of her, eyeing Marty coldly.

Marty thanked the woman and placed her wrap in the cart. She started away, telling herself that the woman was obviously just a grouch.

Then she heard someone, and she had no doubt it was the grouch, say, "I've seen prettier."

One of the men, undoubtedly the one proficient in sign language, said, "Well, you ain't seen her in them sexy little nighties and whatnot. She looks some sweet."

"Hmmpf," the grouch said, obviously dubious.

Marty kept walking, pretending she didn't hear, but inside she was seething. Not that she hadn't experienced this reaction before; she had. For some reason, people thought they could talk about her as if she were an object. Just a face on a magazine, not a real person. And it hurt. And she hadn't expected it to happen here.

She wasn't going to let a few thoughtless people ruin her good mood. Determinedly, she continued to browse the aisles for a few peaceful minutes before she overheard a hushed voice saying, "You'd never know that was her."

Marty didn't pause in reaching for a box of tea, choosing to believe that the stranger's observation wasn't about her. But when she turned to toss the tea into her cart, there was no ignoring who the woman was talking about. The whispering lady and her friend were staring directly at Marty, although they did have the good grace to glance away when Marty stared back.

Rather than wheel her cart in the opposite direction and leave the aisle, Marty strolled toward them. The two women didn't look at her, but at the shelves to intently discuss the merits of powdered nondairy creamers.

Marty sauntered by them, trying to look calm, as if she hadn't heard them. But once she was out of their sight, she hurried toward the dairy section to get the cream cheese Ellie requested. Then she headed to the checkout.

After waiting in a long line, she finally reached the cashier and started placing her items on the conveyor belt.

Marty had just finished emptying her cart when her cashier said loudly to the cashier at the register beside hers, "You know, it's hard to believe who they'll put on the cover of those fashion magazines."

The other cashier, a woman maybe a little older than Marty, nodded but looked distinctly uncomfortable.

Marty's cashier didn't. In fact, she glared at Marty, then said, "I swear, some of those models are just downright ugly."

Marty stared at the woman, whose highlighted, overpermed hair and hard blue eyes looked vaguely familiar. She debated what to do, what to say.

"Hi, Marty," a husky voice said so close to Marty's ear, she jumped. She spun around to look into gorgeous amber eyes fringed with long, dark lashes.

Many a model she knew would kill for lashes like that.

Marty blinked again and managed to stop staring into those beautiful eyes only to notice wonderfully molded lips curved into a lopsided smile. Then the eyes and lips turned toward the horrible cashier.

"Hey, Lynette, can you believe you're waiting on Millbrook's most famous native?"

Marty blinked again. Lynette? Lynette. That was who that horrible cashier was! Awful, mean Lynette Prue. And if Marty wasn't mistaken, Nathaniel Peck was trying to make the wretched woman feel uncomfortable.

Chapter 6

Nate had just run into Beckham's to pick up a quick lunch when he spotted Marty at the deli. He also witnessed the locals' reaction to the model in their midst. And he could tell Marty saw it too. She looked uncomfortable—and Nate would swear almost hurt.

When he saw her waiting in Lynette Prue's checkout aisle, he knew he had to step in. Lynette would not be nice—she rarely was.

So without further thought, he squeezed past the others in line, leaned in, and said hello to Marty.

He fully expected Marty to tell him to take a hike. So when her surprised look turned to an almost flirty gaze, he wasn't sure who was more shocked, he or Lynette.

"Hey, you," Marty said and smiled warmly.

Damn, she had an amazing smile.

He simply stared at her for a moment, lost in that gorgeous grin. Then he recovered and slipped an arm around her waist. Or at least he thought it was her waist; it was hard to tell through her giant coat.

Marty stiffened at his touch but didn't pull away,

which also surprised him. And after a few moments, she actually relaxed against him.

Lynette watched them intently, and she didn't, or couldn't, disguise her annoyance.

Marty didn't seem to notice Lynette; her full attention was on him. Her beautiful smile widened, and she said in a soft, inviting voice, "So, did you come find me to take me to lunch?"

Nate didn't hesitate. "Yes."

"Good, I'm starving," she said, the words filled with innuendo.

His body reacted immediately. Man, how he wished she really wanted him to satisfy another type of hunger. He'd been giving that idea a lot of thought since he'd last seen her. A lot of thought.

As Lynette fumbled with Marty's groceries and shot them confused, angry glances, Nate leaned close to Marty's ear. "So are we still on for tomorrow night too?"

Marty looked up at him again. There was a flash of warning in her smoky eyes. He'd definitely pushed this charade far enough, but again, Marty surprised him.

"Of course, baby."

Only he would know her charming grin had changed into something more akin to baring her teeth.

He hugged her tight to his side. Man, he wished she weren't wearing that massive coat. If this was the only time she was going to allow him to touch her, he really could do without the down armor separating them.

"That's going to be $12.84," Lynette ground out through clenched teeth, and Marty quickly pulled out of his grasp to fish for her wallet in her pocket.

"Let me," Nate said, reaching for his wallet, but Marty stopped him.

"No," Marty said firmly, but then tempered it by adding, "I'll order a big lunch."

Nate grinned. "Okay." She really was quite an actress.

Marty paid Lynette, and Nate picked up the plastic shopping bags. They left the store, Lynette staring after them, still stunned.

Once they were out of her line of sight, Marty reached for the bags.

"I'll carry them," Nate told her.

"I don't need you to carry them." Marty reached for the bags again, and again Nate moved them out of her grasp.

"Where's your car?" he asked.

She stopped and braced her hands on her hips. "Nathaniel, I need to go."

"Nate."

"What?"

"Nate, you keep forgetting to call me Nate."

She sighed. "Fine, Nate. I have to go."

He shook his head. "We're going to lunch."

She frowned, regarding him like he was a simpleton. "That was just for Lynette's benefit. I have no intention of going to lunch with you." She held out her hand, waiting for him to hand over the shopping bags.

He attempted to look affronted. "I feel so used."

She seemed confused by him, but then stated, "Well, I think it was officially your turn." She snatched the bags from his hand and walked away from him.

Nate didn't move for a moment. His turn? Had he used Marty? But before he could try to strain the possibly forgotten memory through his sieve mind, he realized Marty was making her escape.

He chased after her, circling around in front of her, forcing her to stop.

"How about just a Steamy Indulgence instead?"

Marty's eyes widened, then her mouth turned down in a distinctly disgusted expression. "No, I'll *definitely* pass on that."

Nate was confused by her reaction for a moment, then quickly said, "Oh no." He chuckled, "No, I didn't mean that like it sounded. It's a new coffee place on Main Street. Lattes, cappuccino, other steamed things—hence the name."

Marty still looked dubious.

"Come on, I faced the wrath of Lynette Prue for you," he pointed out. "Surely you can have a cup of coffee with me."

She regarded him for a moment, then said, "All right."

Nate wondered why she suddenly gave in so easily, but he didn't question her further. He'd been thinking about her far too much to mess up a chance to spend a little time with her. Although in his fantasies, she didn't dislike him quite so intensely. Ah, well, he couldn't have everything.

"Okay. Want to ride there with me in my cruiser?"

"I'll follow you," she said.

"I don't know if I can trust you," he said jokingly, although he did think she would bolt if given half a chance.

"Yeah, well, that makes two of us," she murmured wryly, and he got the feeling there was more that he should understand about that comment. That vague feeling like something was pressing against his brain returned. He ignored it.

"I'll ride with you, then," he said and scanned the parking lot for her vehicle. It wasn't hard to find the silver Jaguar, and he headed in that direction.

The car stood out, gorgeous and sleek, in a sea of ordinary. Even the layer of dirt and salt from the winter roads couldn't hide its classic lines. Nothing could hide that kind of timeless beauty—much like its owner's.

Marty wore gray sweatpants, a giant parka, and running shoes. Her short hair was mussed, her face free of any make-up, but she was still beautiful, absolutely stunning.

"That's why Lynette was so catty," he said over the roof of her car as Marty used the remote to unlock the doors.

"Huh?"

"People notice you. That bothers someone like Lynette."

Marty seemed to consider that, but instead of saying anything, she slid into the driver's seat, tossing her grocery bags over the seat into the back.

He folded into the passenger's side, the vehicle small for his tall frame. His knee protested, throbbing almost unbearably, but he ignored it.

"It's on Main Street?" she asked.

He nodded.

She checked her mirrors and backed out of the parking spot. Both of them were quiet as she pulled onto the street.

"So, are you enjoying your visit?" It was a lame question, Nate realized, but it was hard to be suave when the woman so obviously detested him. And when his knees were practically touching his chin.

"Yes."

"Do you like living in New York?"

"Yes."

"I don't know how I would deal with all the commotion," he said, casting a look at her. "Do you like that—all the hubbub?"

"Yes."

Okay, this wasn't going well at all.

"Listen," he said slowly, "can't we just have cup of coffee and a nice conversation—like a couple of friends."

Marty whipped into a parking space in front of the coffee shop so quickly, his knees slammed against the dashboard.

She turned off the engine and shifted in her seat to face him. "Is that what you think we are? Friends?" Her eyes flashed angrily.

He hesitated, then simply stated the truth. "I honestly don't know what we are. But I know I'd like to be friends."

He'd like to be a lot more, but at this point, he'd take friendship.

"You might have my sisters and my brothers-in-law convinced that you've changed," she said. "But I find that very hard to believe."

"Okay," he said slowly. "Well, I think you might have to wait in line to join that club. There are quite a few people who feel exactly the same way." He jerked the silver handle and opened the car door. "Let's just get a cup of coffee."

Marty watched as Nate unfolded his long legs from under the dash. His movements were awkward, stiff. And she felt a pang of guilt. Whatever had happened, whether he was truly changed or not, he had been through something.

She remained in the car for a moment. Maybe she should just tell him this was a mistake and leave, but when she glanced over at him, she couldn't.

He waited on the sidewalk. He didn't appear angry

or irritated. He looked withdrawn. His amazing amber eyes muted to a dull brown. His lips immobile, all hints of his appealing grin gone. He looked hurt, and tired.

She fought the urge to bang her forehead on the steering wheel. She did *not* want to feel bad for Nathaniel . . . Nate Peck. For all she knew, this was just another one of his elaborate setups to win her trust. To convince yet another person that he was a changed man.

But why? What was the point? For all he knew, she'd be gone from Millbrook in a week. Unless it was just a sick game he liked to play. She'd certainly known men who played sicker games.

She glanced at him again. Ah, hell, it was just coffee. That was a small price to pay for the look on Lynette Prue's face. That was worth coffee *and* dessert.

She got out of her car and offered him a tentative half smile. "Okay, truce."

He regarded her skeptically. "Are you sure? Do you really want to be seen with a conniving ogre like me?"

Marty rolled her eyes. "I wouldn't describe you as an ogre."

His eyes glimmered just slightly, as if a flame was trying to flicker to life in their amber depths. "A monster, then?"

She shook her head. "Not a monster either."

"A cad?"

She considered that label. "Yeah, that one fits."

"And the conniving?"

"You'll get no argument there."

He looked wounded, but this time the expression was obviously affected.

Bells jingled as he opened the door to the coffee shop and held it for her. She entered, immediately enveloped in warmth and the rich, nutty aroma of brewing java.

Paintings done in brightly colored oils and broad brush strokes hung on the walls. Funky, cylindrical lights in different colors hung over the round wooden tables.

Nate led her to one of the tables in the corner. "Is this all right?"

She nodded.

He shrugged out of his brown, police-issue jacket and hung it on the back of one of the chairs. "What can I get you?"

Marty glanced up at a huge chalkboard over the espresso bar. Every flavor and combination of coffee she could possibly imagine was listed in different colored chalk. Overwhelmed, she said, "Just a latte."

He nodded and headed up to the counter.

Marty pulled off her own coat and sat down.

She watched Nate as he ordered. He was in his uniform. The brown material fit his tall, muscular body impeccably, accentuating his broad shoulders and narrow hips. Yet even with the perfect fit, the outfit didn't look quite right. She had no idea why. There was nothing she could place a finger on exactly, but he gave the impression that he was wearing a costume.

She thought about how he had looked at Abby's wedding. He'd been wearing his uniform then too, and as she recalled he'd looked like the model officer. Like he'd been born wearing a uniform. What changed?

That seemed to be the $64,000 question, didn't it? But given that she kept asking it, maybe it was time to admit Nate had changed.

As he walked back to their table, a cup in each hand, she watched him. His movements were easy, loose, even with the limp. His hair was an interesting combination of golden blond and brown with a peppering of ginger. The color made his unusual amber eyes more striking.

"See anything you like?" he asked as he set one of the cups down in front of her.

"No," she said automatically, her face flushing.

He glanced around the room. "I actually like this artist. She lives in Tenant's Harbor. She has a good eye for color." He took a seat across from her and took a sip of his coffee.

"Oh," Marty said, relieved he'd been talking about the artwork rather than her blatant staring.

They quietly sipped their coffees for a moment.

"Why did you grow out your hair?" Marty couldn't believe she asked that.

He glanced up from fiddling with the lid of his cup. "Why, does it look bad?"

"No," she answered quickly—too quickly, she realized. She paused, then added, "I think it looks nice."

His eyes widened in mock surprise. "Did you just give me a compliment?"

Marty shook her head, but a smile tugged at her lips. "I just happen to like longer hair."

"So it isn't me, per se. You'd like long hair on anyone?"

"Right."

As if on cue, the shop door jingled open, and a large man, balding on top but with a long, scraggy ponytail, stepped inside. He walked past them to the counter.

"So, you like his hair too," Nate asked offhandedly.

She shrugged. "It's fine."

"You aren't going to give me an inch, are you?"

She took a sip of her coffee, then said quietly, "I guess I like yours a bit better."

Nate leaned back in his seat, a slightly smug look on his face. "Damn, I think that *was* a compliment."

"Don't let it go to your head."

"I'm sure you won't let it."

Marty started to assure him that was true when a teenage girl approached their table. From the apron covering her pink sweater and low-rise jeans, Marty could tell she was an employee here. The girl colored slightly and brushed a wisp of hair from her cheek that had escaped its ponytail.

"Ms. Stepp?" she asked nervously.

"Yes," Marty said, offering the girl a polite smile.

"Hi, I was wondering if I could get your autograph?" the girl asked, her voice a little breathy and nervous. Again she pushed back the stray hair. It fluttered right back into place against her cheek.

Marty's smiled broadened and she set down her coffee cup. "Sure. Do you have a pen?"

The girl nodded, reaching into one of the deep pockets on the front of her apron. She pulled out a red marker and a small square of card stock, which listed the coffee specials for the week.

"What's your name?" Marty asked.

"Megan."

Marty signed the paper. The marker bled slightly on each letter like lipstick in the wrinkles of an older woman.

Marty frowned at that analogy. Why would she think of that?

"I have one of the Calvin Klein ads you did with Arturo hanging in my locker," the girl said sheepishly as Marty handed the paper back to her.

"Wow." Marty nodded with a sincere grin. "Do you like Calvin Klein's stuff?"

Megan looked down the autograph, then glanced back at Marty. The girl's cheeks were nearly fuchsia, she was blushing so much. "I like Arturo," she admitted, then blurted out, "Did you really date him?"

A wave of disappointment lessened Marty's smile just slightly, but then she laughed. She should have guessed that the girl was interested in Arturo. Girls loved him. Of course, she'd loved Arturo once too. "Yeah, I dated him—for a while."

"What's he like?"

"Very nice. And funny. And he happens to love Calvin Klein."

The girl giggled and blushed even more. "He's so cute. I always watch him on *Day After Day After Day*."

"He is cute," Marty agreed. "And I think he makes quite a believable neurosurgeon." Okay, there might have been a hint of sarcasm in that last statement.

Megan didn't seem to notice. "Me too. He's the best." She then glanced back at the man behind the counter who was presumably her boss. "Thank you so much." She held up the paper.

Marty smiled back. "You are very welcome."

After Megan left the table, Marty glanced over at Nate. He was watching her, his arms folded over his chest, a slight smile curving his lips.

"What?" she asked.

"You dated a soap star named Arturo?"

Marty bristled. "He wasn't a soap star when we were dating."

"Arturo . . . What is his last name?"

"He doesn't use a last name," Marty admitted dully.

Nate bit back a laugh. "Oh, like Madonna or Cher."

Really more like Liberace, she thought, although she didn't say so.

"So how long did you two date?"

"Quite a while."

"Arturo," he said again with a slight smile.

She straightened in her seat. "Like you can give me a hard time. After all, you dated Lynette Prue."

"Well, you do have me there. Definitely a poor choice."

She couldn't help but nod her agreement.

"So why did you and Arturo break up?"

"None of your business. Why are you so interested in this, anyway?"

"Just curious," he said, offering her a benign smile. "After all, if I should ever get the chance to date you, I wouldn't want to make the same mistakes he did."

A wry laughed escaped her. "Oh, I don't think you'd make the same mistakes. But don't worry, we won't be dating anytime soon. I'm not interested in a relationship with anyone."

Instead of looking disheartened, as she had expected he would, he looked almost encouraged. "So it isn't me in particular."

She almost laughed again, this time genuinely amused, but instead she managed to say, deadpan. "Well, I have to admit, you'd be fairly low on my list."

This time he did look hurt.

They both sipped their coffee in silence for a few moments.

"What if I became a soap star?"

The sudden question startled her, then she smiled. "Nope, that wouldn't do it either."

He sighed, but then offered her a quick smile that made his eyes twinkle. He took a sip of his coffee.

It really was too bad she'd sworn off men and that she disliked this one so much in particular. He really was quite cute. Of course, it had always been the cute factor that had gotten her into trouble before.

Chapter 7

"So, what *exactly* happened to Nathaniel Peck?" Marty asked casually as she sat in Ellie's kitchen, licking cream-cheese frosting from a stainless steel beater. Emily sat in her high chair with the other one, although it looked as though more of the frosting was going in her hair than in her mouth.

Ellie stopped, a rubber spatula heaped with icing in her hand, and looked over at her sister, obviously startled. "I told you—he was attacked."

"Yes. But why do you think he has changed?"

Ellie's eyes returned to the carrot cake, and she began to spread the frosting around the sides. "He just has. It's like night and day, really."

Marty waited for her to elaborate, but Ellie didn't. Finally, she prodded. "How so?"

Ellie continued to coat the cake evenly, obviously mulling over the question. "He's just nicer. Less . . . abrasive." She paused. "I can't really describe it, because I didn't honestly know Nate that well until recently. But according to Mason, he is just a whole new person."

Marty held the beater loosely in her hand and pondered Ellie's words. "Do you think it's because of the attack?"

Ellie reached back into the bowl for more frosting, nodding. "I do. He was in a coma—the doctors said he might die." She glanced over at Marty. "Don't say anything about that. I'm not sure if other people know. He told Mason."

"Why?"

Ellie shrugged. "Maybe because Mason has been through a life-altering experience with his alcoholism. I don't know, really."

"But you think he has honestly changed?"

"I do," Ellie said again.

Marty again considered her sister's adamancy. She didn't understand why it should matter to her if Nate had changed or not. But for some reason, it did. Maybe she wanted to believe people really could change. Herself included. She wanted to be more than a face on a magazine—or one of the ugly Stepp sisters. She wanted to be Marty Stepp, whoever that was.

Emily threw her mixing beater on the floor and gave Marty a start. Then the toddler reached out a hand to Marty.

"Well, little friend, you have got to want this, because I know you don't want me to pick you up," Marty said, referring to the beater she was still holding. "Do you want this?"

The sticky little girl smiled a big, gap-toothed grin.

Marty handed it to her, and Emily replied with a happy bit of babble and a kick of her chubby legs. Then she proceeded to add more icing to her already well-frosted curls.

"You nut," Marty scolded affectionately as she picked up the tossed beater and placed it in the sink.

Ellie stopped scraping out the last bits of frosting from the bowl to smile at her daughter. "She is that. Aren't you, Emmy-Lou?"

The toddler kicked her legs again and giggled.

Marty sat back down at the table and watched Emily, but her mind was still on Nate.

"So why are you so interested in Nate and whether I believe he has changed?"

Marty looked up at her sister, then reached over to swipe a bit of frosting from the edge of the mixing bowl. "I'm just curious," she said after licking her finger.

Ellie nodded in her customarily accepting way—a way that didn't really reveal whether she did believe Marty or not.

Marty ran a finger along the edge of the bowl again. "I actually had coffee with him today, before coming over here." She popped her sugary-coated finger in her mouth.

Ellie stopped fiddling with the cake and gaped at her, blue eyes wide, mouth in a perfect O.

Marty couldn't help finding her expression rather humorous. With powdered sugar on her sweater and spatula in her hand, Ellie looked like a kitchen fairy that someone had goosed. All she needed was a chef's hat and some wings.

"You had coffee with him?"

Marty nodded. "Yes."

"And?"

"I only went with him because he saved me from having to listen to Lynette Prue's catty remarks. She is still awful."

"And she's actually Lynette Nye now. She married Jared Nye."

"Figures."

"Yeah," Ellie agreed, then she asked, "Did you have fun with Nate?"

She had, in an awkward sort of way, Marty realized. But she didn't say that. "It was okay."

Ellie continued to stare at her until she finally said, "So have you forgiven him?"

Marty considered that. "No. It's more like a truce. I still think he owes me an apology. A big apology."

Her sister nodded. "But you can tolerate him now?"

"Yes."

Ellie let out a sigh of relief. "That's good, because I was really, really dreading telling you that he is going to be at this party tonight."

Marty stepped into the huge shower in the bathroom attached to Ellie and Mason's guest room. The rest of their house might be true to the historical integrity of the building, but the bathrooms were very contemporary, with all the modern conveniences any twenty-first-century person might want or need.

The shower, for example, was huge and beautiful, with frosted-glass bricks making up two of the walls and slabs of dark gray granite forming the other wall and floor. Two separate showerheads created a cross stream of pulsating, steamy water.

There was a granite bench against one wall where a woman could sit and shave her legs . . . or whatever.

Marty wiped the water back from her face and hair and glanced at the bench. Suddenly a very clear image of herself straddling a hot, wet, naked man flashed through her head. And she didn't need to speculate for even a second who that hot, wet, naked man was.

She groaned out loud and then stuck her head back under the powerful spray. She clenched her eyes shut, trying to block out the image, but that only seemed to make it clearer in her mind. Long, muscular legs, broad shoulders, a flat stomach, and . . .

She stepped out of the water, opened her eyes, and focused on a bottle of shampoo. She wouldn't think about Nate. Naked or dressed. Wet or dry. Absolutely *no* Nate. In any state.

She squeezed some of the shampoo into her hands and began to lather her short locks. Again, she was bombarded with an image of her fingers sinking into longer, shaggier hair.

"This is insane," she declared to herself, her voice sounding faintly hollow against the shower walls.

She was intrigued by the man, curious about his sudden change. And she was obviously adjusting, rather poorly, to the idea of no men in her future. That was it, end of story.

She rushed through the remainder of her shower, making sure not to look at the bench, and she only once, accidentally, glanced at the shampoo bottle. But when she was in front of the mirror, a plush towel wrapped securely around her, she felt a little more in control again.

She wiped off the condensation-covered mirror with a hand towel and looked at her reflection. Despite her career choice, she'd never been the type to stand in front of the mirror for hours. But today, she forced herself to look—to really see the face that had been the focus of her whole life.

She tilted her head, inspecting her face from a several angles. Then she studied it from straight on.

In her opinion it was an ordinary face. Maybe her lips were fuller than most, and her chin a little pointier, but overall it was just a face. When she thought about herself, she didn't think about her face or her height or her build. But everyone else did. Whether they thought she was beautiful or ugly, everyone reacted to how she looked.

Today in the grocery store had been a prime example of that. And she didn't want to be an object that people felt they had every right to comment on.

She wanted people to know Marty Stepp for something other than her physical appearance. She wanted to be remembered for being someone real, someone good.

Which led her back to Nate, as all things, including shampoo bottles, seemed to do these days. She wanted to understand how he had changed. How he got people to see past the man they all thought they knew and believe the man he'd become. Lord knew, if Nathaniel Peck could change, anyone could.

As Nate stepped into Mason and Ellie's house, he was struck by the cheery holiday spirit of the place. A huge Christmas tree, well over ten feet tall, was in the foyer. Spruce swags with bows and berries decorated the banister up the staircase. The smell of food and evergreens and the happy chatter and laughter of guests encompassed him. Faint notes of a Christmas carol played under it all.

Content, peaceful warmth overcame him. He couldn't recall ever feeling that way before. It could be that he just couldn't remember the sensation, but he had the innate impression that he'd simply never felt this way before.

"Nate," Mason greeted him, shaking his hand and clapping him on the back, genuinely pleased to see him. "Here, let me take your coat."

"All right. Um, this is for you. It's a plant." Nate handed a small houseplant to Mason.

Mason nodded. "Great. I'll put it . . . here." He set it on an antique table by the entrance. Then he turned back and held out a hand for Nate's coat.

Nate shrugged out of the wool dress coat that he'd probably only worn twice before tonight. He didn't used to mingle with the particularly classy members of Millbrook society. And when he had, he'd never made an effort to impress with proper etiquette. Now, he rather liked the coat.

He glanced at the plant sitting forlornly on the table. He needed to work on the appropriate hostess gift, however.

As Mason headed upstairs with an armload of coats, he gestured with an elbow toward the dining room and living room. "Ellie has just set out," he shook his head as if overwhelmed, "I don't know, a zillion different appetizers. Go eat."

"I will." Nate smiled and headed in the direction of the living room. This room was also decorated with another, smaller Christmas tree and other Christmasy odds and ends. Logs burned cheerfully in the marble fireplace, and people sat and stood everywhere, talking and eating.

He stood in the doorway, suddenly feeling a bit out of place. He knew everyone in the room, but none of these people had ever considered Nathaniel Peck a friend.

Fortunately, Ellie noticed him and left the group she was chatting with to approach him. "Hi, Nate," she said with a friendly smile and gave him a quick hug. "Thank you for coming."

He smiled down at her. "Thank you for inviting me. The house looks great."

Ellie smiled, pleased. "I get a bit carried away. Why don't you join us?" She gestured toward the small circle she'd been talking with before she spotted him.

He immediately noticed that Marty wasn't in the group. "I think I'll get something to drink first."

"Please do. There is eggnog and wine in the dining room. And soft drinks in the kitchen."

He nodded. "Great."

He wandered back into the large foyer and then down the hall, saying hello to the few people he encountered, all the while looking for Marty.

It didn't take long to find her. She was in the dining room. Her height made her visible, but it was her gorgeous smile that made her stand out. She stood on the far side of the room, drinking eggnog and talking to Charlie Grace.

Nate sidled into the room, situating himself beside a large china cabinet, hoping she wouldn't notice him and he could just watch her for a moment. He wanted to see if she acted as uncomfortable around other people as she did around him.

She looked fantastic tonight. Unlike most of the women who wore dresses or skirts, she wore a dark green turtleneck tucked into a pair of black jeans. The outfit might have been casual, but on her, it looked as stunning as any cocktail dress. The knit of the sweater clung to her subtle curves, and the jeans made her legs look impossibly long.

Nate noticed her posture was relaxed as she leaned forward to hear something Charlie said—relaxed in a way she'd never been around him. Then she smiled warmly at Charlie, a full smile, not just the slight curve of her lips that she gave him. She laughed at something the man said. Nate could hear the amazing rich tone over the din of all the other guests. She leaned forward again to hear Charlie, and another lush laugh escaped her.

Nate gritted his teeth. Well, Charlie Grace might be funny, but he was a good two inches shorter than Marty.

He immediately chided himself for being so petty. But he wasn't going to deny it, he was envious. He really wished he could walk up to Marty and receive that same easy response from her.

Their coffee today hadn't been as successful as he'd hoped. He hadn't wowed her with his charm. He hadn't made her laugh the same way Charlie Grace seemed to. He'd gotten a few smiles, but now after seeing her full, gorgeous grin, he realized those smiles had been more polite than anything.

He peeked back around the china cabinet to see Charlie leaving, replaced by a taller, dark-haired man. It was Jake Sanborn.

Jake handed her a refreshed cup of eggnog, which she accepted with a polite smile. The same smile that Nate got, when he actually got a smile.

Nate also noticed that her posture was not nearly as relaxed with Jake as it had been with Charlie. He frowned. What could be so different about the two men?

He leaned against the cabinet and watched more intently. Jake touched her arm. Marty stepped back. Jake took another step closer. She excused herself to get an appetizer, which she only nibbled, still looking distinctly ill at ease.

He considered approaching her, feeling the need to

at least try to make her feel a bit more relaxed, but Aaron Peters approached her first.

Again, he noticed that Marty offered him her stiff, polite smile. Then Aaron seemed to follow the same pattern that Jake had, stepping close, touching her arm. And again, Marty reacted the same way. She put distance between them—this time by leaving the room.

Well, he did have his answer. Marty was edgy with other men, not just him. Instead of making him feel better, it made him feel more concerned and intrigued. Why didn't she trust men? Had this Arturo—God, what a silly name—had he broken her heart? Nate wanted to know the whole story. And why didn't Charlie Grace make her feel nervous? Maybe his lack of height was a good thing.

Then he noticed Charlie standing at the dining-room table, placing different appetizers on a plate. He smiled at the woman beside him, and Nate remembered that Charlie was married. Jake and Aaron were not. And Marty's reaction became crystal clear. Marty wasn't wary of married men, only single ones.

"Nathaniel?" A hand touched his arm.

He glanced around to see Josie Nye, Jared's sister, standing close by his side. "What the hell are you doing hanging out in the corner?"

"What are you doing here?" he asked. "This doesn't seem like your type of scene."

She sighed as if she totally agreed, then said, "I'm here with Warren Howe."

Now, that made sense. Warren Howe would be here. He was a town council member and worked with Mason. Warren always had a fondness for younger, flashy women. And with her fire-engine red hair piled high on her head and her low-cut, sparkly cocktail dress, Josie flashed all right—like the sign of a motel that rented by the hour.

Nate couldn't believe that, at one time, he had found Josie very attractive. They had even dated for quite a while. But again, all those feelings and memories seemed like they belonged to another person.

"So, you planning to try and make poor old Warren into Mr. Josie III?"

"Why? You jealous?"

He didn't feel the need to respond. They both knew how their relationship ended, and it hadn't been Josie who'd done the ending.

"So," she said once she realized he didn't intend to take her bait, "you've been getting pretty chummy with Mason and Chase and the Stepp sisters."

"They are nice people."

"Mmm," she said, not hiding her disdain.

Irritation immediately coursed through him, but he kept his voice calm and even as he said, "Then maybe you shouldn't be taking advantage of their hospitality."

"Mmm," she said again, this time like she was considering his suggestion.

Nate, hoping the conversation was over, crossed to the table and ladled some eggnog into a glass. He was just about to take a sip when Josie reappeared at his side.

"Lynette told me that you and the tall Stepp sister are dating. Is that true?"

Before he could answer, a hand touched his arm, causing him to jump slightly.

"I'm sorry," Ellie immediately apologized, offering him a sheepish smile. "I didn't mean to startle you. I just meant to tell you when you arrived that a lot of the appetizers are vegetarian. Just avoid the white dip." She pointed to a bowl in the center of the table. "That's clam dip, and the silver platter, those are crab balls. Other than that, I think you should be able to tell which ones have meat."

He grinned down at her. "You didn't need to do anything special for me."

Ellie shrugged and said in her kind way, "It was no trouble. I wanted to do it. And it was fun. I love trying new recipes."

God, Ellie was like a breath of clean, clear air when compared to Josie.

The small blonde looked around him and gave Josie a shy smile. "Josie, thank you for coming. Did you get a drink?"

Josie held up her glass of wine but didn't bother to respond any further.

Nate clenched his teeth. Had he actually liked this person at one time? Even more disturbing, had he acted like her? He knew he'd acted worse.

If Ellie noticed Josie's rudeness, she didn't react. Instead she excused herself and went to talk to Ginny Harris, Mason's secretary, leaving him alone again with Josie.

"It was fun. I love trying new recipes," Josie said in a grating, sickly sweet voice, then she eyed Ellie from across the room. "From the looks of her, I think she needs to lay off the new recipes. You know, the ugly Stepp girls are just as weird as they ever were. You and Marty Stepp. People say you're brain damaged—now I know it's true."

Nate turned to Josie, and this time he couldn't keep his anger in check, although he did manage to keep his voice low. "The Stepp sisters are 100 percent classier than you. They certainly wouldn't attend a party you were hosting and bad-mouth you. Maybe you should leave."

Josie looked unimpressed. "I don't think that is up to you. I'm here with Warren and I'll leave when he wants to leave."

She turned and sauntered from the room.

Chapter 8

Marty ducked back into the hallway as Josie Nye exited the dining room. The redheaded woman didn't even notice her as she stormed toward the living room.

Marty remained still, her back flat to the wall, trying to comprehend what she'd just witnessed. She'd been walking into the dining room to get more eggnog, hoping the rum would make Jake Sanborn and Aaron Peters more tolerable, as both men insisted on following her all evening. Then she saw Nate and Josie.

They were standing close together, and at first, Marty had assumed they were having a friendly chat. After all, Josie was Nate's best friends' sister.

But she quickly saw that neither of them looked particularly happy. Josie sported the nasty sneer that Marty remembered well from school days. And Nate looked irritated. A muscle in his jaw kept popping like he was clenching his teeth to keep his mouth shut.

Marty was about to forgo the eggnog to avoid them when Ellie joined the two. Nate's whole demeanor had transformed. He grinned down at Ellie, and he seemed so genuinely pleased to talk with her. But when Ellie left, Josie got really nasty.

Marty heard her say something about the ugly Stepp sisters, and Nate became obviously furious. He glared at the other woman with hard eyes, his lips in a firm line. Marty heard him coldly tell Josie that he thought she should leave.

And Josie had, anger clear in her eyes and in the set of her jaw.

Marty moved back to the doorway and peeked into the dining room. Nate still stood at the table, an eggnog glass clutched in his hand.

She moved back into the shadows, once more leaning heavily against the wall. She had no idea exactly what Josie had said, but it didn't matter. All that mattered was that Nate defended her and her sisters to Josie. He never would have done that before . . . before whatever happened to him.

She carefully moved to watch him again.

"Oh, for heaven's sake, just talk to the man."

Marty jumped and spun around to see Abby standing beside her, following her line of vision.

"My God, you scared me!" Marty muttered.

"You two need to talk to each other," Abby said, not apologizing for nearly giving Marty a heart attack. "You two have been sneaking around watching each other half the evening."

"No, I . . . he was watching me?"

Abby nodded. "Almost since he got here."

"Seriously?"

"Do I look like a woman who feels well enough to make up stories?"

Marty noticed that Abby did look a tad green even in the shadows. "Can I get you anything?"

"If you are so intrigued by the guy, talk to him. If he's still truly a jerk—well, don't talk to him anymore."

Spoken like a woman who didn't invariably get involved with the wrong men, Marty thought. But she didn't want to get involved, she wanted to see if he had really changed.

"Okay," Abby said, "I've given you my two cents. Now I need to find Chase and a saltine."

Marty smiled sympathetically.

Abby headed toward the living room, where Chase met her in the doorway with a concerned expression and the ever-ready cracker.

Marty smiled to herself and then peeped around the door frame. Nate still stood at the table, although he looked a tad calmer. His lips weren't compressed. They were back to being almost pouty, and sinfully sexy.

Okay, thoughts like that were not why she wanted to talk to Nate. They weren't. She wanted to understand this drastic change. She wanted to understand so she could begin to change her own life.

She took a deep breath, pulled back her shoulders, and walked into the dining room. Nate saw her as soon as she entered and greeted her with one of his lopsided smiles.

"Hi," he said as she approached.

"Hi."

"Is our truce still on?" he asked.

She nodded. "I believe it is."

"Good. Would you like some eggnog?" he asked.

"I would love it." She offered him a smile.

"Okay," he said, his gaze dropping briefly to her lips before turning to the punch bowl. He set down his own drink and then reached across the table to scoop some creamy liquid into a glass for her.

When he handed it to her, she couldn't help noticing that he appeared almost absurdly pleased.

"What?" she asked, confused by his expression.

"I really like your smile," he told her, the comment a frank observation.

Marty's heart jumped in her chest, the sudden movement stealing her breath for a moment. She found the forthright remark far more flattering than a long, colorful homage.

"Thank you."

He smiled back, and Marty couldn't help thinking that she really liked his smile, too.

"Hey, there you are." Aaron Peters joined them, once again standing far too close to her.

She shifted away, which brought her closer to Nate. Her arm actually brushed against his, but she didn't feel the need to move away from him.

"Yes, here I am." She could barely keep the exasperation out of her voice.

"Peck, how are you?" Aaron said, reaching forward to clasp Nate's hand.

"Doing well, Aaron. And how are you?"

Marty couldn't tell how Nate felt about the other man from his polite greeting. But it was rather easy to see how the other man felt about Nate.

"Fine, Peck, fine. I still can't get used to seeing you in settings like this. I've always seen you as more of a bar sort of guy. You know, beer and peanuts over eggnog and hors d'oeuvres."

Nate smiled, the gesture still polite if somewhat stiff. "I guess I'm a bit of both."

Aaron raised an eyebrow as if that idea never occurred to him. Then he turned to Marty. "Ellie was telling me that you are staying through the holidays. I was wondering if you would like to go to Bangor with me tomorrow evening to see a performance of *The Nutcracker.*"

Marty smiled courteously but then said, as she placed a hand on Nate's arm, "I would normally love to, but I actually have a date with Nate tomorrow night."

Both Aaron and Nate gaped at her, but Nate recovered quickly. He grinned at Marty and then shrugged at Aaron.

Surprise continued to widen Aaron's eyes, but he managed to mumble, "Well—well, I thought I would ask."

"Thank you," Marty said, although she felt far too satisfied about shocking the pompous man to look properly sincere.

"I believe I'll go . . . go speak to Mason now." Aaron hurried away, obviously desperate to leave them.

"Why do I get the feeling you're using me again?" Nate said wryly as soon as Aaron was gone.

"Do you mind?"

"That depends. Are we really going out on a date tomorrow night?"

Marty pretended to think about the question. "Sure. Why not."

"Then no," he said with a satisfied grin. "I don't mind being used at all."

"You have a date with Marty Stepp?" Sam repeated back slowly what Nate had just told him. "*The* Marty Stepp?"

"Yes."

Sam collapsed into the metal-framed chair on the other side of Nate's desk. "I can't believe she would go out with you."

"Thanks," Nate said flatly.

Sam straightened up a bit, staring intently at Nate.

"She's a friggin' supermodel. You do remember that, don't you?"

"Yes. I remember that."

Sam slowly nodded and looked duly impressed. "Wow, I really can't believe she agreed to go out with you."

Nate considered being offended by his brother's utter amazement, but then decided it was truly incredible. "Nor can I."

"Wow."

"Yep."

"So, where are you going to take her?"

Nate frowned. He'd been wondering the very same thing for hours. He glanced at the clock on his office wall, and he only had three hours to decide.

Last night, Nate had been so startled when she announced to Aaron Peters that she already had a date with him—and then so thrilled—that he hadn't given any thought about where to take her. Before tonight, a date had been just a necessary evil before he got the woman he was interested in back to his place and into the sack. That was not the objective with Marty. Oh, he definitely wanted her in his bed, but he'd just be happy with a second date at this point.

"I have no idea where to take her," he finally said.

"Well, she's used to fancy, expensive stuff, I bet, being a model and all. You've got to take her someplace upscale. So Heady's is out."

Nate might not have had a clue about where to take a classy woman like Marty, but he was smart enough to realize Heady's, with the peanut shells on the floor and the stale smell of beer permanently steeped into the walls, was not class. The waterfront bar was the hangout of rough locals, not famous supermodels.

"How about someplace in Bar Harbor?"

Sam shook his head. "Everything is pretty much closed for the winter."

"The Millbrook Inn?"

"Yeah." Sam nodded. "I hear they have great food, and they have dancing."

That sounded like the place to Nate. They could have a nice meal, a few dances, and maybe he could charm her enough to get her to agree to another date.

He wanted to get to know Marty. He was intrigued by her. Intrigued by her mistrust of men. Intrigued that while she seemed to readily run from most men, she had stood up to him more than once. Even when he could tell it had been difficult for her. There was an audacity in Marty. She was strong, but yet, he didn't think she saw it.

Maybe he was so fascinated with her because he felt a bit the same way. Like there was someone inside of him that couldn't quite get out. And of course, there was the fact that she was beautiful, but he didn't want to just hop in bed with her. He wanted to understand her—and in some weird way, protect her.

Had he ever felt this way before?

"Yep," Sam said definitely and Nate blinked up at him, thinking he was answering that question for him—and with the wrong answer to boot. Then Sam continued, "I think the Millbrook Inn is the way to go."

Nate released a pent-up breath, relieved Sam couldn't read his mind. His little brother was annoying enough without being in his head. "Yes. I agree."

Sam stood up, running a hand down his legs to straighten the creases out of his uniform trousers. "Well, it sounds like you have a plan, then."

Nate nodded, hating the nervousness that still churned in his gut. He'd never been the nervous type. But then again, he'd never really cared. If something didn't work out, then he'd move on to the next thing. But he wanted this to work out.

Sam headed to the glass door that separated Nate's office from the other officers' cubicles. "Good luck," he said as he left, then he stuck his head back in the doorway and added, "Man, this really proves you're not gay. A supermodel. Damn."

Nate shook his head as Sam promptly closed the door behind him.

A few moments later, Sam stuck his head back inside the door. "Bring her flowers. I bet she expects that."

"Right," Nate said.

After the door swung shut again, Nate sat there for a minute. How did he get flowers? Did he call? Did he stop by the florist on the way to Marty's house? He'd never in his life gotten flowers for a woman.

Then he remembered Aaron Peters and Jake Sanborn. As soon as those two men had pushed Marty, she'd fled. Flowers might be too pushy. Maybe it was just better to stick with the dinner and dancing.

He got the distinct feeling the worst thing he could do was push Marty. Something had happened to make her wary of men. He had to play this right if he hoped to keep seeing her. If there was a date number two, then he'd figure out the whole flower thing.

Marty was just brushing on a coat of raspberry-colored lip gloss when she heard a knock at the back door. She checked her image in the compact one last time, snapped it shut, and threw both the mirror and the lip gloss back into her tote bag.

Her heart pounded erratically, the sound loud in her ears. She wasn't sure, but she thought she might have actually shushed it on the way to the door—as if her heart would listen to a verbal order better than a mental one.

All day she'd told herself this wasn't a big deal. It wasn't a real date. It was half reimbursement for not having to go out with Aaron Peters and half research.

She paused with her hand on the door handle. Again she reprimanded her pounding heart, this time silently. But the rebellious organ just didn't seem to believe her reimbursement/research reasoning. She took a deep breath and slowly blew it out. She took another one, and managed to get her skeptical heart calmed down.

That was, until she pulled open the door.

Nate stood on the back stoop, looking—wonderful. He had on a black wool dress coat, beige scarf, and tailored black trousers. His shaggy hair was tamed slightly, although wayward locks still fell over his forehead in rebellious waves. His lips were quirked into that crooked half smile that looked both sweet and sexy at the same time.

"Hi," he said. Then the half grin slowly unfurled to a full one.

It took her several seconds, or maybe minutes, she really wasn't sure, to realize he was smiling because she was just standing there, staring.

She blinked, then stepped back so he could enter the kitchen. "Hi. I'm sorry. Come in." She shut the door, and then without looking at him, went to the table and gathered up her cell phone and a few other items, adding them to her tote. Under the pretense of getting ready to go, of course.

When she did finally glance at him, he'd taken off the black overcoat. And if she thought he looked wonderful before . . . Wonderful didn't even begin to describe how he looked now.

He wore a dark blue dress shirt that fit his broad

shoulders perfectly and tapered down to hug his lean, muscular torso. The shirt was tucked into the waistband of his black pants, which emphasized the narrowness of his hips and the length of his legs. He looked like he'd walked straight out of a designer clothing ad. He was magnificent.

Breathe, she told herself, and tried to pry her gaze away from him. Her heart thumped wildly against her breastbone and she realized, belatedly, that she should have listened to it earlier. There was no way this date was going to be a simple way to figure out if he'd changed. Not with him looking like that.

But she forced herself to take a huge breath and chanted, *Stay focused. Stay calm,* over and over to herself.

Finally she said in a voice that sounded impressively composed, "I think I'm very underdressed."

"Well, maybe I'm overdressed," he said easily. "I thought we might go to the Millbrook Inn for dinner, but I'm up for whatever you want to do."

Marty hesitated. Part of her felt like she should offer to go change so they could go where he'd planned. But she knew she couldn't be with him in a romantic place like the Millbrook Inn.

She fully intended to keep this light and friendly. This wasn't a real date. It was research. To see if she honestly believed Nate had changed, and if so, how he did it. She had to keep telling herself that. She had to stay focused.

"The inn sounds lovely, but I'm more in the mood for something less formal." She tugged at the hem of her sweater. "Obviously." She laughed. The sound wasn't as self-possessed as she'd hoped, but rather brittle—and almost desperate.

He didn't argue, but she did think she saw a flicker of disappointment in his eyes.

Again, she fought the urge to dash upstairs and change. No! She couldn't get into a situation where either of them thought this was a serious date.

She did plan to have fun with him. Against her better judgment, she had to admit she enjoyed his company. But no romantic thoughts or feelings. None!

"Where would you normally take a girl?" she asked, then bit her tongue. She had a pretty good idea where the old Nate took his dates. An image of a bed and tangled sheets flashed through her mind.

Stay focused.

She centered on his face.

He didn't seem to be having the same lascivious thought. His eyes were narrowed and he appeared to be pondering the question. Then he said, somewhat sheepishly, "I haven't really been out much since I was injured."

"Where did you go before?"

He laughed humorlessly. "Oh, you really don't want to go there."

She perked up, forgetting for a moment that he was drop-dead gorgeous and that she absolutely could not be attracted to him. Why wouldn't he want to take her to his old haunt? Well, it was easy to convince a few select people that he'd changed, but he couldn't convince everyone, could he? Maybe his close friends knew that he hadn't really changed.

"Oh, come on," she cajoled. "Let's go there. I'd love to see it."

Nate gave her a look that stated quite eloquently that she was nuts, but then after a few seconds said, "Okay, if you really want to. But I think I should warn you—now we're both overdressed."

Chapter 9

Nate continued to tell himself that he should have just refused to bring Marty here as he pulled his cruiser into the parking lot of Heady's.

The old, wooden building teetered right on the edge of the waterfront. It literally looked as though a precise gust of wind and a slight shove would topple the whole place right into the cold, greenish water of Fiddlehead Bay.

Nate turned off the engine and stared at the dilapidated building. The roof was missing shingles, and it sagged in the middle. The windows were dingy and paint was chipped from the frames. A backlit sign that read Heady's in red lettering with black outlining hung over the doorway. It had a jagged break in the glass where one of the regulars—either Eric Dunton or Barry Roy—had thrown a beer bottle at the sign when Carl Hoyt, the owner, kicked them out for being drunk and disorderly. And it took a lot to get kicked out of Heady's.

This bar was so far from classy that Nate would be willing to bet it belonged on its own continent.

He glanced at Marty. She stared at the building, her eyes wide and uncertain.

"Are you sure you really want to go here? There's a great seafood restaurant just down—"

"No," Marty said abruptly, then offered him a tenuous smile. "I want to go here. It looks . . . interesting."

She could say that again. But instead of arguing that neither of them really seemed to want to be here, he just unlatched his door and stepped out of the car. He came around to her side to open the door for her, but she was already getting out.

She still eyed the building with obvious qualms.

He didn't have the heart to tell her the outside was the nice part.

As they approached the entrance, the front door swung open and two drunken men, arm in arm, staggered out, singing at the top of their lungs. One of them almost stumbled into Marty but caught himself and then gave her a wide grin, which revealed a few missing teeth. He winked and started singing again.

"Would you believe those two were the most refined of the people who come here?" Nate asked.

Marty gave him a disbelieving look.

"They aren't," he assured her, "but they're close."

Nate pushed open the door, and the stink of stale beer, cigarette smoke, and other things he didn't want to think about assaulted them. Despite the stench, the place was packed.

Loud music played on a jukebox and some of the patrons danced on a tiny raised platform at the back of the room. A dozen or so booths lined two of the walls, and a rectangular bar took up the center of the room. Patrons were seated all the way around it, while two bartenders, both female, rushed around filling people's drinks.

Nate started into the crowded room and was surprised when Marty slipped her hand into his. Her fingers felt long and slender and clasped his as though he were her lifeline.

Nate wove through the people, nodding at a few patrons he knew. Relief washed over him as he located an empty table near the makeshift dance floor. At least they could get a little privacy seated in a booth. Of course, it was far from cozy, as they were so close to the music they would have to practically shout at each other to talk.

He waited for Marty to slide in on one side, and then sat down across from her. The remnants of peanut shells and wet rings from beer glasses dotted the tabletop. So they both sat with their hands in their laps, waiting for one of the waitstaff to appear and wipe the table down.

"Are you really sure you want to be here?" he asked again.

She nodded. "It's fine. I really like this song."

Nate didn't recognize the song, but he did recognize that closed-mouth, polite smile she'd just given him. And he hated it. It meant she felt uncomfortable.

"Oh my God!" a loud, abrasive voice shouted, and Nate turned to see Wanda Blanchard approaching the table. Her bleached blond hair and heavily made-up face looked exactly the same as it had the last time he'd seen her, nearly six months ago.

Wanda carried six bottles of beer, three balanced in each hand. "Don't you move one of those cute little butt cheeks," she warned Nate as she passed. "I need to serve these, and I will be right back."

Nate agreed, although his first instinct was to grab Marty's hand and run. What was he doing back here, much less bringing Marty with him?

"I take it you know her," Marty said, leaning out of

the booth slightly to watch Wanda totter off on her spiked heels.

"Yeah. She's waited tables here for a couple years."

Marty nodded, although she didn't quite look like she believed that he only knew Wanda in the context of a waitress.

"Oh my God," Wanda said again when she returned, slipping into the booth seat next to him. "Look at you." She immediately touched his longer hair. "Look at you!" She laughed, loud and piercing, like he imagined a dog whistle might sound. Had she always laughed like that?

"Your hair!" Wanda exclaimed, again running her fingers through it. Then her hand dropped to the front of his shirt. "And these clothes! You look like an actor or something. Or even—"

"A model," Marty supplied in a matter-of-fact tone.

"Yes!" Wanda said and smiled at Marty. Her smile promptly disappeared. Her lids lowered until her eyes actually disappeared and only thick, dark eyeliner and sparkly blue eye shadow seemed to remain.

The blonde turned back to Nate. "So is this what's been keeping you so busy?"

"No," Marty assured Wanda before he could answer. "We're just friends."

Wanda's eyes seemed to magically reappear, although Nate noticed she still looked a little skeptical. "Oh. How do you know each other?"

"We went to school together," Marty said matter-of-factly, and Nate studied her, trying to figure out what that dry tone meant.

"Yeah? I went to school in Palmyra. You know Palmyra?"

Marty nodded.

"Listen," Wanda said, facing him directly, so there was no doubt that she was only talking to him. "I got to get out a couple more rounds. But then I've got a break. You need to tell me why you haven't been coming around. And you need to dance with me. I miss your dancing, baby. And in these clothes—the women will be crazy."

She touched his cheek, and he jerked away. Wanda didn't seem to notice She turned back to Marty. "You ever danced with him?"

"I have, actually."

Nate frowned at Marty. When had he ever danced with her?

"He's got some sweet moves—on and off the dance floor." She winked at Marty, and Marty, surprisingly, winked back.

"Okay," Wanda said as she got up from the seat, using the table to balance herself back onto her insanely high heels. "Don't go anywhere."

Nate nodded, just wishing she would leave. And then, hopefully, he and Marty could leave.

"Why haven't you been here since your—attack?" Marty asked as soon as Wanda wobbled back to the bar.

So she knew what had happened to him. He figured her sisters would tell her, which didn't bother him. He just wished he could tell her the whole story.

"I just . . . haven't." He shook his head, trying to find a way to explain what had happened to him without having to say the extent of the whole experience. "The accident changed me. And I don't seem to relate to the same things I once did."

"Like women with bottle-blond hair and make-up from the seventies." Marty immediately bit her lip, looking very contrite. "I'm sorry. That was rude. She is your friend."

"That's the thing. She was my friend, but now, I feel like I barely know her." He sighed, frustrated. Frustrated that he couldn't tell Marty what happened. Frustrated that he didn't completely understand it himself. Even frustrated that he couldn't just go back to the way he used to be. In some ways, it would be so much easier. "I—I sometimes feel guilty about the way I feel, because I don't want someone like Wanda to think I dislike her now or something. She is a very nice person. I . . ." Again, he struggled for the right words. "I just wasn't—always very nice."

Marty watched him, her eyes locked with his, intense as she seemed to absorb his words. "It's about changing yourself for the better. About you being someone different."

A sense of relief flooded him. She understood. "Exactly. Unfortunately, a lot of the people I considered friends were not much nicer than I was, so I've sort of cut myself off from them."

"I can understand that."

Relief rushed through him.

Wanda appeared back at their table and placed a beer in front of him and a glass of pink wine in front of Marty. "I know what Nathaniel drinks, but I had to guess on yours. You look like a blush kinda gal to me."

Marty took a sip of the wine and only made a hint of a face at the taste. "Perfect," she assured Wanda.

Nate watched Wanda head across the room to deliver more drinks. "Let's just finish these and get out of here,"

Marty pouted, her full lips perfect for such a ploy, and Nate fought the desire to lean over the grungy table and test their rosy fullness.

"I wanted to see your dance moves with Wanda," she told him.

"Speaking of which," he said, the mention of dancing reminding him that he still couldn't recall when they had ever danced together, "when did we—"

"Holy shit!"

Marty yelped as a solid weight literally slid her across the booth seat and trapped her against the wall.

When she recovered her balance and her breath, she saw that Nate was in much the same position on the other side of the table. Except the guy on the other side of the table clamped a wiry arm around Nate's neck and began to grind his bony knuckles on the top of his head. His pleased smile revealed crooked teeth, which matched his sparse, uneven mustache.

Marty cast a wary look at the large guy beside her. God, she hoped he didn't decide to do that to her. The huge guy just watched the antics on the other side of the table with no discernable emotion.

"You old dog, you! I didn't think we'd ever see you around these parts again," the man gripping Nate yelled as he rubbed. The hair that Nate had tried to tame stuck out every which way.

Nate, who was actually much bigger than his crazed buddy, easily shook off the other man. Then he said in a subdued voice, as if he hadn't just been mauled, "Hey, Kenny."

"'Hey, Kenny'?" Kenny nudged Nate with his shoulder. "'Hey, Kenny'? Can you believe this guy?" he asked both Marty and the man beside her.

She shook her head automatically.

"He's acting like he just saw us last week." Kenny shook his head. "When's the last time you saw him, Jared?"

Marty looked back to the barrel-chested man beside

her. Was this Jared Nye? He had a square jaw visible under his tightly trimmed goatee, thin lips, and a bald head. She remembered Jared as a skinny teenager with a mullet and not even the first signs of facial hair. But as she studied his profile, she saw the stoniness of his eyes and the deep grooves on either side of his mouth.

She remembered Josie Nye had that same harsh look. If this was Jared Nye, the Nye family trait seemed to be living fast and living hard.

He said to Nate in a deep voice devoid of any emotion, "I haven't seen him for a while."

"So, what? You avoiding us?" Kenny asked.

Marty watched Nate's reaction. There was absolutely no missing the guilt in Nate's eyes. "I've been busy—trying to get things caught up at work. And I also have physical therapy three times a week."

Kenny listened, a genuine look of concern on his face. "Have you gotten any leads on who attacked you?"

Nate shook his head and took a sip of his beer.

Marty frowned. "But you are looking, right?"

Jared shifted in the seat, his knee bumping hers under the table.

Then Marty realized that three pairs of eyes were on her as if the men all just realized she was there.

Kenny was the first to react, immediately hopping up as much as the booth would allow and extending a hand to her. "Kenny Boroughs. Pleased to meet ya."

Marty accepted his hand. His fingers were rough and even from a distance smelled like gasoline and motor oil. "Marty Stepp."

"You're that model, ain't ya?"

When Marty nodded, Kenny let out a low whistle and gave Nate an approving look. "So she's what's keeping you away." He grinned back at her. "Can't say I blame ya."

Nate gave Marty a pained look that wordlessly apologized for Kenny's comment.

Marty smiled reassuringly. Kenny didn't bother her. It was the silent hulk beside her who was making her uneasy.

For whatever reason, Jared Nye made her exceedingly uncomfortable—and it wasn't just his size. Maybe it was her memories of him in high school. Or maybe it was how he kept slanting sidelong glances at her. Glances that while only brief seemed to strip her bare.

She focused her attention on Nate. He was visibly uncomfortable too, fidgeting with his beer bottle, his eyes occasionally straying to the exit.

Again, she was struck by the same feeling she'd had at the coffee shop, when he'd looked so out of place in his police uniform. His clothes tonight suited him impeccably. But this place, a place where he had once been a regular, seemed completely unnatural. If she hadn't known the old Nate, she'd never have believed that he ever hung out here.

She had disliked Nate when she'd first seen him again. She'd been angry at him. Distrustful of him. But he'd never given her the creepy vibe that Jared did. Jared made her feel downright nervous.

Unfortunately, Jared picked that moment to shift in the seat, his leg now pressing fully against hers. "Marty Stepp," his voice rumbled, and even if the sound wasn't really menacing, it sure seemed that way to her. "I wouldn't recognize you now."

She looked up at him, forcing herself to look directly into his cold eyes. "I wouldn't have recognized you either."

He smiled, and Marty saw that he had straight, white teeth. She remembered he'd had braces in high school.

Almost as if it were in slow motion, he reached forward and tugged one of the messy locks of her hair. "You look good with short hair. Not many women do."

Nate cleared his throat. "You know, we have to go," he said coolly, and Marty got the impression that he didn't like Jared touching her. Maybe almost as much as she didn't like it. "I promised Marty a nice dinner."

Jared dropped his hand and placed it on the table. His fingers were huge, like thick sausages, and his knuckles were riddled with faint white scars. They looked like hands that had been used to inflict lots of pain.

Marty shuddered.

Nate took out his wallet and started to throw some money on the table when that beefy hand reached across and stopped him.

"Let me pay," Jared said. "Since this is the first time you've been back here."

Nate hesitated, then put his wallet away. "Thanks."

Jared nodded, his thin lips curving into a smile that looked more like a sneer. "What are old friends for?"

Marty looked back and forth between the two men, trying to figure out if there was an undercurrent to their words. Or if she was just perceiving something that wasn't really there.

To her relief, Jared slid out of the seat, releasing her from her tight corner.

Kenny was still jabbering on about this and that as he stood to let Nate out. But Nate appeared to be only half listening; he was watching her, worry creasing his brow.

Without hesitation, she hurried away from Jared to stand close to Nate. She slipped her hand into his, and he squeezed her fingers reassuringly.

"It was real nice to meet you," Kenny said with a friendly grin, and Marty smiled back. She did think Kenny was a genuinely nice guy.

Jared sat back down and eyed their linked hands for a moment. Then he said, and there was no mistaking the undertone this time, "Yes, it was very nice to see you again, Marty. Maybe I'll see you around."

Marty restrained the urge to tell him she hoped she never saw him again. Instead she smiled, if she could call it that. It was more a pained curl of her lips.

"Okay, see you all later," Nate told the men, and quickly led her back through the crowd to the door.

Once outside, Marty took a deep breath. The faintly fishy smell of the waterfront suddenly seemed so clean and fresh.

Then she looked over at Nate, and he appeared as shaken as she did.

"I'm sorry I made you come here," she said, and she sincerely meant it. Now her plan to test him seemed really stupid. His friends did certainly verify that Nate had changed, but the whole incident had been uncomfortable for both of them. Nate didn't deserve that.

"That's okay," he said as he unlocked his cruiser. "Although I think I should get to pick where we're going next." He still looked a bit shaken.

Marty forced a smile at him; she was such a schmuck. Then his words sank in—*where we're going next*. And for some reason that she didn't want to question too closely, she felt relieved that things didn't have to end here, on this poor note.

"Deal."

Chapter 10

The tenseness had already started to seep out of Marty's limbs as Nate pulled the cruiser out of the bar's parking lot. She never in a million years imagined that she would be relieved to be alone with Nate Peck. Much less that she would feel safe.

She thought of Jared. She instinctively knew that he was the "not nice" friend whom Nate was trying to avoid.

She shot a sidelong glance at Nate. She knew that Nate and Jared used to be inseparable, but now she couldn't see it.

"Do I have a peanut shell on my face?"

Nate's question startled her. Then she blushed, realizing that he'd caught her staring. "No," she said quickly, facing forward. After a few moments she asked in a falsely composed voice, "So where are we off to?"

"I thought I'd take you to that seafood place down the road. Does that sound okay?"

"It sounds great."

Nate smiled over at her, his grin incredibly handsome.

You're not getting involved, she told herself. *You're just having fun.*

Just then the police radio on his dashboard crackled to life, red lights blinking. "Hey, Nate, you there?"

Nate frowned at the machine, but he picked up the handset. "What is it, Sam?"

"Can you come over to Frank Moody's? He's been robbed again."

Marty saw a quick flash of the muscle in Nate's jaw, then he pressed the button on his mouthpiece and said, "Sam, can't you just write up a report and tell him I'll stop by tomorrow?"

"I know it's your night off." Sam's voice sounded tinny, but even over the radio, Marty could make out the supplication in his voice. The line went dead for a moment, then Sam added, "Frank is really insistent about seeing you."

Nate held the receiver for a moment, sighed, and then said, resigned, "I'll be there in a few minutes."

He hung up the mouthpiece and glanced at Marty. "Sorry about that—Frank Moody is a determined old guy, and if he gets it in his head he wants to see me, well, he won't let it go. He'll keep Sam there all night."

"That's okay," Marty said. "Was that Sam as in your little brother, Sam?"

"Yeah, it was," he said with a slight nod. He sounded disappointed, but she didn't think his response had anything to do with his brother. Then he said, "I'll run you over to your house first."

Marty suddenly understood his disappointment. She didn't want the date to end either. "Is it okay for me to go with you? I mean, I won't compromise the case or something by being there?"

Nate chuckled. "No, you absolutely will not compromise this case."

"Then I'll go."

Nate looked over at her, giving her a heart-melting grin. "Good."

A few minutes later, Nate pulled his car up to the front of an outdoor skating rink set up on the edge of the town park. Trees decorated with multicolored Christmas lights lined the rink's edge, and Christmas music was being piped out of a small trailer at the entrance. Kids and parents skated around on the blade-marked ice. The trailer was open on the side like an ice-cream truck and offered skate rentals and an assortment of hot treats.

Sam, or at least Marty assumed it was Sam, stood beside a stooped-over man with a head of thick, white hair and ruddy cheeks. The man waved his arms and appeared to be shouting.

As they approached, the elderly man rushed up to Nate with surprising agility. "They did it again!" he shouted. "They stole it again."

"Okay, Frank," Nate said soothingly, "calm down."

"Those little bastards did it again."

"Frank," Nate warned, jerking his head toward the skaters.

"The bastards are probably out there on the ice right this minute," Frank hissed, although he did lower his voice considerably. "You got to do something."

"Frank," Nate said, keeping his voice quiet, "I told you before, this is just the prank of some kids, and I don't want them to get in any real trouble, do you?"

Frank thought about it, then shook his head, although he still looked as if he'd like to see them swing from his highest signpost.

"The thing is, Frank, the kids are going to keep stealing your sign as long as you insist on putting out the same one."

"It ain't the *same* one," Frank said, his voice gaining

volume again. "I got to make a new one every time them little bas—them kids steal it."

Nate nodded as if he were quite sympathetic to Frank's ongoing war, but Marty noticed a hint of a smile tugged at his lips. "What if you just reword your sign, as I suggested the last time this happened?"

Frank was already shaking his head before Nate even finished the suggestion. "That sign gets people in here to my Santa." He pointed at a rather bedraggled Santa Claus seated in what looked like a white resin lawn chair at the end of the rink. An equally scruffy mechanical reindeer bobbed its head up and down. A hand-painted sign reading "$5 a photo" was propped against his legs. "That Santa makes me a pretty penny during the Christmas season. Who's gonna know he's here if there ain't no sign?"

Marty suspected all of Millbrook and the surrounding area already knew about Frank's lawn-chair Santa.

"I do understand that, Frank, but I'm sure another sign could get the people in too." Nate still remained very calm.

Frank actually seemed to consider Nate's suggestion. Then he said dubiously, "I don't know, it's a catchy sign."

"It is," Nate agreed, "but I think you're going to keep having the same problem until you change it."

Marty noticed Sam had joined them, standing behind Frank. He rocked back and forth on his heels and looked as if he was biting back laughter.

"I just don't get what is so damned interesting to them bas—kids about that sign." Frank scratched his head, his gnarled fingers disappearing into his white mane.

Nate nodded sympathetically.

Sam did laugh, although he managed to hide the chuckle behind a loud, somewhat strangled cough.

"So, everything is okay?" Nate asked as he shot his brother a warning look.

"I reckon," Frank said, but he looked more than a little dissatisfied. "I better get back to work." He headed back to the trailer, then he stopped and said crankily, "I sure as hell liked it better when you was a hard-ass." He nodded, indicating he'd said his piece, and disappeared into the trailer.

Sam let out the laughter that he had mostly managed to keep inside throughout their talk.

"Be nice," Nate warned.

"I'm trying," Sam said, wiping a hand over his face like he could wipe away his amusement.

"Marty, this big idiot is my brother," Nate said. "Sam, this is Marty."

Sam did manage to get his laughter under control and smiled at her, extending his hand.

As Marty accepted it, she noticed that Sam looked a lot like his older brother, although he was a couple of inches shorter and his smile didn't have nearly the same effect on her pulse as Nate's.

"Did I end up interrupting your dinner?" Sam asked.

"No," Marty said. "We were just on our way, actually."

"Really?" He gave Nate a questioning look.

"We went to Heady's," Nate admitted.

Sam groaned and shook his head like Nate had failed him in some way.

"It was my idea," Marty said abruptly, feeling the need to defend Nate. "Not one of my best."

"Yeah," Sam readily agreed and opened his mouth like he was about to add to that comment when his walkie-talkie buzzed on his belt. He answered it, made a few comments, and then returned it to his belt. "Speaking of Heady's, there seems to be a fight going on there. Gotta go."

"Be careful," Nate called after his brother as Sam jogged to his cruiser.

They watched Sam leave the parking area, hitting the main street before he flipped on his siren.

"Will he be okay?" she asked.

"Sure. He has two other officers for backup."

Marty nodded, but suddenly the realization that Nate was a cop hit her. Even in a small town, the job could be dangerous.

Her eyes found the scar, only half visible, curving with the contour of his cheekbone, the other half hidden under his unruly hair.

His career choice was hardly her concern. Maybe if he were her boyfriend—or her husband . . .

What are you thinking? Are you a complete nut? Thoughts like that were pointless and not what she wanted anyway. She needed to get a grip!

She stopped staring at the line marring his cheek and wandered over to the edge of the rink to watch the skaters.

Burl Ives sang "Holly Jolly Christmas," and she had to smile as a little girl in a Santa cap did shaky spins to the music.

Nate came up beside her, smiling at the same little girl. After a few moments, he asked, "Are you ready to give dinner another try?"

Suddenly a quiet dinner seemed too private, too intimate. And as much as she'd have liked to say she had control of her attraction to him, she couldn't. Christmas music, people, a lawn-chair Santa, and a ratty reindeer suddenly seemed a lot safer than a restuarant.

"Let's stay here. Let's skate."

Nate glanced back out at the busy rink. "I don't know. I haven't skated in a good ten or fifteen years, and even then it was hockey skates."

"I've only skated once in my life. Let's try. If it's too hard, then we'll just drink cocoa and watch."

Maybe he heard the desperate edge to her voice, or maybe he was just being nice, but he said, "Okay. What size do you take?"

It took her a second to realize he was referring to skate sizes. "Ten," she admitted with embarrassment.

"Tiny. I'm a thirteen." He started toward the trailer, his gait uneven and a tad slow.

Her gaze dropped to his leg. How had she forgotten? "Nate." She chased after him, placing a hand on his arm to stop him. "I forgot about—about your knee."

He looked down at it as if he'd forgotten, too. "I'll be careful. And lean on you a lot."

She started to say no when she saw the resolute glint in his amber eyes. "Okay," she agreed, still a little tentative.

He grinned at her and headed off to the trailer like this had been his idea to begin with.

Marty walked over to a bench and sat down. It was a beautiful night. The sky was clear, a sharp purple-black color dotted with pinpoints of light. The air held a sharp chill, but it wasn't unbearable and there was not even a hint of a breeze.

She could so easily get used to living back here.

"The last pair of tens," Nate said, sitting down beside her and handing her a pair of battered white skates. His skates were black and slung over his shoulder so he could also carry a cardboard tray with two steaming Styrofoam cups, four foil wrapped hot dogs, and tons of condiment packets.

"I'm starving," he admitted.

"Me too." Marty laughed.

He peeled open the end of one of the hot dogs, checked it, and then handed it to her. "That's yours."

She frowned. "Are they different?"

"Mine are just rolls," he told her slowly.

"Just rolls?"

"I'm a vegetarian." He said the word like he expected her to throw her skates at him and run.

She didn't have that reaction, but she did have to admit she was rather surprised. "I'd never picture you as a veggie."

He nodded. "Yeah, well, I didn't used to be. I used to be a die-hard carnivore. But this seems to be another side effect of my injuries."

"Oh."

"Crazy, isn't it."

"Nah," she assured him, "I once knew a model who only ate things that were white, because her guru told her that was her nutritional color. She had colors for everything. She never wore anything but yellow; that was her personal color. Unless of course she had a fashion shoot—she would wear other colors for those. But then right back to the yellow. See, that's much stranger."

He nodded, but she got the odd feeling he still considered his vegetarianism stranger. But after a few moments, he asked, "Did she eat marshmallows? Because those aren't nutritious at all."

Marty laughed. "Probably."

"Well, she could eat my hot dog rolls."

She lifted an eyebrow, eyeing with distaste the meal he was making. "Not with all that ketchup, mustard, and relish on it."

He took a big bite of his condiment sandwich. He chewed and swallowed with a grimace. "Yeah, not my best vegetarian creation. But ole Frank didn't have much to work with."

"Speaking of Frank, why do kids keep stealing his signs?"

Amusement danced in his eyes like fire in a glass of bourbon. "He insists on putting out these hand-painted signs that say, 'Moody's is the place to go—for the best Ho Ho Ho.'"

She coughed, nearly choking on her hot dog. He gently thumped her back until she caught her breath and managed to utter, "He's right; that is catchy."

Nate nodded in full agreement. "Can you really blame the kids?"

"No. I really can't."

Nate watched Marty as she contentedly ate her hot dog and sipped her hot chocolate. She occasionally smiled over at him about one of the skater's antics. And not the closed-lip, polite ones that actually meant she was miserable; these were the real ones. The ones that made her face glow and stole his breath away.

He'd really believed that tonight was a wash. After Heady's and especially after the encounter with Jared, he'd figured that Marty would leave the bar and demand to go home. He couldn't believe it when she asked to come with him after Sam's call. If there had been a perfect out, the police call had been it.

She popped the last bite of hot dog in her mouth, then brushed the crumbs off her jeans.

He noticed her fingers were as long and slender as they'd felt in his hand. Beautiful, elegant hands.

"Okay," she smiled, "ready to do this?"

He nodded. He could feel her smile to the soles of his feet. It took him a full thirty seconds to stop watching her and struggle with his own skates.

Marty finished first, standing up on the worn artificial turf that surrounded the seating area. She wobbled slightly, then got her balance. She grinned down at him proudly. "This isn't bad—after all, I've made my living off teetering around in high heels all day."

He joined her, also unsteady for a moment. "But did you slide around on your high heels?"

She considered that. "Occasionally, but only by accident."

He offered her his hand, and noticed her fingers were frozen. "Do you have gloves? Your fingers are like ice."

She released his hand to dig around in the pocket of her suede jacket, which he noted was at least lined with shaggy, faux fur. She materialized the pair of rainbow-colored mittens that he remembered from the grocery store. She slipped them on and took his hand again.

He was glad her fingers would be warm, but he missed the feeling of her skin, even cold, against his.

"Okay," she breathed. "I'm ready."

They teetered to the edge of the ice, and both hesitantly stepped onto the cloudy blue-white surface.

Slowly, they began to move, more in awkward, slippery steps than actual gliding.

About halfway around the rink, the feeling of the ice and how to control the skates came back to Nate.

He began to move smoothly, or as smoothly as he could with Marty clinging to him—which was much, much nicer than skating anyway.

"No fair," she said as she half slipped and half skittered to a stop. She released his hand and glared at him, hands on her hips. "You're good at this."

He laughed, then showed off just a bit by skating a circle around her. "I'm sorry. It just suddenly came back to me."

She pouted, but her dark eyes twinkled. "Well, this is no fun. We were supposed to be bad at this together."

He skated a few feet away and held out his hands. "You can do this."

She eyed him dubiously. "This *is* harder than high heels."

"Oh, come on," he coaxed. "I'll catch you."

She hesitated, but then pushed off and slid toward him. Just as she reached him and his arms curled around her waist to steady her, his knee gave out. And with a shocked squeal from Marty, they both toppled to the ice.

They lay there for a fraction of a second, dazed. Then Marty, sprawled on top of him, began to giggle, the sound not silly and girlish, but rich and infectious.

He grinned up at her. "Are you all right?"

"I'm fine," she said breathlessly. "You make a pretty good cushion."

He raised an eyebrow at that. Parts of him were certainly not staying soft. But rather than inform her of that, he shifted slightly and said, "I wish I could say the same for the ice."

"Oh," she said, concern immediately dousing the merry glittering in her eyes. Much to his dismay, she promptly scrambled off him.

He sat up and braced a hand on the ground to lever himself to his feet. He gained his balance and then extended a hand to her.

She started to stand, her hand gripping his, when suddenly her feet slid back out from under her again and she landed on her back. This time he landed on top of her, his legs entwined with hers, his face level with her face.

She stared up at him, her eyes wide, and more breathless laugher escaped her luscious lips.

He couldn't seem to tear his gaze away from those lips. They looked so plump and rosy pink, and he imagined, despite the cold, she would taste like ripe, warm summer berries.

Suddenly, he realized her laughter and smiled had faded. His eyes moved up to hers. The deep chocolate brown of her irises seemed to become darker, almost a black, and for a split second, her gaze strayed to his mouth. Her lips parted, looking moist and inviting.

He started to lean forward just to test them, just to take a small taste. But just when he was just centimeters away, he stopped.

Then, as if he were pulling away from a powerful magnet, he slowly lifted his head and gradually rolled off her.

He lay there for a moment, letting the frigidness of the ice seep through to his skin and sober him. He wanted to groan out loud. He wanted to grab Marty and kiss her senseless, but he did neither. He just lay there, telling himself he was doing the right thing, no matter how maddening it was.

He couldn't rush Marty. He'd seen over and over again how she reacted to men who were pushy and forward. If he wanted a relationship with this woman, and God, he did, he had to let her set the pace.

Even if his entire body was telling him to take his *go slow* theory and shove it.

After one more deep breath, he sat up and leaned over Marty—from a safe distance.

"Are you okay?"

She nodded, her eyes dazed and her delectable lips still parted temptingly. She pushed up to a sitting position, and they just stared at each other for a moment.

Finally, he said, "Maybe we should just go back to watching from the sidelines."

Marty nodded. "Yeah, I think the sidelines are much safer."

And Nate had the feeling they were talking about more than just skating.

Chapter 11

Marty threw her small suitcase in the trunk of her car and then got in the driver's seat. She started the ignition and backed out onto the street.

As she drove, she fiddled with the radio, finally stopping on a station that was promising to play continuous Christmas music. Although it didn't, but rather went into a weather report, which predicted flurries for Santa's big trip tonight.

Then it returned to the Christmas music. She hummed along, glad to be out of her grandmother's house and headed to Ellie's. She would spend Christmas Eve with her family and hopefully be so busy with her niece and holiday stuff, she wouldn't have time to think about anything else.

The original plan of staying at the old house so she could have privacy and time to gather her thoughts was not working out as she'd envisioned. Now, she had too much quiet, too much time to think.

And was she thinking about her future? No. Was she thinking about whether she should retire from modeling? No. Was she figuring out what she could do if she wasn't a model?

Nope. Nope. Nope.

She was thinking about Nate Peck. That was it. That was all.

She spent hours rehashing all the events of their evening together—from his behavior at Heady's to the moment on the ice when she'd been certain he was going to kiss her. But he hadn't.

Why hadn't he?

She rolled her eyes, angry with herself for even thinking about this again. If he had been going to kiss her, she should just be thankful he didn't. What would have been the point? He might have thought she was interested in him, which she wasn't. He might have asked her out again, which he hadn't. And he might . . .

She sighed, feeling that familiar heaviness in her chest. He hadn't asked her out again. He hadn't called. Nothing. Okay, it had only been two days, if she counted today. And it *was* the two days before Christmas. But still.

"Argh," she growled, the sound blending in with the "Gloria" part of "Angels We Have Heard on High."

She wasn't going to do this. She did not want a relationship. Not with anyone, and certainly not with Nate Peck. So he was so different from the man she remembered. So they had laughed and talked and had fun. She couldn't trust him—because he was a man, plain and simple.

She pulled into Ellie's driveway, parking beside her sister's small SUV.

Nate was just another untrustworthy man, no different than Arturo or Rod.

She paused, her hand on her keys, which still

dangled from the ignition. Had she ever really laughed with Rod? No, not often. And they had never talked about much of anything outside of photography and modeling. Rod took himself very seriously. He wasn't much fun at all.

And Arturo . . . Well, he had been fun. They did talk about tons of things, and they laughed a lot. He was very silly, very outrageous. It was really just the man part he had issues with. Or rather he was fine with being a man, he just wished Marty were one, too.

She sighed and got out of the car. She used her keyless remote to pop the trunk and retrieved her suitcase.

She glanced up at Ellie's house and saw her sister with Emily in her arms. Ellie waved Emily's hand at Marty. Marty waved back and slammed the trunk closed.

She was going to have a nice, fun Christmas Eve. And she wasn't going to think about Nate anymore. After all, with her abominable taste in men, Nate Peck was probably certifiable. These days he just hid it well.

Nate sat in a brown plaid chair that had been there, in the exact same corner of his father's living room, for as long as he could remember. The Christmas tree, with its old-style, screw-in bulbs and bubble lights, glowed in its proper place in front of the window to the left of the television.

Nate put his feet up on the hassock that matched the plaid chair and took a sip of beer. He studied the whole room, from its dark wood paneling to its sort of gold and brown swirled shag carpet. Nothing had changed since the seventies. Actually, nothing, with the exception of a television replaced sometime in the nineties, had changed since September 13, 1981.

That was the day that Nate's mother had left them. She ran off with the apple man, a guy who came around selling fresh-picked apples in the fall.

Since he only came by once a year and lived somewhere outside of Fryeburg, it was hard to believe his mother had been able to strike up such a significant affair with the man. Significant enough to leave her husband and kids. But then, Daisy Peck had always been a free spirit.

After that, they received one postcard from her from Arizona with a picture of a cactus dressed up like a lady on the front. Skirt, hat, purse, the whole thing. Daisy had joined some sort of new-age commune there, and they were building things that looked like jungle gyms—her words—to communicate with aliens.

And there was never another word. Nate sometimes wondered if the jungle gyms worked.

He had been almost ten when his mother left. And even though he didn't know it at the time—and probably wouldn't have known it at all if he hadn't died on that operating table—she had been the main influence on how he'd felt about women.

He hadn't been good to the women he dated. He never did anything abusive, but he had certainly left a trail of bruised and broken hearts in his wake. And he'd never felt bad about it, because he didn't care. He wasn't invested in those women for anything outside of a good time. He'd never been in love with any of them.

Now, he wondered if maybe he didn't fall in love because he was afraid of ending up like his father—pining for someone he couldn't have.

But now that had changed. From the moment he had slipped on the ice and stared into Marty's bottomless, dark eyes, he knew he'd done more than just fall on her—he'd fallen *for* her too.

It hadn't been fireworks or bells or anything like that. It had been as simple as staring into her eyes and knowing this was someone he could so easily fall in love with. So easily.

The problem was he had no idea how to do that— how to be a real boyfriend. Especially when the woman he wanted didn't trust men and had told him, more than once, that she wasn't interested in a relationship.

And then there was the fact she could head back to New York any day. Leaving him.

"Hey, what are you doing in here, sitting in the dark?" His father stood in the doorway, silhouetted against the hall light.

"I'm just enjoying the Christmas lights."

His father nodded and then sat in his chair, a vinyl recliner with silver duct tape over cracks in the arms. "The tree turned out pretty this year, I think."

Nate nodded and took a sip of his beer.

They sat in silence for a few moments, then his father said, "So what are you really doing sitting in the dark?"

Nate smiled at his father's casual shrewdness. "Thinking."

His father nodded and took a drink of his own beer. It was several seconds before he asked, "Anything you care to share?"

Nate hesitated, then asked, "Do you ever regret marrying Mom?"

His father didn't answer right away, and Nate thought maybe he wasn't going to. They never talked about her.

"No. I don't."

"Even though she left?"

He shrugged. "I'd have been happier if she hadn't left, but what can you do?"

Nate cracked a slight smile. His ever-practical father.

"Why the question about your mother?"

Nate took another sip of beer. "Just curious."

More silence, except for the quiet hum of the television, the volume so low it was unintelligible.

"You know, if there is some girl you're interested in, you can't let your mother leaving affect that."

A half smile curved Nate's mouth. When had his old man become so insightful?

"Mom isn't affecting how I feel about her. But I don't know how to handle the situation. I haven't had any women in my life that I really thought I could care about."

"I 'magine that's partly my fault. I didn't provide much in the way of female influence for you boys. Couldn't really face another relationship after losing Daisy."

Nate knew it had been hard for his father, raising two kids on his own. Especially a difficult kid like he'd been. But it also must have been very lonely for his dad.

"You shouldn't be giving me the pep talk, Dad. I should be giving it to you."

His father chuckled. "Ayuh, I reckon you should. Maybe we should just both go for it."

The clock on the shelf over the television read a few minutes after eight. Marty was probably over at Mason and Ellie's with her family, getting her little niece excited for Santa's visit tonight.

He finished off the last of his beer and stood up. "You don't mind if I take off for a little while, do you?"

His dad shook his head. "Nope, I was planning to go next door to Widow Haynes's anyway. She invites me over every year for a piece of her mincemeat pie and a cup of eggnog, and I never go. This year I decided maybe I'll take her up on it."

Nate nodded, happy for his father. Maybe they were both changing. "Well, have fun."

His dad winked. "You too, son. You too."

Marty was just heading back into the living room, where her sisters and her brothers-in-law were lounging around the fire, playing with Emily, when there was loud knock at the door.

"I'll get it," she called to the others.

When she opened the door, her first thought was that the weather report had been right. Then her second thought was that snow flurries had never, never looked so amazing.

Nate stood on the porch, snowflakes clinging to his hair and his broad shoulders, melting on his long lashes.

"Merry Christmas," he said with a grin.

She blinked. "Hi." The word was barely a hoarse whisper. "Hi," she said again, this time more determinedly—not like some besotted ninny who had been dying to see him for nearly two days.

"I hope I'm not interrupting anything."

"No, nothing important." *Just the blood flow to my brain.* "We're just hanging out, talking. Come in."

Nate had just stepped into the foyer and had taken off his coat when Emily galloped around the corner. Her gait was sort of sideways and out of control, not helped by the slipper feet in her red Christmas sleeper, but she managed to stumble to a stop when she saw him. Her neck craned as she stared up at him with wide, round eyes.

Then to Marty's amazement, Emily held her arms out. "Up," she demanded.

Nate chuckled and scooped her up. She settled into his arms, looking like a baby doll against his large frame.

"Unreal," Marty complained. "I have to bribe that kid to let me hold her."

Emily touched his nose with a chubby little finger. "Nozzz," she announced.

"Man, and she even does tricks for you." Marty grimaced at him and tried not to think about how adorable he looked holding a child.

"What can I say—I've got a way with the ladies," he boasted, but then had to cringe as Emily threatened to poke out his eye.

"Eyzzz," she proclaimed proudly.

"Hey, Nate," Mason said, coming out into the foyer. "Good to see you. I see Emily already found you. Come on in."

Nate graciously agreed and chatted with his friend as they joined the others.

Marty followed.

Nate greeted everyone and then settled on the floor in front of the screened fireplace. The little girl left him to go over and lie down next to Chester, Chase and Abby's sweet-natured golden retriever. Marty sat in a chair opposite him.

"Are you spending the night over at your dad's?" Chase asked Nate.

"Yeah," Nate said, stretching his long legs out in front of him, resting back on his elbows.

After that Marty kind of lost track of what everyone was talking about. All she could focus on was the way the fabric of his jeans encased his legs, showing every sinewy muscle. And how the way he was leaning back pulled his black turtleneck sweater tight against his well-developed chest and flat stomach.

A hand tapped her shoulder, and she jumped. She frowned up at Ellie, who was holding Emily.

"Sorry," her sister said with a shrewd little smile and cast a quick glance at Nate, who didn't notice because he was chatting with Chase. "I didn't mean to interrupt, but we're taking Emily up to bed. I thought you might want to kiss her good night."

Marty noticed Mason over her sister's shoulder; he also sported a knowing smile.

Marty stopped glowering at them both to smile at her niece. "Can I get a kiss?"

The baby leaned forward to offer her cheek like some European royal, which Marty did kiss, but then she grabbed the toddler and tickled her until she giggled gleefully.

This time Emily gave her a tight hug before going back to Mommy's arms.

When Marty turned back to the conversation, she saw that Nate was watching her. His eyes seemed to glow in the firelight. Their gaze held for a moment, and then he smiled.

Her heart did a somersault in her chest.

"Well," Abby said loudly, effectively ending the moment. "I think maybe we should head home."

Chase gave her a confused look.

Abby not so subtly jerked her head in the direction of Nate and Marty.

Understanding dawned on Chase's handsome face. "Yeah, yeah, we should go. Before the roads get too slick or my wife falls asleep."

Abby stuck out her tongue at him.

Nate sat up. "Yeah, maybe I should head home, too."

"No," Abby said quickly, then she added in a more leisurely way, "There is no need for you to rush off just because I'm an old pregnant lady who has to be put to bed by ten. Stay, keep Marty company."

"Do you want company?" Nate asked Marty.

Marty glanced at Abby and Chase, who appeared to be eagerly awaiting her response. "Sure," she said slowly. "Why not."

Nate leaned back on his elbows. He appeared as pleased as everyone else.

"Okay," Abby said. "See you tomorrow morning. No need to walk us out."

Abby and Chase disappeared.

"Do you feel like there have been bets placed?" Marty asked, not bothering to even try to act like nothing odd had just happened.

"Maybe a little. Do you want me to leave?"

She shook her head no. She didn't want him to leave at all. But it was hard to act relaxed now when she felt like she had 5-to-1 odds placed on her.

"Want to go for a walk?" he suggested.

That sounded great. She felt warm and flustered. Cold air and snow seemed like just the thing to clear her head.

Plus, he'd put on a coat, she thought as she watched the muscles in his shoulders ripple as he levered himself up.

The night was very quiet as they walked out onto the porch. Snow drifted to the ground through the air, unhurried, peaceful.

"Wow, it's so dark," Marty said, as she stepped off the porch and started down the driveway. The old snow crunched under their feet, and their breath puffed out in front of them.

"I forget how dark it gets here," she said, looking up at the sky, snow clinging to her cheeks. "It's never dark in Manhattan. Unless, of course, you're about to be mugged. Muggers can always find the only dark places."

"Have you been mugged?" he asked sharply.

"Only once, and it was rather uneventful. He asked for my purse, which I gave to him. But I didn't have my wallet in it, only some cash and my apartment keys. Then he asked for my shoes, which I also gave him. They were from a fashion show I'd done that night, and they were hideous and horribly uncomfortable. I was rather glad to be rid of them."

"Your shoes?"

Marty nodded. "I guess they looked expensive. Or he had a foot fetish."

Nate smiled slightly, but there was an unsettled look in his eyes. "You did change the locks at your apartment, didn't you?"

"I did," she assured him.

"So you really like New York, huh?"

She thought about the question, really thought about it. "I loved it when I first moved there. It was so different than Millbrook. It was exciting and fast paced—and I liked being anonymous. But now . . . I guess I still like it. But then there are nights like this. Quiet and tranquil, if not a little cold." She shivered.

His pace slowed. "Do you want to go back?"

"Just up to that next light." She pointed, not wanting to give up and head back. The snow felt magical.

"Okay."

They were silent for a few moments.

"I actually think I'd like to move back here one day," she admitted.

"Really?" Nate seemed surprised.

"Maybe." She still didn't know what she was going to do, hadn't come to any definite conclusions. But it felt nice to tell someone just a bit of what she'd been thinking about.

"That would be . . . nice."

Marty frowned at his reaction. It wasn't exactly an excited response, but she felt he hadn't said what he really wanted to—like he wanted to say more but didn't feel comfortable about doing so.

"It's really just a thought."

He nodded.

They reached the streetlight and she stopped, looking up at the snow reflecting in the light. It swirled and shimmered, creating a halo against the inky black sky.

"It's just so beautiful."

"It is," he agreed, but when Marty looked at him, he wasn't watching the snow. His unusual amber eyes burned into her.

She could feel that gaze like a touch, brushing away the cold and leaving delicious heat in its wake.

He stepped toward her, and she didn't back away. She couldn't. She was trapped by the desire she saw in him and felt in herself.

But just when she thought he would reach for her, he stopped.

"Should we head back?" Suddenly his eyes were unfathomable, the desire sunken back into their whiskey-colored depths.

She released a shaky breath, then nodded.

On the walk back, the silence of the night was more grating than pleasant. She wrapped her arms around herself to stem the cold and the breathless frustration that seemed to be skittering through her.

No, not frustration. But rather that thundering sense

of relief like when you catch yourself right before you fall. That feeling that steals your breath and makes your heart race.

Definitely not frustration. If she *was* frustrated, it was because he kept making her think something was going to happen—then it didn't. It wasn't a disappointed frustration, but rather a "stop toying with me" frustration.

Was anyone believing this?

As they climbed up onto the porch, Nate stopped in front of the door.

She expected him to tell her that he was going to go. But instead he faced her and gave her one of his endearing grins. Then he said decisively, "I'm going to kiss you now. Because it's Christmas Eve, and we are standing under the mistletoe."

Marty looked up to see a softball-sized sphere of mistletoe hanging from a brass hook over the front door. She'd never noticed it.

Her gaze left the ceiling and locked with Nate's as he moved closer, stopping only inches from her. His smile disappeared, and she could see melted snow glistening on his full lower lip.

Slowly he leaned forward, his lips so close she could practically taste the small beads of moisture there, and he murmured, "I've already passed up the opportunity way too many times to miss this one."

His mouth captured hers, his lips cool and damp—and wonderful. He coaxed her and teased her with gentle insistent pressure until her hands came up to rest on his chest, to steady herself, to find an anchor in his sweet, snowflake-flavored onslaught.

Then his tongue teased the seam of her lips with nothing more than darting sweeps of sizzling heat. But those brief, tantalizing touches were more than enough to start her insides on fire.

She opened her mouth to him. Her tongue slipped past his cool lips to taste the heat within. Her hands slid up his chest and circled around his neck. She pressed herself harder against his solid, lean body.

He groaned and pulled her tighter, his arms warm and deliciously strong. She clutched him in return, her fingers tangling in his hair, her mouth molding fully to his, tasting him. Devouring him.

This was it. This was the kiss. The kiss she had dreamed of, the kiss she never got.

Out of nowhere, Nate's words played through her brain. *I'm going to kiss you now.* Except instead of his husky, marvelous voice, she heard the voice she remembered from high school, not yet matured into that wonderful roughness. But saying the very same words. The words that had set her up and made her a laughingstock.

Suddenly, she was furious with herself. One great kiss and she'd forgotten everything. Forgotten how he used her. Set her up. Lied. Was she ever going to stop being attracted to men who hurt her?

Marty pushed at his chest and jerked out of his grasp, backing away from him until she was flat against the door.

Nate watched her, his breath coming in harsh bursts, confusion clear in his eyes. "Marty—"

"Don't," she hissed, holding up a hand. She turned, her hand on the door handle, her intent to escape, to hide. But she paused and glared back at him.

"So who dared you this time?"

When Nate stared back at her, no comprehension on his face, she shoved open the door, stepped inside, and without looking back, slammed it in his bewildered face.

Chapter 12

"Hey, Nate," Sam said as Nate walked into their dad's kitchen and went straight to the refrigerator.

Nate grunted in response and then began to dig through the fridge shelves looking for a beer. Maybe two.

"Did you know Dad went over to Mrs. Haynes's for pie?" Sam asked, but continued on before Nate responded. "Unreal, huh? After all these years, she finally got his attention."

Nate grunted again, shoving a giant jar of mayo out of the way. Finally, after moving old containers of this and that, he located a silver can of light beer behind a jar of bread-and-butter pickles. Light, no wonder it was buried way in the back. He cracked it open anyway and downed half of it in one swallow.

"Whoa, what's up with you?" Sam asked.

"I don't want to talk about it. Night."

Sam shrugged. "Night."

Nate left the room, beer can in hand. He was such a fool. Every instinct had told him that he couldn't rush things with Marty. And he hadn't intended to. He'd decided taking things nice and easy was the best bet for both of them.

Then he'd spotted the mistletoe dangling like a clear, harmless invitation from the porch ceiling. The small ball of herbs seemed like fate, especially after he'd resisted kissing her twice before. It was Christmas Eve, after all, and if there was a more perfect time to kiss under the mistletoe, he didn't know it. It seemed the right thing to do, so he'd gone for it.

And the kiss itself had been amazing and absolutely right. He couldn't remember any woman feeling so good in his arms, so perfect. And the kiss he'd intended to keep gentle and sweet had ignited. He knew he could have kept things under control if Marty had seemed cautious or uncertain, but she hadn't. She responded with the same fiery need he'd felt, the same hunger. But suddenly everything shifted. The burning desire he'd tasted on her had turned to burning rage in a split second.

Who dared me? He'd tried to understand that question all the way home, but he still didn't have any idea what it meant.

He paused on the narrow back stairs to his old bedroom. Maybe Sam would understand what she meant. Maybe it was something he'd forgotten—although he couldn't imagine ever forgetting a kiss like that.

He returned to the kitchen. Sam still sat at the table, snacking on pretzels and reading the newspaper.

"Do you remember someone daring me to do something like, say, kiss a girl?"

Sam immediately nodded, although he didn't look up from his paper. "Sure. Jared and Derek Nye would dare you to do all kinds of dumb things."

"They did?"

Sam lifted his head to look at him. "I can't believe you could forget this. You guys did tons of stuff. Pranks, dares—most of which were pretty mean."

If the anger Nate had seen in Marty's eyes tonight was any indication, whatever he'd done to her had to have been more than mean, it had been downright cruel.

"Did—did they dare me to kiss Marty Stepp?"

"Yep, at a dance, in front of everyone. Don't you remember? You all used to call her 'the fifty-foot freak' and 'the giant—as tall as she was ugly.' And then one of you, probably Jared, bet that no one would dare to kiss her in front of the whole school. And you took the dare."

Nate shook his head, unable, or unwilling, to believe what his brother was saying. But even as Sam told him all those awful things, memories started to reverberate in his head. Those cruel names, said in his own voice, like they were echoing down a hallway, slowly becoming clearer.

Shadows of sitting next to Marty in a classroom . . . study hall. And of talking to her and laughing as if they were good friends. The whole time setting her up. The whole time laughing behind her back with Jared and Derek Nye.

Nausea roiled in his gut. Had he been that cruel? Had he really set out to hurt people? Because what he was remembering was more than a thoughtless prank—he planned it, in vicious detail. And all to impress Jared Nye.

He collapsed into a chair and stared unseeingly at Sam. Then he asked, not sure if he wanted to hear, "Did I do a lot of cruel things?"

Sam pondered that and then shrugged. "I don't think you knew how mean you were being. I think you just followed Jared's lead."

"But I should have known better."

"You were a kid. You know better now."

Now being the operative word. What would he still be like if he hadn't undergone such a life-altering experience? But he couldn't know.

Again he felt sick.

"I thought you knew all this. That's why I was so shocked you had the cojones to ask her out. But what shocked me even more was that she said yes."

Nate frowned. Why had she said yes? Was it to show him exactly how it felt to be attracted to someone and have that attraction thrown right back at him? Had she played him—at the party? At the skating rink? Tonight?

Maybe that was why she was so insistent on going to Heady's. Maybe she had planned to kiss him there, so his "friends" could see his embarrassment once she rejected him. If so, it was far less than he deserved.

No, that didn't make sense. She'd pulled away from him, expecting that she was being set up again. That he was going to humiliate her. She simply didn't trust him—just like she didn't trust other men.

Had he been the beginning of her distrust? If so, how on earth did a person apologize for something that had plagued another person her whole life? Was it possible?

"So did Marty dump your ass?"

Nate glanced at his brother. "Sort of."

"You should have taken her to the Millbrook Inn."

"Yeah," Nate agreed flatly. He should have done a lot of things—like apologize to Marty years ago. Or better yet, never hurt her in the first place.

Marty sat on Ellie and Mason's sofa, her long legs curled to her chin, watching the orange embers smolder in the fireplace, a cup of cold tea forgotten on the coffee table.

Ellie and Mason were in bed. They had been in the living room stuffing Christmas stockings and arranging Emily's gifts under the tree when Marty had stormed back into the house.

Concern had been clear on both of their faces, but they hadn't pressed her. Ellie just offered her tea, and Mason rambled on about all the different toy kitchen sets they'd looked at for Emily. She knew they were both being kind, trying to distract her. It didn't work, but she did appreciate the effort.

She was also thankful when they decided to go to bed. Marty didn't think she could have held back the tears much longer.

Now, the tears had dried, and she just felt confused. Confused and stupid. Part of her was still angry at Nate for what he'd done all those years ago. Hearing his voice so clearly in her head had startled her. But really, that wasn't why she had pulled away or why she had lashed out. She wished it were—it would be so much easier if she really did hate him for the things he'd done. But she didn't. She hated herself for responding to him.

No, she hadn't just responded. *Respond* sounded like an ordinary, uncomplicated reaction.

She responded. Done. Finished.

But nothing had been either ordinary or uncomplicated about her reaction to Nate's kiss. That kiss had set her on fire—*whoosh*—up in flames like an inferno, completely and utterly burning for him.

Even now, after all the emotions, all the tears, she still burned. Not the explosive, combustible fire she'd felt in his arms, but the low, sizzling burn like the orange embers falling through the fireplace grate. A spark waiting for Nate to return and rekindle the roaring blaze inside her.

She closed her eyes and rested her forehead on her knees. What was she doing? She'd come home because she had no idea what she was going to do with her life. The only thing she'd known absolutely, positively was that she was swearing off men.

That was her vow, and in less than a week, she'd kissed a man. The very last man she needed in her life. And she had *responded* to him like she'd never, never responded to another man—ever.

She'd been ready to jump Nate's bones right there on her sister's porch.

She groaned.

She had to leave. That was the only answer.

"What do you mean, you're going back to New York?" Ellie asked, stunned. "It's Christmas Day."

Marty stopped lining up Emily's pretend food in her play kitchen. "I've decided I should probably go do that show I pulled out of. Feeling guilty, I guess."

Ellie frowned. "Does this have anything to do with last night?"

Marty handed her niece a red plastic frying pan, which the little girl put on her head.

"Hat," Emily declared.

"It is a hat," Marty agreed, then balanced a blue plastic saucepan on her own head.

Emily grinned.

"Did Nate do something?" Ellie persisted.

"We kissed." Marty kept her tone offhanded, as if the whole experience hadn't affected her to the very core.

"Oh my, really?" Ellie didn't look like she knew how she should react. "Was—was it a good kiss?"

"It was fine." Lord, that was an understatement.

"Is that why you're leaving?"

"I've had hundreds of fine kisses. One more isn't anything to get worked up about."

Ellie now looked confused and worried.

Marty sighed, guilt rising in her chest. She did owe her sister some explanation for her erratic behavior. "I've been thinking about—maybe quitting modeling."

"What? Why?"

Marty paused, then handed Emily plastic fries, which the toddler then stuck into her pretend microwave. "Why? Do you think that's all I can do?"

"No," Ellie immediately said. "No. I think you can do anything you want. But why do you want to stop modeling?"

Marty faced her. "I want to do something else. Something I can be really proud of."

Ellie's blue eyes widened. "You should be very proud of yourself. How many people have done what you've done?"

"Anyone with a face that is in at the time."

"It's more than that. You are talented."

Marty snorted, not at all the sound people would expect from the face that beamed or pouted or peeked coyly from the covers of magazines. "You promote literacy. You help kids learn. Abby does research. She could find the cure for cancer one day. I convince people to buy products they don't need. I promote bulimia. And I give boys inspiration while they are in the bathroom."

"Marty," Ellie scolded. "You do so much more than

that. And frankly, I don't want to think about that last one."

"It's true."

Ellie shook her head, dismayed.

"Hat," Emily said, shoving a fake pancake at Marty. Absently, Marty placed it on her head.

Emily giggled.

"Well, if you're thinking about quitting modeling, then why go back to do this show?" Ellie asked.

"Because I can't think here." Marty wasn't going to add that she didn't intend to do the show. She just wanted to go back to her apartment, where things didn't remind her of . . .

"Is that because of Nate?"

"No," Marty insisted quickly, vehemently. "One kiss from a guy I knew in high school isn't enough to send me packing, believe me." Who was she asking to believe—Ellie or herself?

"But this is a guy you've had strong emotions about forever," her sister pointed out.

"Yeah—hate."

"Well, that would be enough to confuse anyone, kissing someone you hate."

"When did you become the little psychoanalyst?"

Ellie ignored that but did have her blasted look of understanding sympathy. Hell, she *could* be a shrink—all she need was a notepad and bust of Freud.

"It was just a kiss. One kiss. Very uneventful."

The sympathy turned to skepticism. "Well, I had 'one kiss' with Mason, and it changed my whole life. And I bet if you asked Abby, she had that 'one kiss' with Chase, too."

Marty growled with annoyance.

Emily gave her a quizzical look.

"All right," Ellie held up her hands. "I'll drop it. But please tell me that you are honestly okay. That you just need to think."

"I just need to think."

Doubt lingered in Ellie's eyes. "Well, I'm glad that we all got to have Christmas morning together."

Marty nodded. Other than her inner turmoil or her insanity, as she'd come to think of it, the morning had been nice. Emily played with the presents Santa Claus left, jabbering with excitement. Ellie made a huge breakfast of waffles and bacon and eggs. Mason sang Christmas carols loud and off-key all morning. Abby and Chase arrived with more gifts and lots of Christmas spirit.

And even though Marty did feel a tad jealous of the love her sisters had found, she also felt at home. They never made her feel like a fifth wheel. Her brothers-in-law were her family, too, and it was the first real Christmas she'd had in years.

But despite their sincere happiness about her being here, she couldn't hang about in her sisters' lives. They had their own families. Marty needed to find her own way. She needed to find what made *her* happy.

Marty scooted forward on the hardwood floor, where both she and Ellie sat with Emily. She hugged her sister. "I know you worry, but I'm fine. I just need to figure out some stuff."

Ellie returned the embrace, squeezing her tight. "Sometimes the answer is right there in front of you. Just remember that."

"I will."

Marty finished drying the last teacup and placed it on the shelf with the others. Closing the cabinet door, she turned around to look at the room. The large kitchen was spotless, as if she'd never been there.

She glanced at the ancient clock shaped like a teapot that had hung on the kitchen wall for as long as she could remember. It was almost five o'clock; if she left now she could be back to her apartment by midnight or one.

She started to take one more walk through the house to make sure she had everything when someone knocked at the back door.

Her heart jumped, and she immediately scolded herself. She didn't want to see anyone. She was in a hurry. She needed to get on the road, or she wouldn't get back to New York until the wee hours of the morning.

When she pulled open the door, she was greeted by a wall of flowers, all types, all colors, like someone went to a hothouse and uprooted as much as they could possibly hold. She couldn't even see around them to distinguish the person holding them.

Until the bunch lowered slightly and one unmistakable amber eye peeked through the sprays of baby's breath and ivy.

"Truce?" a husky voice asked sheepishly.

Marty stared at him for a moment, then despite her better judgment she said, "I don't know," rather than shut the door in his floral-hidden face. She knew she should. She was too vulnerable to this man.

Nate lowered the mammoth bouquet. "May I please come in?"

Again, her body rather her brain seemed to react. She stepped aside.

After wrestling the flowers inside ahead of him, he walked to the kitchen table and set the bouquet down.

Marty half expected the table to creak under all that weight.

"I just wanted . . ." He noticed her luggage piled up next to the door. "Are you leaving?"

She nodded.

He sighed, the sound bleak. "Well, at least I caught you before you left. I owe you a huge apology. I am so, so sorry for being the jerk I was in high school. I know what I did was unforgivable. But I just want you to know that if I could take it back, I honestly would."

She had waited for these words forever. But the satisfaction and the closure she'd expected to feel from his words were overshadowed by his presence. As much as she didn't want to be, she was happy to see him again.

She really was a fool—a hundred times over. It was a good thing she was leaving.

"I would have apologized before this," he continued, obviously taking her silence for lack of acceptance. "I would have apologized that first night, here in your upstairs hallway. But I didn't remember."

She frowned.

"I know that sounds stupid, like some lame excuse. But since the attack, I don't remember things, and I have no idea how I forgot something so awful, but I did. I am so sorry."

"How did you remember?" she asked quietly.

"Sam. He told me when I got home last night. I didn't understand what you meant when you asked who dared me this time. So I asked Sam."

Marty nodded. "I accept."

"He—" He stopped explaining and stared at her. "You do?"

"Yes."

"Thank you." He glanced around the room as if he

didn't know what to do next. "Well, I guess I should go and let you . . . go."

He started for the door when Marty said, "Tell me about all these flowers."

He stopped, again with uncertainty in his eyes. But he returned to her side. They both looked down at the giant, wild bouquet.

"Um, I've never actually gotten flowers for a woman before," he confessed.

"Not even Lynette Prue?"

He seemed startled by the question, but slowly his eyes began to sparkle as he realized she was teasing him. "Nope, not even Lynette Prue. Anyway, I wanted to get you something perfect. Flowers that I thought you'd really like, but I couldn't decide. So I just started taking a couple of each. And I left with this."

Marty shook her head. It really was an amazing bouquet. Roses and carnations in several colors. Lilies, foxglove, white daisies, mums, Gerber daisies, sunflowers, even a couple of birds of paradise.

"Where on earth did you find a florist open on Christmas Day?"

"Sam knows a woman who owns a shop in Bangor, and she was willing to meet me there. Fortunately, she had a large selection in the cold storage."

"A very large selection," Marty agreed.

"It's kind of . . . tacky, isn't it?"

"No," Marty assured him. "I'm just not sure I could actually carry it by myself."

"Well, this is my first attempt. I think I could do much better next time."

Marty continued studying the flowers, but her heart raced. Was that an invitation? A promise? It didn't matter, as she'd be in her car heading out of town in a few minutes.

Without looking, she could tell his gaze was on her. She could feel him. His mere presence was like a physical touch.

They continued to stand there, her eyes locked on the flowers, his on her.

Until he cleared his throat and made a big show of checking his watch. "Well, I'd better go. My dad is making Christmas dinner. And you need to get on the road."

"Yes," she agreed, but not with the vehemence that she intended. "Before it gets too late."

Nate nodded, and she could see the regret in his eyes—for his behavior in the past or for her leaving, she wasn't sure.

He took a deep breath, then headed for the door. Then he paused. "You know, it is getting rather late. You won't even get to New York until after midnight. How about joining my family for dinner?"

She hesitated. She should leave—now. But there was such a look of sincerity in his eyes. And it was late. Did it really matter if she left now or tomorrow? No.

All that mattered was that she kept her heart safe from this man. Having dinner with his dad and brother wasn't going to risk that.

"Just as an added apology," he cajoled.

"I am hungry," she admitted.

He smiled, a wide victorious grin that for a split second almost made her change her mind.

But then he said sincerely, "Thank you."

She nodded and went to get her coat.

Chapter 13

Nate really believed she was leaving and that would be it. Over. Done.

So when she agreed to stay for dinner, which he'd just thrown out there as a desperate attempt to keep her close even for a few more minutes, he actually felt weak with relief.

She pulled on her coat, but then paused at the kitchen table. "Let me put these in water."

She went to the sink, put in the stopper, and turned on the faucet. Then she returned to the flowers, scooping them up in both arms, and put them in the water-filled sink. The bouquet barely fit.

She stared at the monstrous jumble of flowers for a moment, then glanced at him. There was incredulity in her eyes. "I've never received a sinkful of flowers before."

His heart thumped in his chest. Maybe he had done something right. Maybe the gesture had truly touched her.

"Then again, I don't think many people have received a sinkful of flowers," she added.

"I try to be unique."

She smiled, this one different than her others, this one almost bittersweet. She plucked out a few of the flowers—a red rose, a few white daisies, and some greenery—and came to stand beside him at the door.

"What is that for?" He gestured to the bouquet.

"I can't show up for dinner empty-handed."

He smiled at her. She was adorable, sweet, generous. The perfect woman. And she was leaving. Maybe he had been right to close off his heart all his life. This sucked.

If he'd hoped meeting his family would somehow convince Marty to stay, Nate feared this wasn't going to do it. Frankly, if he didn't have an obligation to be there, he would have run, too.

He had expected his father and brother to be fine with a guest joining them. Polite. Friendly. They were all those things. To the extreme. In fact, they were treating her like the fiancée brought home to finally meet the family.

"So you live in New York," his father said to Marty.

"Yes, in Manhattan. Mr. Peck, this is delicious." Marty gestured to her plate with her fork.

Nate swore his father blushed as he gave his thanks.

Nate glanced at Sam, who watched Marty like her every move was the winning play of the New England Patriots in the Super Bowl.

Nate didn't recall Sam being starstruck at the ice rink, but maybe it was seeing her in the bright light of the dining room. Or it was just that she was in his house, period. Whatever the reason, both men were besotted.

"So, you are a model?" His father had asked that question twice already.

But Marty didn't show any signs that she noticed. "Yes. For over ten years now."

"That's something," his father said, shaking his head, as impressed as he had been the first two times.

"So you really like my brother, eh?" Sam suddenly asked, and Nate wished he had just continued to stare at her.

Marty shot a quick look at Nate. "Sure."

Sam shook his head. "That's amazing. A beautiful woman like you actually dating my brother."

"Sam, cool it," Nate hissed.

"We're not really—" Marty started, but his dad cut her off.

"Forgive Sammy. This is the first time Nathaniel has ever brought a lady home. And the first time a lady has joined us for Christmas dinner in a long, long time."

Marty smiled graciously at his father, and then she looked at him, curiosity and surprise mixed in her eyes.

"Ten years as a model," his father said. "Nate has been in the police force for a little less than that. Did you know he's the youngest chief of police in the state?" His father's chest actually seemed to puff up as he said that.

"No," Marty said, shooting Nate an impressed look. "I didn't know that."

"He is." His dad also gave him a proud tip of his head.

"Speaking of which, I never did tell you about the fight at Heady's the other night," Sam said, then politely added for Marty, "I hope you don't mind a little shop talk."

Marty quickly swallowed a bite of potato. "Not at all."

"I went to break it up and the only one who was still there was Jared. He had a split lip, and Wanda and another waitress were cleaning up broken glass. But when I asked him what happened, he said nothing. That there wasn't any fight. I asked Kenny. Wanda. I even asked Carl Hoyt, and he was the one that phoned in the complaint. Every one of them acted shifty, and I'd even say a bit scared, but they backed Jared's story."

Nate didn't respond other than to eat a forkful of squash.

"What do you think is going on?" Sam pressed him, obviously irritated that his brother didn't seem concerned.

"I don't know," Nate said. "It sounds like Jared has them covering up something."

"Something isn't right there," his father agreed.

"I think you should call Jared in to the station," Sam told Nate.

"On what grounds?" Nate asked. "That he's hiding something?"

"Sure," Sam said, the color in his cheeks rising like it always did when he was irritated. "You've brought in people for less."

"I don't want to talk about this now. It's Christmas. Let's just enjoy a nice evening."

Sam started to silently eat his dinner, but then stopped, setting down his fork with a clatter. "I can understand wanting to have a nice Christmas dinner, but you never talk about our work. Whenever I try to ask you anything about the job, you just put me off."

Nate sighed and put down his fork, too. "I do talk to you about work, but I like to keep it just that—work. To be discussed when we are at the police station and we're on duty."

The table was silent. Marty glanced back and forth between the brothers, looking a bit uncomfortable.

Sam glared at Nate, and Nate simply stared back.

"More potato?" their father asked Marty, who accepted even though she still had a full portion on her plate.

"I just don't get you," Sam said. "You don't seem the least bit interested in your job anymore."

Nate didn't answer. Again he busied himself with his meal.

"Ten years as a model," his father said to Marty. "That is something."

Right after they finished dinner, Nate offered to give Marty a ride home. She got the distinct feeling that his family was making him uncomfortable. He didn't say much on the drive and neither did she. She was too busy trying to digest all the information she'd learned during the dinner.

But once he had pulled into her driveway, she turned to him.

"Was I really the first woman you ever brought home?"

Nate nodded. "Yes."

"Why did you bring me?"

"Because I wanted you to stay here a little longer."

"Why?"

"I want to get to know you."

The blood in her veins raced, but she forced herself to ignore it.

"You know," she said slowly, not sure if she should share this, "I came home because I was thinking of quitting modeling."

He shifted in his seat as much as the steering wheel would allow. "Really?"

She nodded, pleased that he didn't ask why. "Have you really lost interest in your job?"

He sighed, the sound tired. "Yeah."

She could see the tightness in his jaw, and she thought that was all he was going to be willing to say. But then he added, "Since the attack . . . the experience . . ." The words evaded him.

She knew how he felt, understood that he couldn't make the words come. The decision was huge, and sometimes it was just too hard to talk about. She'd barely been able to tell Ellie, and even then Ellie didn't understand the whole story.

Nate's indecision about his job was a bond between them. Immediate, strong. He could understand a facet of her life that no one else could. And even though they weren't talking about why either of them wanted to make such a life change, just the knowledge that someone felt the same way was comforting.

"I'm thinking I might stay here a while longer," she said suddenly.

"You are?" She could see, even in the dim light, his amber eyes seemed to brighten to a golden color.

"Well, I mean, a week or so."

The gold in his eyes faded slightly.

"I think we could be friends," she told him.

"I do, too."

"But I don't want anything more. I don't want a relationship. Just friends, or we can't hang out."

He nodded, but the gesture was one of acceptance rather than agreement. "Okay."

"So," she said with a wide grin. "Want to take me to the Millbrook Inn for dinner tomorrow night?"

"As friends?" He looked skeptical.

"Yes, as friends," she told him.

He mulled it over. "I don't know . . . That's a romantic place. Not a 'just friends' sort of place."

"It may be romantic," she informed him. "But I *know* it's expensive, and you owe me. An apology, flowers, and a turkey dinner ain't gonna do it, bud."

"No, you're right." But there was no teasing in his voice as there had been in hers. "I do owe you more than I can probably ever give."

His eyes were dark now, all the gold gone. He looked so disheartened that Marty couldn't resist reaching out to touch him.

"I might go easy on you," she murmured as her fingertips brushed over the scar on his cheek. Lightly, she traced the ridged line up to his temple. "I think you've experienced enough."

He sat perfectly still, allowing her to touch him but not making any motion to touch her back.

She felt his silky hair tickle the backs of her fingers and she felt that tickling in the pit of her belly—and lower.

She snatched her hand away, shaken that such a simple touch could arouse her so easily.

She took a deep breath, and then managed to say with only a hint of a quaver in her voice, "But I won't take it easy until you treat me to a dinner at the Millbrook Inn."

He grinned, no indication on his face that her touch had had any effect on him whatsoever. "You got it. Should I pick you up here?"

She nodded.

"At seven?"

"Seven," she agreed. But as she got out of the car

and headed up her back steps, she wondered at the wisdom of this idea. She'd originally suggested it as a fun thing to do with her friend. But romantic *anything* needed to be avoided if she was to remain unaffected by this man.

She waited on the top step until he backed out of the driveway and drove down her street. She didn't want a relationship. She didn't.

But despite her protests, it still took several more minutes in the frigid night air to cool her sizzling nerve endings.

Chapter 14

"So are you staying because of Nate Peck?" Abby asked as they browsed through the aisle of women's clothing in a small boutique.

"No," Marty said defensively, irritated by the question, partly because she didn't like the idea that her sister thought she was so needy. And partly because she, too, worried she was that needy.

You aren't. You are just having fun, she assured herself. *No harm in that.*

"How about this?" Ellie held up a dress that looked very mother-of-the-bride-ish.

Marty shook her head. "Too formal, and too matronly."

Ellie gave the dress a critical look, then shrugged and hung it back up.

"So why are we going to every shop from here to Bangor looking for the perfect dress?" Abby asked in her usual pragmatic way.

"I just want to look nice. Is that a crime? Does that mean I'm looking to get lucky?"

"Shh," Ellie hissed, casting an embarrassed glance around the small shop.

"No, it doesn't," Abby answered. "I've just never seen you get so persnickety about clothes."

"I am a model," Marty pointed out, but she knew that argument didn't quite ring true. And she felt a bit like a hypocrite using that excuse. After all, just the other day she was exalting in the fact she didn't have to dress up. That she was tired of dressing up.

Darn Abby.

"So, you are just staying to visit?"

Marty glared at Abby. "What, do you want me to leave?"

"She doesn't want you leave," Ellie assured her quietly.

"I just want to stay for a while. I'm tired of New York. And I'm enjoying being home—although right at this moment, the reasons are eluding me."

They picked through the racks in silence, the slide of clothes hangers against metal the only noise.

"Are you honestly considering retiring from modeling?" Abby asked.

Marty glared at Ellie. Her middle sister continued to busy herself with shuffling through the racks.

"You used to be the trustworthy sister," Marty muttered at her.

Ellie looked offended. "I didn't know it was a secret."

"I didn't know I had to specify."

"Why shouldn't I know?" Now Abby was offended. "And why is Ellie the trustworthy one?"

Marty rolled her eyes.

Once more they fell quiet, although this time the scrape of hangers on the racks sounded more brusque and forceful.

"I'm tired of modeling. I want to do something different."

"I think it's great," Ellie said in her quiet, supportive way.

Abby frowned at Ellie. "I think it's great, too. If it's what you really want to do. And you're doing it for the right reasons."

It was Marty's turn to frown. "For what other reasons would I be doing it?"

"I don't know," Abby said. "And I'm not saying you *are* doing this for the wrong reason. Just be aware."

Ellie, ever the peacemaker, interrupted by holding up another dress. "This is the one."

Marty, irritated by Abby's typically practical and grown-up response, didn't even look at the dress that Ellie was waving like a surrender flag before almost rejecting it outright.

She was glad she didn't; the dress was perfect. Subtle, stylish, and a wonderful, brilliant red.

"That is it!" She rushed around the racks, took the dress, and examined it. Then she hugged Ellie. "It's perfect."

Then she held out an arm to include Abby. Her oldest sister couldn't help it if she was so annoyingly sensible.

You are doing the right thing, Marty told herself as the three sisters embraced. She was going day by day; there was nothing impractical about that. It was quite sensible, really. And she was having a bit of fun while she decided what to do with her life. Also a very rational thing to do—unhappy people made poor choices.

She lifted the dress up a bit to admire it even as she continued to hug her sisters. And this dress was perfect.

A friend could still want to look pretty for another friend. There was nothing wrong with that.

How could Nate be so nervous over a nondate? But if anything, he felt even more uptight about this evening than he had the first time they went out.

And what did he call this, anyway? A nondate didn't sound right. It wasn't even a real word. They were going out—but that seemed to imply more, too. They were grabbing dinner? They were hanging out? Nothing seemed to fit. It was the event that would remain nameless.

He paused in front of the back door to comb his hands through his hair, pushing back the pieces that seemed determined to fall in his eyes. He brushed his hands down the front of his coat and then he knocked.

As soon as Marty opened the door, his nervousness disappeared, replaced by outright, unadulterated lust.

Damn, she was breathtaking.

But he shoved his attraction away as best he could and said calmly, "Hi."

"Hi," she said as she stepped back to let him in. The hem of her cherry red dress swirled around her trim ankles.

She had great ankles.

She wore shoes made up of little more than a few silver straps and a pointy front piece to cover her toes. The shoes, like the dress, accentuated her lovely ankles.

But it was the rest of the dress that was almost too much to handle. The red material was fitted at the top, revealing her long, willowy torso. Then the neckline scooped into a vee, hinting at cleavage without showing too much. Sleeveless, it did show the pale skin and graceful curves of her shoulders. It reminded him of something that Audrey Hepburn would have worn in a dance scene in one of her movies.

Her hair, however, was very modern in its usual tousled disarray. Tonight, she wore small glittery clips throughout the mussed locks. Although modern, it worked. She looked charming. She looked more than charming, she looked . . .

"You look gor—great." He didn't want to overstep his friendship boundaries by complimenting her too much.

Marty smiled, her full lips colored just a shade lighter than her dress. "You're looking pretty dapper, too."

Dapper. He liked that. "Are you ready to go?"

She nodded, going to get her coat, and then she also picked up a small black purse and shawl from one of the chairs.

"Okay, ready," she said, her voice a little breathy. Apparently, she was nervous, too.

Once in the car, Nate turned off his police radio. "Just in case," he told Marty.

"I don't think I can skate in this outfit."

When Nate cast her a sidelong look, she understood it immediately. "Don't you even say it. I could skate—with a little more practice."

He nodded.

"I could."

"I know you could," he agreed, but they both knew he was just humoring her. Nate liked the banter between them. It was comfortable and helped him control his raging libido.

Of course, the dim light of the car also helped.

He glanced over at her. Her clips twinkled in her hair

and the streetlights glinted off her glossy lips. His body reacted immediately.

Okay, forget the car theory.

"I really did like your dad. He was sweet."

It took him a moment to focus on what she'd said and not his pounding pulse. "Sweet, huh?" He was pleased his voice sounded calm. "I don't think as a tough, old lobsterman that he has ever been called sweet."

"Well, he is. And Sam is great, too."

"Pushy at times, but he is great."

"I have one of those myself. Abby."

"Really?" Nate was surprised. Abby always seemed so refined to him.

"She's not really pushy, just practical and direct."

"And what is Ellie?"

"Shy and sweet."

"I can see that. So which sister are you?"

She was quiet for so long, he glanced over at her. "I'm opposite of Abby and Ellie."

He frowned at that description. "So you think you are impractical and rude."

She shrugged. "Maybe just impractical and mouthy."

"I don't see that at all."

"Wait until you get to know me better."

He cast another look at her. Her mouth was set in a grim line, almost none of her lush, glossy lips visible. He immediately wished he hadn't asked her to label herself. She obviously found the topic awkward—and upsetting.

"Sam would say I'm dull and possibly gay." He could not believe he just said that.

But it did get the reaction he wanted; she was instantly snapped out of her troubled mood.

She gaped at him. Even out of the corners of his

eyes, he could tell her dark eyes were round circles. "He does? Why would he think that?"

"He thinks that because I haven't seen anyone since my attack, there's something wrong with the machinery."

"Is there?"

"No," he assured her. It was on the tip of his tongue to offer to prove it, but he didn't think she would consider that a friendly gesture—or rather, *too* friendly a gesture.

"But we went out."

"Well, since you don't want a relationship, I told him today that we are just friends. You could see the flicker of disappointment and concern in his eyes as I said it."

"I'm sorry." She winced. "I had no idea I was ruining your reputation."

"You are. And not in that fun, involves-a-shotgun-wedding-afterward way."

She laughed. He loved her laugh; it was rich and spicy and warm, like mulled wine. And just as intoxicating.

"Well, here we are," he said, pulling into the inn's parking lot. The place appeared relatively busy, if all the cars were any indication, which was probably good. The more people, hopefully the more distractions.

He came around to her side of the car, but Marty was already pushing open her door. He held out a hand to her.

"You know, for someone who has to be used to limos and such, you sure don't let a guy open the door for you."

She smiled and gave him a pained look. "I've been known to do the same thing to the chauffeur. It's habit."

"Haven't you ever dated any gentlemen?" He swore silently to himself as soon as the question left his mouth. First of all, if her mistrust of men and reluctance to have a relationship were any hint, then no, she hadn't. And secondly, he'd never opened a door for any woman but her in his life, so who was he to suddenly consider himself a gentleman?

"Like I said, habit." She didn't seem upset by the question, but he still couldn't help wondering if his question made her think about her past boyfriends. Even though they were just friends, Nate still didn't want her thinking about other men when they were together.

But once they stepped into the foyer, he knew all thoughts of other men were definitely gone.

She twirled around in the center of the domed-ceiling vestibule, taking in all the Christmas decorations.

"Wow," she breathed. "This is beautiful."

He glanced around at the spruce swags and old-fashioned glass ornaments, white lights, and poinsettias, but his gaze came right back to Marty. Her eyes, wide with wonder, and the happy smile on her lips were far more beautiful than any of the decorations.

"I've only been here once, for Abby's wedding. It was beautiful then. But these decorations are unbelievable."

"They are," he agreed. He watched her for a moment longer, then held out his arm. "I've never been to the dining room, but I believe it's this way."

She accepted his arm and followed him down the hallway in the opposite direction from the ballroom where Abby and Chase's wedding reception had been.

The Millbrook Inn restaurant was not large, but rather a cozy room with a blazing fireplace and authentic gaslights on the walls. The gaslights, although they gave the illusion of being the primary light source, were only for atmosphere. Recessed lights were discreetly placed around the ceiling and didn't interfere with the historical feel of the room.

"Chase did this room," Marty said proudly.

"He really does amazing work," Nate said, thoroughly impressed. Chase was the best carpenter around, perhaps the best in Maine.

The hostess came forward to take their coats and hang them up in a closet near a small bar.

It was a bit easier to not stare at Marty when she had the coat on. But now, with it gone, he could again see her lovely, bare shoulders, golden in the soft light.

He forced himself to look away. He could do this. Friendship was good. He liked friendship.

Fortunately the hostess returned quickly, which was some distraction but not much. He was pretty sure everyone in the place was looking at Marty in that dress. It was stunning.

"So this is the first time you've been here, too?" she asked as the hostess led them to their table situated under one of the gas lamps.

"Yes." *Meet her eyes. Don't drool.*

"You didn't bring Lynette Prue here?"

That got his attention. He smiled. "You aren't going to let this Lynette Prue thing go, are you?"

"Nope."

"Hi, Nathaniel," a female voice said, just after they got seated. He looked up to see Jeannie Moore.

"Hi, Jeannie. Nice to see you. Are you having dinner?"

"Yes, with Derek Nye." She gestured to where Derek sat a few tables over. She waved for him to join them.

Derek seemed reluctant, but he did finally stand up and head toward the table. As he got closer, Nate could see that he had a black eye, not a terrible one, but there nonetheless, and a small cut on his cheek.

"Derek," Nate greeted him, holding out his hand.

Derek hesitated before accepting it. "Nathaniel."

"How have you been? Long time no see."

"Yeah—yeah," Derek said, crossing his arms over his chest. "Um, I'm good. And you?"

"Can't complain," Nate said, watching the other man closely. Derek was definitely uncomfortable, just as he had been the two times he'd seen him since Nate got out of the hospital.

Why did he make his old friend uneasy? Had Sam told him how much Nate had changed since the attack? He doubted it. Did his limp and scar make Derek nervous for some reason? They weren't much more noticeable than his own black eye and cut.

Nate suspected that Derek was uneasy because of the falling-out Nate had had with Jared. He supposed he couldn't blame Derek for not knowing how to react to him now—now that Nate couldn't stand his older brother. But Jared was very bad news. He'd remembered that even when so many other things had disappeared from his memory.

"Do you both remember Marty Stepp?" Nate asked.

"I knew that was who you were!" Jeannie exclaimed, grabbing Marty's hand and pumping it enthusiastically. "I told you, Derek."

Marty smiled.

"The people in Millbrook are just so proud of what you've achieved," Jeannie gushed. "You are a real success story. And you are just as beautiful as your pictures."

"Thank you," Marty said, but Nate could see her smile stiffen. Not enough that Jeannie would notice it, but just enough that he could tell Marty wasn't comfortable. He couldn't imagine why Jeannie's compliment would make her ill at ease.

"Well, we'd better get back to our table and let these guys enjoy their night," Derek said.

"Nice to meet you," Jeannie told her.

But just as they started toward their table, Nate had to ask, "What happened to your eye, Derek?"

Derek stopped dead in his tracks, but he didn't turn around right away. When he did, he wore a slight smile, but his eyes didn't quite meet Nate's. "Just a stupid accident. Up at the mill."

"That's what I figured," Nate said, not bothering to hide his disbelief.

Derek nodded and then quickly ushered Jeannie back to their table.

Marty leaned forward and asked softly, "Do you think he was involved in that fight at Heady's?"

"Definitely."

"What do you think they are hiding?"

Nate shook his head. "I have no idea. But Jared can be very underhanded. Derek isn't as bad. Unfortunately, he's stuck under his brother's thumb."

"I thought you and Jared were best friends."

"We were. But our friendship started to get rocky once Jared married Lynette about three years ago now, I guess. We didn't stop hanging out altogether, but things did become strained, especially when Jared would drink. He's an extremely jealous guy, and he had it in his head that Lynette was really in love with me."

"Do you think she is?"

"No. If she was smart, she wouldn't be. I was a terrible boyfriend. Not to mention that it's been years since we dated."

"I don't know. Love can easily last through both terrible and time," Marty said as if she knew from experience. But the waiter arrived to deliver menus and take drink orders, and Nate couldn't ask her more.

"Do you think Jared had anything to do with the attack?" she asked as soon as the waiter left.

Nate's head shot up. "No!" His voice calmed. "Jared is a jerk and he can be a nasty drunk, but he'd never get that violent. Especially not to me. Even if we don't get along now, we were buddies for a long time."

"Okay," she said, letting the idea go. "You're right. I shouldn't have suggested that." She looked down at her menu.

Nate glanced over to where Derek sat. He was eating his meal, but he saw Nate's look and his fork hesitated for just a second on the way to his mouth. Then Derek turned his full attention on Jeannie.

Could Jared have been involved with his attack? No, he didn't believe it.

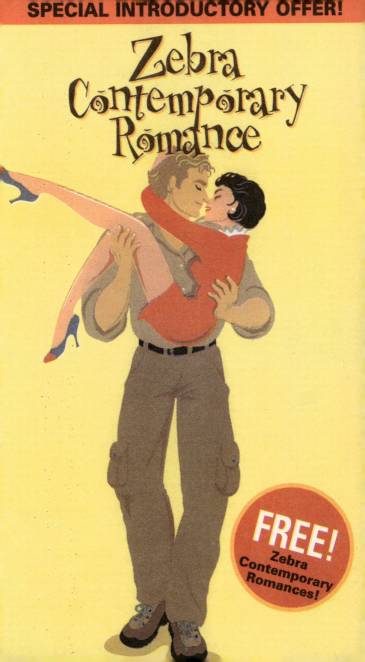

Zebra Contemporary

Whatever your taste in contemporary romance – Romantic Suspense ... Character-Driven ... Light and Whimsical ... Heartwarming ... Humorous – we have it at Zebra!

And now Zebra has created a Book Club for readers like yourself who enjoy fine Contemporary Romance written by today's best-selling authors.

Authors like Fern Michaels...Lori Foster... Janet Dailey...Lisa Jackson...Janelle Taylor... Kasey Michaels... Shannon Drake... Kat Martin... to name but a few!

These are the finest contemporary romances available anywhere today!

But don't take our word for it! Accept our gift of FREE Zebra Contemporary Romances – and see for yourself. You only pay $1.99 for shipping and handling.

Once you've read them, we're sure you'll want to continue receiving the newest Zebra Contemporaries as soon as they're published each month! And you can by becoming a member of the Zebra Contemporary Romance Book Club!

As a member of Zebra Contemporary Romance Book Club,

- You'll receive four books every month. Each book will be by one of Zebra's best-selling authors.

- You'll have variety – you'll never receive two of the same kind of story in one month.

- You'll get your books hot off the press, usually before they appear in bookstores.

- You'll ALWAYS save up to 30% off the cover price.

SEND FOR YOUR FREE BOOKS TODAY!

To start your membership, simply complete and return the Free Book Certificate. You'll receive your Introductory Shipment of FREE Zebra Contemporary Romances, you only pay $1.99 for shipping and handling. Then, each month you will receive the 4 newest Zebra Contemporary Romances. Each shipment will be yours to examine FREE for 10 days. If you decide to keep the books, you'll pay the preferred subscriber price (a savings of up to 30% off the cover price), plus shipping and handling. If you want us to stop sending books, just say the word… it's that simple.

If the FREE Book Certificate is missing, call 1-800-770-1963 to place your order.
Be sure to visit our website at www.kensingtonbooks.com.

FREE BOOK CERTIFICATE

Yes! Please send me FREE Zebra Contemporary romance novels. I only pay $1.99 for shipping and handling. I understand that each month thereafter I will be able to preview 4 brand-new Contemporary Romances FREE for 10 days. Then, if I should decide to keep them, I will pay the money-saving preferred subscriber's price (that's a savings of up to 30% off the retail price), plus shipping and handling. I understand I am under no obligation to purchase any books, as explained on this card.

Name _____

Address _____ Apt. _____

City _____ State _____ Zip _____

Telephone ( ) _____

Signature _____
(If under 18, parent or guardian must sign)

Thank You!

Offer limited to one per household and not to current subscribers. Terms, offer and prices subject to change. Orders subject to acceptance by Zebra Contemporary Book Club. Offer Valid in the U.S. only.

CN075A

Zebra Contemporary Romance Book Club
Zebra Home Subscription Service, Inc.
P.O. Box 5214
Clifton , NJ 07015-5214

Chapter Fifteen

As Marty watched Nate cut doggedly into his salad, she really regretted suggesting that Jared Nye could be involved in Nate's attack. The idea obviously troubled him, and it wasn't manifesting itself in just his attitude toward his salad. His whole demeanor had changed.

Before, he'd been charming and funny, and now he'd grown silent, preoccupied.

She finished the bite of her own salad and said lightly, "Did I ever tell you about the time I had a photo shoot in Ecuador?"

Nate looked up from his greens, frowning as though she were a madwoman.

"I know I've never told you," she informed him. "I'm trying to make blithe and amusing conversation. Work with me."

He smiled slightly. "Why, no, you haven't ever told me about your photo shoot in Ecuador."

She feigned surprise. "Really? I could have sworn I had. Well, let me tell you now. I was on a shoot in this remote village near a national park beach called Los Frailes, which is where the actual shoot was taking place. Los Frailes is unbelievably beautiful, with white sand beaches, blue, blue water, and these soaring sandstone bluffs.

"But the village where I was staying was really amazing too, with cabins made out of materials like bamboo cane and tagua palm leaves. Some of the cabins were actually built in the trees. It was so wild, but so beautiful. The village didn't actually have any running water except for a sort of bathhouse/laundromat on the outskirts of the town—and by laundromat, I mean big tub-type thing to both bathe in and hand wash your clothes."

"Is this a true story? Or are you just making this up for my amusement?"

"It's true," she assured him.

"Models don't get better digs than tree houses?" he asked skeptically.

"Don't knock it until you've tried it," she told him, then continued on with her story. "So, I had gone to the bathhouse/laundromat with a sack full of laundry to wash. The bag wasn't too heavy on the way there. But once the clothes were wet, they were considerably heavier."

"There wasn't a dryer in this place?"

"Well, if there were, don't you think I would have used it?" she pointed out reasonably.

"I don't know. Did you have enough quarters?"

"Shh," she warned. "You're ruining the mood of the story."

He clamped his lips together in a great show of being quiet.

She watched him for a few moments just to be sure he would continue to behave himself. A hint of a smile tugged at those beautifully shaped lips, revealing a brief glimpse of the appealing creases that bracketed his mouth when he smiled fully.

Focus, she told herself and forced her gaze to his eyes. They glittered like topazes at the bottom of a glass of champagne.

She stared at his shoulder.

"So . . . Where was I?"

"At a bathhouse with a heavy sack."

She focused on his face and found him grinning outright. God, he had a gorgeous smile. But she quickly reprimanded him again. "Eew! You're making this story sound really disturbing."

"Sorry." He suppressed his smile and looked appropriately contrite.

"So, I picked up this bag, which now required me to use both arms, and headed back to my lodging, which was on the other side of the village. As I struggled along the rutted road, this elderly indigenous man came up to me, literally stopping right in front of me. So I had to stop, too.

"He was short, only coming up to about my shoulders, with thick, gray hair and craggy, leathery skin. But he had wise, dark eyes and a friendly—if somewhat toothless—smile. He kept gesturing to my face and then indicating that he wanted me to lean down.

"So I did, assuming that I had something on my face and since I was carrying this heavy bag of wet clothes, I figured he wanted to wipe the dirt or whatever off for me. But instead, he captured my cheeks between his two calloused hands, and he kissed me—right on the lips."

Nate's look of amusement was replaced by an expression of appalled bafflement. "This *is* a disturbing story."

"No, it isn't. Listen to the rest. So after the man kissed me, he looked up at me with those wise eyes and said . . ." She stopped. "You know, this isn't a very good story after all."

"Wait, you can't stop a story there."

"It's a boring story," she insisted, and reached for her wine.

"Nope, I need to know what he said."

She sighed, staring into her glass. Finally she said evenly, although she could feel heat burning her face, "He said, 'So beautiful.'"

Puzzlement still filled his eyes. "Does this sort of thing happen to you often? Strange men coming up and kissing you?" He seemed genuinely concerned.

"That isn't the point, really." Although Marty didn't think she wanted to share the point now. She wished she hadn't shared the story, period. Either he was going to think she was telling him a tale about how beautiful she was, or worse, he'd figure out how she really felt about the story.

"You're right, I don't get the point. Some old guy used the fact you had your arms full as an excuse to plant one on you. You should have called the police."

"Nate, this is a remote village on the coast of Ecuador. There aren't any police." She frowned. "You really are missing the point."

"Explain it to me," he said, his eyes searching hers as if he needed to understand this story—for his own peace of mind, if nothing else.

Despite her better judgment, she explained her reasoning. "It's a beautiful story because I was in the middle of nowhere, where no one knew who I was. I hadn't showered. I had on no make-up, and I'd just done laundry—by hand. And this man who was so old and wise and had seen so much beauty in the place where he lived thought I was beautiful."

Nate stared at her for a moment, then to her dismay, his amber eyes lit with a dawning understanding.

Of course he would understand the story. She should have just left it the silly story of a lecherous old man. Instead, he knew it was the story of a silly woman who didn't feel like people ever really saw her—the real her.

She covered up her consternation with her best saucy smile. "Gotcha! I totally made that up. Although an old guy on the subway once copped a feel while I had my hands full with grocery bags."

Nate regarded her for a moment, then laughed. "You did get me. I totally believed you there for a minute."

She forced a laugh in return.

She was relieved as the waiter arrived with their entrees. But as they ate, she glanced up at Nate and caught him watching her.

He smiled, a compassionate little curl of his lips.

She returned her gaze to her food. She had been wrong about her self-description in the car on the way there. She wasn't mouthy, she just had a big mouth—a *very* big mouth.

By the end of their dinner, Nate felt like they'd both loosened up again. All topics like old men and inner beauty and unpleasant friends and jealousy were easily avoided. And although there was an empty bottle of wine sitting in the middle of the table, he didn't think it was the pinot grigio that had them feeling so relaxed. They honestly enjoyed talking to each other.

Marty told him about some of the other trips she'd made for her modeling. She had traveled all over the world and had amazing stories.

They joked, mainly about the fact that Nate had

ordered an entree that he didn't even know what half the stuff in it was. Some sort of pasta with Belgian endive and capers and arugula, that last of which he was pretty sure was a spinach-type green.

Marty decided "arugula" was Belgian for "phlegm." Which Nate had to admit wasn't too appealing, but fortunately the food was delicious, so he could overlook the possible germ exposure.

And they laughed. Sometimes Nate would stop, under the guise of taking a drink of wine or a bite of pasta, and just listen. Her laughter was so amazing. Velvety and inviting, it seemed to create a cheerful cocoon around them.

Several times, he noticed people at other tables watching her, charmed smiles on their faces, too, as if they just couldn't help but join in her merriment.

He watched her now, as she took a sip of her cappuccino, and then sighed. Marty let her gaze wander over the rest of the room, a happy smile curving her lips. He couldn't remember ever enjoying someone's company so much. His old tactic with women had been to rush through the date—if there even was anything that could be considered a date—jump in the sack, and then decide in the morning if he liked the woman enough to suggest getting together again.

This was all new to him.

On the other side of the room, a pianist played, the notes barely reaching their table.

"Do you want to dance?" he asked, wanting to hold her, even though he knew the touch wouldn't lead to anything more.

She set down her cup, and with a determination he didn't understand said, "I would."

He rose and reached for her hand. "I should warn you, I'm not a great dancer."

She slipped her fingers in his and stood. "That's not what Wanda says."

"Women from my past are just going to keep coming back to haunt me, aren't they?"

Marty paused, causing him to stop, too. She held out her arms slightly, their fingers still linked, and gave him a flip little grin. "Hey, I think I might be one of those women."

He didn't return her ironical smile. "You can haunt me all you want."

Her grin faded, and for a split second, he thought her gaze dropped to his lips. Even if they didn't, his body sure as hell reacted like they did. His pulse raced, all blood heading somewhere it really, really shouldn't.

He started toward the dance floor with more purpose, as if holding her tight against him was going to help his current situation. Not likely.

Only one couple was dancing, an older man and woman who twirled in sync as if they'd danced together for years.

Nate stopped on the other side of the dance area and pulled Marty against him. She kept the one hand tucked in his and placed her other hand on his shoulder. His free hand automatically found the slight indentation at the base of her spine, and they began to move.

This close, he could smell her perfume, subtle like wildflowers with just a hint of grapefruit. He leaned his head in closer, his cheek almost touching hers, and breathed deeply.

"You smell wonderful," she whispered as if she'd been reading his mind. Her breath stirred his hair and tickled his ear.

They swayed, their heads close together. Their bodies brushed, then drifted apart, the rhythm incredibly arousing in its innocence. Clothes against clothes. Hands in proper places. Mouths only inches apart.

He lifted his head and looked into her eyes. Desire swirled in their dark depths, and he could barely stop himself from leaning in to taste that longing.

Then the music stopped, and the older couple clapped.

Dazed, Nate stepped away from Marty, looking around. The couple was applauding the pianist.

When he looked back to Marty, she appeared as overcome as he was. He stepped forward to take her back in his arms, but she held up her hands and then made a great show of fanning herself. "I'm sorry. I'm really warm."

"Do you want to sit down?"

"Yes, I think so."

Once they reached the table, she seemed to have control of herself. Nate wished he could say the same thing.

"Wanda was right. You are a good dancer."

He smirked at her as he sat down.

"You are. Definitely better than high school."

His hand paused halfway to his wine glass. High school. Their one terrible dance. Here he'd thought he saw desire in her eyes, while she was busy recalling that horrible school dance. Obviously his hunger for her was so strong, he was seeing things that weren't even there.

"I'm sorry," he said. Both for that dance years ago and his own almost uncontrolled desire now.

If he had expected her to be hurt or offended or even

forgiving, she surprised him again. "Yeah, well, I guess you'll just have to take me out for coffee tomorrow."

He stared at her for a moment, completely dumb-founded. Then he chuckled. "You are absolutely right. Coffee is the only option."

Chapter 16

"Tell Jared," Josie ordered Derek as soon as their brother walked through the door to her house.

"Tell me what?" Jared asked, heading directly to Josie's fridge to get a cold beer.

"It isn't that important," Derek said and tried to concentrate on the evening news showing on the small television on the kitchen bar.

"Derek saw Nathaniel at the Millbrook Inn with Marty Stepp," Josie told Jared as she stirred a steaming pot on the stove top.

"Derek's right. That's not important." Jared collapsed onto one of the stools beside Derek and also started to watch the TV.

"The hell it's not," Josie said as she lifted the lid off another saucepan. She stirred the contents of that one, too.

"You've just got your panties in a twist because of what happened at that Christmas party," Jared said.

"He ordered *me* to leave the party Warren brought me to," she said. "I think that is a good reason to be mad."

Jared snorted. "You would have gladly gone if you thought Nathaniel would have left with you."

Josie glared at him. "Speaking of which, where is your lovely wife? I hope *she* hasn't gone to see our good chief of police."

"You shut your mouth," Jared warned her.

"Come on," Derek shouted. "Can't we have one nice dinner?"

"Oh," Jared said in an irritating babyish voice, "I'm so sorry, little brother. You are the birthday boy, aren't you?"

Derek gave him a dirty look and turned back to the television. How had he let Josie convince him to come here tonight? His family made the Manson family look almost nice.

"Your eye looks better," Jared commented.

"It's fine," Derek said flatly.

Josie stormed around the kitchen, slamming cabinet doors, clattering lids on and off the pots on the stove. She was always subtle when she was annoyed. And she always got annoyed when her brothers ignored things she thought were important.

Jared finished his beer, then checked his wristwatch. "Where the hell is Lynette?"

Derek wouldn't blame the woman if she'd just run away. Jared was ridiculously jealous and controlling. Lynette wasn't a particularly nice person, but she didn't deserve the crap his brother put her through.

But Lynette arrived just moments later. "I'm sorry I'm late. No one was at the deli to put the lettering on Derek's cake."

She brought the cake over for Derek and Jared to see. It was decorated like a snowy scene. Little plastic trees lined a road with a matchbox tractor on it, which Derek didn't really understand.

"They didn't have any snowplows," Lynette explained.

"And we've been out of lobsters and boats for, like, a month."

"It's real nice," Derek told her.

She smiled, then turned to her husband. "Like it?"

He grunted, but when she started to walk away to place it on the kitchen counter, Jared caught her arm and placed a rough kiss on her mouth.

She smiled when they parted, but Derek noticed the smile didn't quite reach her eyes.

"You have to hear this," Josie said as soon as Lynette came around the bar to set the cake down. "Derek saw Nathaniel at the Millbrook Inn with Marty Stepp."

Lynette looked as appalled as Josie. "Really?"

Josie turned to Derek. "Tell her what you saw."

Derek shook his head, amazed that his innocent comment to his sister had turned into this big scandal. "They were having dinner."

"Well, duh," Josie said impatiently. "Tell her about *how* they looked."

"They," Derek said slowly like he was building up to something really thrilling, "looked like they were having a good time."

If he thought that response would aggravate the two women, he was wrong. Josie and Lynette exchanged knowing and peeved looks.

"Why the hell would you care if Peck is seeing that model chick?" Jared asked both women, but he eyed his wife in particular.

"Well," Josie answered, "if it hasn't occurred to you, that woman has a ton of money. And if Nathaniel marries her, he'll have a ton of money—and there will be no way in hell he'll sell his property."

"Wait a minute," Derek said, amazed his sister could possibly head in this direction from him casually mentioning he saw Nate at the inn, "I said they looked like they were having fun. How do you get they are going to get married?"

"It could happen," Josie insisted. "If Nate has money, we might as well kiss *our* money good-bye. No land developer is going to want our land without Nate's property, too, for the water access."

"How do we know he needs money to keep his land?" Derek couldn't believe his sister was making all these assumptions. "He wouldn't—" He was so amazed by this train of thought that he couldn't seem to wrap his mind around it. "He wouldn't have pulled out on the sale if he needed money."

"But he's *never* going to sell if he has plenty of money," Jared said contemplatively, following their sister's way-out reasoning. Of course, Jared would. Both of Derek's siblings were greedy.

"You don't think he'd really marry her, do you?" Lynette asked. "I mean, he hated her in high school. She's not that attractive now—I mean, without all that make-up and stuff."

"Worried your pretty lover boy is going to be lost to you forever?" Jared asked mockingly.

"Jared—" Lynette said, her voice low and pacifying.

Jared cut her off and added, just to be nasty, "Apparently you saw a different woman than I did. She's friggin' hot. I'd do her now—in a heartbeat."

Lynette looked like Jared slapped her. She busied herself by getting plates out of the cupboard.

"This is definitely something to keep an eye on," Jared said.

Josie nodded.

"If he gets too serious, we have to put a stop to it." Jared got up to grab another beer.

Fear rose in the back of Derek's throat. Fear and disgust. "What, are you going to beat Marty Stepp within an inch of her life, too?"

Jared straightened from reaching into the fridge, his eyes boring into Derek. "Me? As I recall it, you were there, too."

Derek glared back for a few moments, but then looked away like the coward he was.

"No, we won't beat Marty Stepp. But I do think we can come up with something to make her run," Jared said, his voice sounding low and sinister.

Derek took a sip of his beer and closed his eyes for a moment. Guilt tore through him. He needed to stop Jared. He couldn't make up for what his brother had already done, but he could stop anything else from happening.

He opened his eyes and looked at his brother, leaning on the kitchen counter talking to his wife.

Derek could make up for what Jared had done—if he weren't so torn and such a damned coward.

"You're seeing Nate again tonight?" Ellie asked, more pleased than surprised.

"Yes," Marty said. "We're—well, it's a surprise, so I don't actually know what we're doing."

"Very mysterious."

"Yes," Marty agreed, grinning stupidly. She was having a great time staying in Millbrook, and a lot of her happiness had to do with Nate. They'd seen each other every day since going to the Millbrook Inn, and every day she was more and more amazed at what a great person he was. He was funny, fun, and just really nice.

"So you two are honestly just friends?"

Marty paused, the piece of cheese she'd been getting Emily forgotten in her hand. That was the only difficulty she had with Nate. Her pesky, outrageous attraction to the man. But what woman wouldn't feel it? He was great and drop-dead gorgeous. She'd have to be dead herself not to feel attracted. But she was trying with all her might to also remain smart. Men always seemed fantastic—and then you got involved with them.

"We're just friends. Even if it kills me, we are just friends."

Ellie looked impressed—mildly confused, but impressed. "I never could have stayed that strong with Mason. But willpower has never been my long suit."

"Well, I don't want to ruin this. This is one of the best friendships I've had in a long time."

Emily snatched the cheese from Marty's hand, giving up on waiting for her distracted auntie to give it to her.

Marty laughed. "Sorry, baby." She tweaked one of Emily's curls. "Okay, I have to go."

"Got to get ready?"

"Nope," Marty glanced down at her faded green sweatshirt and jeans. "This is how he told me to dress."

"Casual and mysterious—right up your alley."

"Gotta love it." Marty gave her niece a hug and then skipped over to give Ellie a hug, too.

Ellie laughed. "This really is the happiest I've seen you in . . ."

"Forever," Marty provided for her. "I know."

"Any thoughts on what you plan to do about your career?"

Marty frowned. "Let's not talk about that right now. I'm still in my just-having-fun phase."

Ellie smiled, but Marty couldn't help seeing there was a glimmer of worry in her sister's blue eyes.

Marty hugged her again. "I'll call you later."

"Okay, have fun!"

Marty met Nate where he told her to, at the old Dunn farm out on Route 1. When she got there she was surprised to see him waiting in the yard, and he was not alone but with two kids.

"Hi," she called as she approached. "Who have you got there?"

Nate grinned and pointed to a boy of about twelve or thirteen on his left. "This is Peter Knowles. And this," he squatted down beside the other boy who appeared to be about seven, "is Freddy Knowles. They are my little brothers."

Marty frowned at that. "Little brothers?" Then she realized he meant they were children he mentored.

"Cool. I'm Marty." She first offered her hand to Peter, who shook it but looked slightly embarrassed. Then she offered her hand to Freddy, but the boy didn't accept it.

Instead he said with a slight lisp, "You're tall and you have a boy's name."

"Freddy," Peter scolded.

"It's okay, Peter," Marty assured the mortified older boy. "I am tall, but I don't actually have a boy's name. My real name is Martha. My nickname is Marty."

Freddy thought about that, then nodded. "My name is really Frederick."

"Really?"

He nodded.

She smiled at him and he gave her a shy one in return.

"So," she turned to Nate, whose eyes twinkled with

pride and excitement, "what are we doing way out here at a deserted old farmhouse?"

"I'll show you. But first things first." He went to his car and opened the back door. He handed her a brown paper bag.

"What's this?"

"Open it," he told her.

She peered inside and saw the bag contained a rather large shoebox. She pulled the box out and took off the lid. Inside was a pair of fur-lined snow boots.

"I'm tired of seeing you tromping around in the snow with nothing but sneakers on."

Marty stared at the boots, her heart swelling. As far as gifts went, boots weren't at all romantic. But there was something so sweet about a guy being concerned about the welfare of her freezing toes.

When she didn't respond right away, he added, "It's not real fur."

She laughed. "Well, thank God for that. I wouldn't want you going against your moral beliefs for my feet."

She sat down in the car with the door open and put on the new boots. They fit great.

"Okay, now here is the fun part." He led her and the boys, who were already grinning, so they were obviously in on the secret, to the trunk. He unlocked it and revealed three big, inflated rings with handles. One red, one blue, and one orange.

When Marty stared at them quizzically, Freddy announced, "We're going tubin'."

She looked up at Nate with dubious surprise. "Tubin'?"

"Come on, grab a tube. The best hill in Millbrook is behind this old farm."

Everyone except Freddy pulled an inner tube out of

the trunk and they all followed Nate around behind the ramshackle building.

He stopped at the summit of what was a surprisingly steep hill, which eventually flattened into a field. Dead grass and weeds spiked up through the snow.

Nate dropped his inner tube, catching it with his foot before it slid away. "You ready?"

Marty eyed the steepness again. "I don't know."

"It's much easier than skating. You just sit. I know you can do that."

She frowned. "What are you implying?"

"Here." Nate took her tube and held it steady for her. "Sit."

She did, shimmying herself around into a comfortable position.

Peter already sat on his, waiting, watching the two adults as if they were nuts.

Nate sat down on his tube and held out his arms for little Freddy to join him. The boy jumped on.

"Okay," Nate said. "Ready?"

Marty nodded. With a cautious push, she shoved herself over the edge, and even though she didn't put any real strength behind her send-off, she flew down the hillside, screaming all the way.

Finally, after mowing down many weeds, she glided to a stop, her tube spinning so she was facing back toward the hill.

Nate and the boys were shouting and laughing as their inner tubes skidded to a halt at the bottom, several feet from her.

They bounded over to her, all three sinking through the snow occasionally on the trek.

"Wasn't that great?" Freddy asked with unbridled excitement, his still-baby-round cheeks rosy.

"It was," Marty said and meant it. "It's almost like flying."

She looked at Nate, whose grin was as wide as Freddy's. The breeze ruffled his hair and made it shimmer like gold and copper and bronze all combining together. He was stunningly beautiful—just looking at him gave her the sensation of flying down that hill again. Her pulse rushed, her breath caught in her throat, and she felt so alive.

"Need help up?" Nate offered his hand, a big hand with long, nicely shaped fingers and a broad palm. She wanted to feel those hands on her bare skin.

"I got it," she told him, using the side of the inner tube and the ground as leverage to get up herself. She couldn't trust herself to touch him, even with her mittens on. Even with munchkin chaperones.

"Why don't you have mittens on?" she scolded him, once she was on her feet. Not only was clothing a necessary barrier against the cold, it seemed a necessary barrier between them.

"Got 'em," Nate said, materializing a pair of gloves from his jacket pocket.

"Well, put them on," she told him.

He did, like a dutiful child, but there was an amused twinkle in his eyes. She got the feeling he knew why she really wanted those gloves on.

Then he grabbed her hand. His gloved thumb rubbed the bare skin just inside the wristband of her jacket as he started dragging her back up the hill. She was sure he knew her real thoughts.

And the glove did nothing to protect her from the yearning shooting for him.

Fortunately, Freddy was there and he proved a far better distraction. He caught her other hand.

"Can I ride with you this time?" he asked.

"Sure, honey."

"Man," Nate grumbled, "thrown over for the pretty girl."

"She's okay," Freddy said with ingenuous honesty. "But, man, her tube is super fast."

Both Marty and Nate erupted in laughter.

"Then you must ride with me," Marty told Freddy.

Nate climbed the step onto Marty's front porch, where she stood in the doorway waving good-bye to the Knowles brothers as they got into their mother's ancient, rusty sedan.

Snow was beginning to fall, leisurely floating to the earth.

"They are such great kids," she said, then she waved again. Two little faces and hands appeared in the windows.

"Aren't they?" Nate agreed, turning to join her in a final wave.

"When did you become their big brother?" she asked as she pushed open the front door and they stepped back into her warm house.

"About two months ago."

"That's all?" She glanced over her shoulder at him. "You seem so close to them."

"I am," he said. "But that just sort of happened the first time I met them. And I see them at least twice a week. More, if my work schedule permits." He followed her into the kitchen.

"Want more cocoa?"

"Nah."

"How about coffee?"

"Mmm, yeah, that I could go for."

She started filling the coffeemaker while he cleared the boys' empty hot chocolate mugs.

"So what made you decide to mentor Freddy and Peter?"

Nate washed out the two cups. "I just wanted to make a difference. To help people."

Marty joined him at the sink, bumping him with her hip to nudge him out of the way. "You're the chief of police. Out there 'to serve and protect.' Isn't that making a difference?"

Nate shrugged. "It is, but I just wanted to help some people before I have to serve and protect someone else from them."

She finished filling the coffeepot, but didn't leave. Instead she leaned against the counter and regarded him. "Could Freddy and Peter grow up to be criminals? Is their home life that bad?"

Nate finished putting the clean cups in the dish drainer, then looked at her seriously. "No, I hope not. But they don't have a father in the picture, and their mother is a really nice woman, but she has to work two jobs to support them. That leaves them alone a lot." He shrugged. "I know kids with easier lives, more stable lives, who ended up taking the wrong path. I just want to help them if I can."

She studied him for a moment, and then with her free hand she touched his hair, brushing it back from his face. Her fingers lingered slightly at his temple. He longed to capture them and press kisses to each of her fingertips.

She dropped her hand and rushed back to the coffeemaker. He continued to watch her, his gaze drifting down to the snug fit of her jeans.

She looked fantastic. He desperately wanted to know if she felt as good as she looked. Tasted as good as she looked.

"All I can find in the cupboard is decaf," she said. He promptly stopped perusing her attributes and met her eyes. She didn't seem to be aware of what he'd been doing.

"Decaf is probably better anyway." His overactive mind and even more overactive libido didn't need any more stimulation than they already had.

"Are you still not sleeping?" she asked, concerned.

He shook his head. "Too much on my mind."

"Anything you can talk about?"

"Nothing you want to hear about." Especially since his late-night thoughts almost always involved her. Often in very compromising positions.

"Have you ever considered something like yoga?" she asked.

He chuckled. Now that was eerie. A lot of those fantasized positions certainly looked similar to yoga.

She frowned at him. "I'm serious. Yoga is very relaxing."

There wasn't anything relaxing about the positions he had in mind. Not until the position was over, anyway.

"I'll think about it." He tried to keep the lascivious look off his face.

"If they have any classes around here, I'd be glad to come with you."

He wasn't going to touch that comment with a ten-foot pole.

He wandered to the window. The snow was starting to fall harder.

He heard Marty moving around behind him. She

opened and closed a cupboard, then she went to the fridge.

The snow looked beautiful in the waning light. His thoughts drifted back to this afternoon. Marty had been so gorgeous today. She had sparkled as she played and joked with the boys, covered in snow and silliness. Her cheeks rosy from the cold. Her short hair wild and tousled. And her wonderful laughter filling the valley around them.

"Wow, it's really coming down."

He started, her voice right beside him.

"Sorry. I didn't mean to startle you." She leaned into him playfully, but instead of pulling away, she stayed, slipping an arm around his waist.

His breath caught.

"I didn't realize you were so close," he finally managed to say. He put an arm around her, brushing his fingers over the slight indentation of her waist.

She still didn't pull away. In fact, her fingers brushed just slightly against his waist, seemingly mimicking his touch.

"I think the coffee is done," she murmured, looking at him, her eyes big and dark, her lips inviting.

He had to put some space between them before he did something he'd regret. Damn, he wanted her. But he didn't want to ruin their friendship pact and risk her leaving.

"I'll get it." Okay, he did regret letting go of her.

The warmth of the house had thawed out the ache in his knee. Between that and the rather insistent arousal he was trying to hide, his limp was more pronounced than usual.

"No, no, no," she said, cutting him off, practically

bumping into him. "Sit. Your knee is killing you. I'll get the coffee."

He hesitated, but did as she said, again to put space between them. She was wreaking havoc on him today. He was reacting to her every move, wanting her.

She always did drive him to distraction, but tonight, she seemed to be standing closer, holding eye contact longer. Touching him.

He couldn't do the friend thing with temptations like this.

She filled their mugs, added milk, and brought them to the table.

"Here you go—with just a dash of milk."

Her fingers brushed his as she handed him the cup. His erection pulsed.

This was torture.

For just a brief moment, he thought he saw a glimmer of yearning in her coffee-colored eyes, a flash of heat. Then the heat was gone, evaporated away like the steam rising from his mug.

Now, she appeared totally unaffected. No sign whatsoever that she knew the effect she was having on him. Maybe the level of contact they'd had today was just an expression of friendship to her.

She sipped her coffee. "It really is coming down," she said again, shaking her head. "I think the weather report said six to eight inches."

"I heard that, too." *Talk weather. Talk weather.*

She took another sip of her coffee. "Maybe you'd better spend the night here."

He nearly choked on his coffee. He hadn't stayed here since that first night. He could not stay here tonight. Not with her in the next bedroom. No way.

"No, I'll go home. Or maybe I'll stay with my dad."

"You can stay here," she offered again.

No, I really can't.

He set down his cup. "You know, I actually should probably go now. I need to swing by the station and see Sam about . . . something."

"Really?" She set down her own mug, disappointed.

He stood. "But I'll see you tomorrow night."

"First Night." She grinned. "Millbrook's answer to New Year's in Times Square."

"Right—and almost as exciting. I'll pick you up at seven." He retrieved his coat from the coat stand.

"Okay. Night. I hope you sleep well."

"Thanks," he said, but he knew there was no chance in hell of that.

Chapter 17

"So you are going to First Night with Nate?" Abby asked, not looking up from the baby blanket she was knitting.

"Yeah." Marty eyed the crooked, rather holey-looking creation skeptically, deciding her sister really couldn't afford to not watch what she was doing. Then again, maybe it would help.

"Ellie says you two are just friends. But you sure sound like you're dating to me."

"Well, we aren't. We're definitely just friends." Marty was beginning to doubt that Nate was even attracted to her anymore. Which upset her more than she wanted to admit.

After going sliding with the Knowles boys yesterday, she had started to think maybe she could share something beyond friendship with him. She had wanted to get closer to him. To share affection. Just for a while.

But every time she'd gotten close, he'd pulled away. She'd even been bold enough to suggest he spend the night. And he'd left. Not the reaction she'd hoped for. Maybe she should see his refusal as a sign.

"Chase and I tried to do the friend thing," Abby said. "Now look at me." She held up the blanket and looked down at her belly, which wasn't actually showing yet.

Marty smiled, but then pretended to misunderstand her sister's meaning. "I really hope that sex with Nate wouldn't inspire me to knit a baby . . . net."

Abby seemed to see the blanket for the first time. She frowned at it. "This *is* terrible," she finally said.

"It," Marty cringed, "has a few problems."

"It looks like moths have gotten to it." Abby scrutinized it for a moment longer, then chuckled and set it aside. "A domestic diva, I am not."

"But you know it, and that's half the battle."

"True." Now that Abby didn't have the knitting, such as it was, to distract her, she studied Marty. "Do you want to be more than friends?"

She should have told her the blanket looked great, Marty realized belatedly. She sighed. "There are brief bouts of insanity. But I know this is best. I don't have good luck with men."

"I never did either. You do remember Nelson, right?"

"You had one bad-luck beau. I'm the queen of bad-luck relationships."

"Sometimes it takes more than one to find Mr. Right. But once you find him, it's amazing." Abby smiled, a dreamy look in her eyes. Even though Marty had seen that look before, it still amazed her. Abby had never been dreamy, ever, until Chase.

"It's worth dating a few duds to find him," Abby assured her with a satisfied smile.

Marty smiled back. "Some women don't find Mr.

Right. I'm willing to accept I might not be one of those women." Even as she said it, she knew it wasn't true. She did want her perfect someone, her soul mate.

But part of her, despite her enormous attraction and new respect for Nate, still didn't trust he could be her soul mate. She didn't know if trust was something she would ever be able to give—and how was she going to have a lasting relationship without it?

But that didn't stop her from wanting to jump Nate's bones. Damned sex drive!

Abby had picked up the baby blanket again. "Do you think I'd be better at crocheting?"

"I think you'd be better at buying."

Abby sighed, but then smiled, not offended. "You're right. And I did sew a little fleece baby bunting, which—" She pulled the outfit out of a sewing box on the coffee table and held it up. The sunny yellow bunting was also sort of lopsided and the stitching was puckered a bit on one side. "Which is pretty awful, too. I think I need to stick to biochemistry."

They laughed.

Marty watched as her sister spread the bunting on her lap and brushed the soft material flat. The faint smile on her lips and distant look in her eyes made Marty think she was contemplating all the wonderful things the future would hold.

A smile also curved Marty's lips. Even though she'd given herself and Abby her standard "no relationships" pep talk, she knew that she hadn't quite given up on the idea of having a little fling with Nate. And the sexy dress she'd purchased earlier today was testimony to that. She wanted to knock Nate Peck off his feet tonight—even though she knew she might be asking for more than she could handle.

***

Nate waited in Marty's living room, flipping through the channels on her television. She'd shouted down to him that she wasn't quite ready. It was a first. She tended to be a go-as-you-are type, which worked very well for her. She didn't need to primp; she looked lovely however she dressed.

Nate stood as he heard her coming down the staircase, and when she turned the corner, he nearly collapsed back into his chair. She looked great all the time, but tonight she was . . . He was speechless.

Her hair, even though he knew it was short, gave the illusion it was longer and was arranged on her head in dark waves, held in place with little jewels. She rarely wore make-up, but tonight she had on smoky eyeshadow that made her eyes look darker, exotic. Red glistened on her full lips, luscious and captivating.

Her satiny dress shone different shades of black in the light and clung to her lithe curves. The top was sleeveless like the red dress she'd worn to the inn, revealing her lovely, pale shoulders.

But it was the neckline that caught his attention and held it. Unlike the red one's, this dress's neckline was quite low. The material draped to create a deep valley that ended between her breasts but still covered their firm roundness. The dress was daring, almost naughty, yet still showed very little—although it certainly fueled his imagination quite nicely.

"So what do you think?" She twirled, and he saw the back of the gown also plunged low, leaving her whole back bare to just above her firm little butt.

The air was sucked from his chest. She was beyond breathtaking, beyond beautiful.

"All the men are going to die of coronaries."

She laughed. "I highly doubt that. You don't think it's too outrageous? I was going to wear the red dress, but then I saw this, this afternoon, in a shop down on Main Street. I thought it would be fun."

He nodded with reverence. "It's very fun. And I think it is absolutely stunning. I cannot believe I am going to be seen with you. I've died and gone to heaven."

"Really?" She seemed so unsure. How could a woman who looked like she did be worried?

"You are the most gorgeous woman I have ever seen," he said softly, honestly. "That I will ever see."

She released a shaky breath, then leaned forward and kissed his cheek. "Thank you."

He knotted his hands to keep from touching her. Instead he simply nodded. "Are you ready?"

"Yes." She went to get her coat, which Nate took and held out for her. His knuckles grazed the soft skin of her shoulders as the coat slipped into place.

"Ready," she asked.

He released a shaky breath of his own, then nodded. Tonight was going to prove exactly how much willpower he really had.

Nate was trying not to stare at her, Marty realized as they reached the Old Mill Tavern where First Night was held. He took her coat to give to the coat-check girl, all the while his gaze traveling everywhere but to Marty.

She shouldn't have worn this dress, she realized. It was too wild, too over the top. It honestly hadn't been her intention to even buy a new outfit for tonight. She'd just happened to go downtown before going to Abby's, for a large latte and a new book. As she'd walked down

Main Street to the bookstore, she'd seen the dress in the storefront of Millbrook's only high-fashion boutique, ironically named Flair, just like her fashion agency. And she'd immediately fallen in love with it. The style reminded her of a dress she'd worn on the cover of *Mod* magazine. And even though she wasn't a clothing enthusiast, she had loved the cut and the material of that gown. She'd felt good in it.

She'd peered at it through the plate glass, trying to talk herself out of buying it. She had the red dress. She wasn't dressing for a boyfriend. It was too sexy.

But then a contrary, niggling voice had pointed out it was New Year's Eve, and if there was ever a time to wear a dress like that, it was tonight. So she'd bought it.

This time, unlike her unsuccessful attempts yesterday, she had gotten his attention. When she'd entered the living room, Nate had been floored. He had practically devoured her with those remarkable amber eyes. But it had been his words that had sent a delighted shiver straight through her.

You are the most gorgeous woman I have ever seen. That I will ever see.

She could still hear his low, husky voice, thrilling every cell in her body. He wanted her. That knowledge made her dizzy and weak. Weak enough to give in to her desire.

She watched him as they waited for the hostess to seat them for dinner. He still didn't look at her, and the set of his jaw and his stance clearly showed that he didn't feel comfortable.

The sharp tang of selfishness at the back of her throat made her swallow. She wished she had just worn the red dress after all. She wanted to have fun tonight, not to make things awkward. Not to send him mixed signals.

"I'm sorry," she said softly, leaning toward him so he could hear her over the din of the other revelers.

He glanced at her, a frown pulling his eyebrows together. "Why?"

"I shouldn't have worn this. It's not appropriate."

"Sure it is," he said, his frown still in place. "It's New Year's Eve."

"But I'm making you feel awkward."

He obviously misinterpreted what she meant by awkward. "Are you kidding? You couldn't look more beautiful. I feel like the luckiest man here."

She smiled slightly, loving his compliments. "No— I mean that I am making it hard for both of us to keep our thoughts platonic."

Understanding lit his eyes. "Yes," he agreed. Then another insight came to him and his eyes twinkled. "Did you say *both of us*?"

She hesitated, then nodded. "You look pretty beautiful yourself."

And he did. Tonight, he had on a tailored black suit that emphasized his broad shoulders and muscular body. Underneath the suit coat, he wore a simple white shirt and a plain black tie. His skin was golden and warm against the crisp whiteness of his shirt, and his eyes shone like rich, sun-warmed honey—so striking she couldn't look away from them.

"Do—" He paused, obviously unsure whether he should ask. "Do you want to take this to another level?"

But before she could answer, Sam and a petite woman with auburn hair joined them. "Hey, you two, did—" Sam stopped short as he really looked at Marty. "Marty. You look—unbelievable."

Marty could feel the heat burning her face. This dress was too much. "Thanks," she did manage, then she wondered if "unbelievable" was really a compliment.

The group remained silent for a moment, Sam staring at Marty, the redhead glaring at Sam, Marty feeling distinctly uncomfortable.

Finally Nate said to Sam's date, "Brittany, you look very nice tonight."

Brittany smiled wanly. "Thank you."

Sam, thankfully, regained his senses and smiled down at his date. "She looks like a million bucks," he agreed.

Brittany's sickly expression colored to a flushed grin. "Oh, Sammy." She was obviously infatuated with him.

The hostess approached their group and asked if they wanted to be seated together.

Before Nate could respond, Sam told the woman yes.

"This was great timing," Sam beamed as they wove through the crowded tavern to their table.

That little muscle in Nate's cheek jumped, and Marty got the distinct impression that he didn't agree.

As for Marty, she wasn't sure how she felt. A part of her was relieved to avoid Nate's question, but another part of her knew it was just a delay. The topic would come up again.

She studied him once they were all seated. He was listening to something Brittany was telling him about the pet-grooming business where she apparently worked.

He smiled, and those smile lines appeared, framing his lips.

Her pulse sped up. If the lines around his mouth were enough to send her heart into overdrive, then the topic was definitely going to come up again. It seemed unavoidable.

Nate glanced in her direction. When he started to look

away again, he realized she was watching him and he turned back. And for a brief moment, their eyes locked and held and nothing else existed but the two of them.

Then the real world intruded again.

"So I painted this poodle's nails blue, like the lady asked," Brittany said, her voice raised to be heard over a burst of laughter from the neighboring table. "But then when she came to get the dog, she insisted that she said pink. So I had to do them all over again. And I was almost late for Sammy."

Sam nodded as if to verify the story. He also had a rather pained look, which seemed to indicate he'd heard this story a few times before.

Marty tried not to laugh.

Brittany didn't even pause for breath as she launched into another story about a cat and a bath. Marty tried to pay attention to the story, but she found herself distracted again—this time by her surroundings.

This was the first time she'd ever been inside the tavern, although she did remember when the derelict building was purchased in the eighties and the refurbishing had begun. Now, it was hard to believe this building had practically been falling down. The wood floors were polished to a high sheen and the walls were painted a warm, mellow cream like fresh butter, the texture of the original beadboard still visible. The ceilings were open to the roof, with the beams visible.

"It's hard to believe this was once a working mill, huh?" Nate shifted his chair closer to her, apparently giving up on Brittany's story, too.

"It is," she agreed.

"This is the dining area—obviously," he added with a cute smile. "And through those large doors," he pointed toward the back of the dining room, where giant double doors stood open, "there is another large room, which they call the ballroom. The New Year's party will be in there."

She nodded. "It's lovely."

He smiled, and again their gazes held. But all too quickly, the outside world intruded once more as the waiter came up to take their drink orders.

For the remainder of the dinner, Marty managed to stay fairly well focused on the conversation, which was mainly dominated by Brittany and her endless grooming stories. But she was rather relieved when the meal was over and Nate asked her if she'd like to go into the ballroom.

"Who knew they did so, so many different things at grooming places," Marty said to him in a lowered voice as they walked away from the table.

"The question is, did I want to know?" Nate said dryly.

Marty elbowed him even as she laughed in agreement.

But Marty stopped laughing as she stepped inside the other room. She had expected this room to have the same warm, yet somewhat rustic ambience of the dining room, but there was nothing rustic about this room. It was pure elegance. The floors were carpeted, with the exception of the center, which was done in dark parquet to make up the dance floor. The ceiling wasn't open like the dining area, but rather vaulted with a huge, gorgeous chandelier twinkling in the center. But the most amazing feature of the room was the giant, arched windows that made up two of the walls.

"I never would have guessed this was so lovely inside," Marty breathed.

"It is, isn't it?"

But when Marty nodded at him, he wasn't looking at the room but rather her.

She shifted slightly, suddenly afraid he was going to ask her again what she wanted from their relationship. And maybe he sensed her nervousness, because he asked instead, "Do you want a drink?"

"Yes," she said with a rush of relief. "Chardonnay, please."

Marty waited at the edge of the dance floor as Nate headed across the room toward a small bar. The dance floor was quite congested with people dancing to the music of a band set up in front of one set of windows.

But because of Nate's height, it was easy to follow his progress through the crowd. Several times, people spoke to him, most of them women. He responded briefly and with a friendly smile but then continued on his way. There were also several other ladies, who while they didn't speak to him, definitely noticed him. He left a sea of turned heads in his wake.

"You have the female population of this room all in a dither," she informed him as he returned with a wine for her and a beer for himself.

"Huh?" He appeared honestly confused.

"Many of the women here were watching you cross the room just now."

Nate grimaced, obviously not believing her. "Well, there is only one woman here whose attention I care about."

Her heart skipped a beat, creating a breathless feeling in her chest. She took a sip of her wine.

"So, should we discuss our relationship?" he asked, his voice low.

She took another sip of her wine—more like a

guzzle, really—then shook her head. "I think we should dance first."

He smiled knowingly. "Chicken."

"Absolutely." She set her glass down on one of the small, round tables situated around the dance floor and reached for his hand.

He put down his beer beside her glass and linked his fingers with hers.

They found a space on the crowded floor and he pulled her against him, his hand hot against the bare skin of her back, his chest solid and warm against her front.

For just a moment, she questioned the logic of getting closer to this man who already had her brain completely muddled and her insides all aflutter. Then she simply laid her head on his shoulder and swayed to the music, reveling in the feeling of him. This was where she wanted to be, and for now, she didn't have to label it. She didn't have to think long term. She could just live in the moment.

Chapter 18

"What on earth is she thinking? Wearing that dress?" Josie muttered to Lynette. "She looks a freakin' street-walker."

Jared raised an eyebrow at his sister's description. Did she really think her skintight, low-cut, cheetah-print dress was any less whorish? He shifted slightly in his seat to get a better view of the dancing couple.

He took a drink of his beer, still watching them over the top of the bottle. One thing was for sure—Marty Stepp might look like a streetwalker, but she looked like a damned sexy one. His dick got hard just watching her.

If she were a prostitute, he'd already have his wallet out and be forking over a pretty penny for a piece of some of that.

"Look at how she's draped all over him," Lynette hissed quietly, and Jared knew she hadn't meant for him to hear her.

But he didn't need to hear her anyway. He already knew Marty touching Nate would upset his wife. After all, that was where Lynette wanted to be . . . draped all over Nathaniel Peck like that lame-ass suit he had on.

Jared nearly snorted out loud. He barely recognized his ex-friend—the man he'd once thought of as a brother. He looked like a damned fairy now, with his hair all shaggy and his fancy duds.

Derek said Nate had some memory loss since the attack, but Jared thought it was worse than that. He thought Nate had brain damage. That was the only explanation for his complete personality change.

Then again, Jared supposed a size eleven work boot to the side of the head would make any person a little fruity.

He polished off his beer. Sometimes he felt a little guilty. Then he realized he *really* didn't like Nathaniel anymore. Didn't like him one bit.

He glanced at Lynette. Longing filled his wife's eyes as she watched those two dance and touch.

He stood up. "I'm going to the bar."

Lynette immediately gave him a pleading look—no longing there. Only apprehension. "Please don't drink too much, Jared. This is supposed to be a fun night."

He snorted. "You two seem to be having a fine time. I don't see why I shouldn't enjoy myself, too." He didn't wait for a response but strode toward the bar. He ordered a shot of whiskey, then turned back toward the dancers.

The song ended, but Nathaniel and Marty didn't leave the floor. They stayed close together, talking and smiling. The band started again, and they returned to each other's arms.

"Aren't you two just darling," Jared muttered sarcastically under his breath.

Then he saw the expression on Nathaniel's face. The brain-damaged idiot gazed at Marty as if she was some priceless treasure.

Josie's theory came back to him. Marty Stepp was a

priceless treasure—or rather, as a model, she surely had made a fortune. A fortune that could possibly keep Jared from ever getting his own little chunk of change.

Of course, Derek was right, too. There wasn't any proof that Nate needed money to keep his land—but why risk it?

He asked the bartender for another shot—a double. He growled as the strong liquor burned its way down the back of his throat, ignoring the woman beside him who gave him a disgusted look.

His hard stare returned to Nathaniel and that sappy look on his face. Then he stared at Lynette. She wore the same sappy expression, but was it directed toward her husband?

No.

How would old Nathaniel feel about his woman thinking about another man when they were together? Marty Stepp did look awfully good in that dress—all pale skin and sleek curves. Maybe it was time to find out how Nathaniel felt about sharing.

Marty reluctantly stepped out of Nate's arms as the last note of the song faded. She could stay pressed tight against him all night with nothing more on her mind than the rhythm of the music and feeling of his hands on her skin.

But the music had stopped—a brief intermission for the band.

"Do you want another glass of wine?"

She shook her head.

"Worried about what might happen if you get a little tipsy?" Nate asked with a teasing smile.

"Should I be?"

"No," he said honestly, his smile fading. "What happens between us is up to you."

"Great," she complained. "Put all the pressure on me."

"No pressure," he promised, but it was hard for Marty to ignore the need in his gaze that promised lots of other things that she really wanted to experience but didn't have the nerve to take.

She started to reach up to brush a strand of hair from his cheek but stopped. Before she could drop her hand back to her side, Nate caught it and pressed a lingering kiss to her palm, his lips warm and so soft.

Desire bubbled through her veins.

"Hey, out there." The lead singer of the band's voice rang out over the crowd. "It looks like we have a celebrity in our midst."

The bubbles immediately evaporated, and Marty's stomach sank.

"Everyone, we have international cover model and Millbrook's very own Marty Stepp here tonight."

The whole room fell quiet and everyone turned to stare at her beside Nate, her hand still held in his.

"And it looks like our chief of police is the lucky man who gets to ring in the new year with her."

Unlike Marty, who still stood there, frozen, like a department-store mannequin, Nate received the attention with good humor, raising his free hand to wave at the rest of the room.

"So, Nate, what do you say? Come on up here and sing your lovely date a song?"

That jarred Marty out of her daze; she blinked at Nate. "You sing with these guys?"

"No," he said with chagrin. "Not unless I've had one too many drinks."

"Come on, Nate!" Now the lead guitarist stepped up to the microphone to coax him.

Suddenly the whole room was alive with cajoling, everyone shouting for Nate to sing.

Marty grinned at him. "I think you have to do it or they'll revolt."

"You're just happy the attention is off you," he said dryly.

"Darn right."

He gave her a wounded frown, but then squeezed her fingers and headed to the stage.

The room erupted into applause, Marty clapping the loudest. She also spotted Sam across the room, using his fingers to whistle.

Nate talked to the four guys on the stage for a moment, then walked to the microphone. "Okay," he said, his husky voice filling the room. "Be kind."

The band started to play, the song sounding distinctly like "Stayin' Alive" by the Bee Gees.

Nate gave the band members an incredulous look. "I don't think so."

Marty laughed, as did the rest of the crowd.

The band stopped, all looking inordinately pleased with their joke.

Then the lead guitarist started strumming again, and Marty recognized it as the song Nate had been singing in her kitchen that first morning she got back to Millbrook—"Ready For Love" by Bad Company.

His deep, almost gravelly tone permeated the air like curls of rich smoke as he proclaimed he was ready for love.

She shivered, feeling each note like a brush of warm velvet, like a lick of smoldering heat.

His eyes found hers, and he sang directly to her—for

her, and the smolder quickly ignited into a flame. Once again she had the sensation they were the only two people in the room. The applause at the end of the song actually startled her, she was so lost in him.

He thanked the crowd and started to step down off the stage when Sam yelled a request. Nate shot his brother a dirty look, but when other people began to tease him, he agreed.

"One more," he said, and again he sought her out, almost seeming to ask permission with his eyes.

She nodded, giving him a puzzled grin. Why would he need to make sure it was okay with her?

He smiled back and then gestured as if he were lifting a cup to his lips.

She nodded, understanding that he wanted a drink. The band began to play again as she walked to the bar. This time she recognized the tune as a song by Eric Clapton.

She relaxed against the bar, watching Nate as she waited for the bartender.

Someone touched her shoulder and she turned toward the person, a smile on her lips. The smile instantly faded.

Jared Nye leaned close to her. "Our guy is something, isn't he?"

She didn't answer, returning her attention fixedly to the stage and Nate. Maybe if she ignored Jared, he'd get the hint and leave.

He didn't. Instead, he ran one of his sausage fingers down the length of her bare arm.

She suppressed a shudder and stepped away from him, bumping into a man wearing a tie that flashed 2005 in red lights.

"Sorry," she mumbled.

The man gave her a friendly, slightly drunken smile and disappeared into the crowd.

Marty debated following the tie guy, but before she could decide, Jared caught her wrist.

She started to pull away, but he squeezed, hard. Hard enough to make her gasp in pain.

Her eyes flew from where his meaty fingers dug into her flesh to his goateed face. His eyes were cold, hard.

"I really think you should come with me."

She shook her head, glancing toward the stage. Nate wasn't looking in her direction. She scanned the room for Sam, but couldn't see him.

"Don't worry, I won't keep you long." He loosened his grip. "And I don't think you want other people over-hearing this conversation."

She hesitated. What was he up to? He pulled her toward the door to the dining room, his hold not tight but insistent.

The room was relatively empty, but apparently Jared didn't think it was empty enough. He steered her down a little hallway near the kitchen.

He released her.

"So you and our boy are an item, eh?"

She frowned up at him. "I don't think Nate considers himself *your boy*. And my relationship with him isn't any of your business."

A sardonic twist, more a sneer than smile, curled his thin lips. "I suppose that is true. It isn't good for a relationship to have an outsider involved." Then he moved forward, boxing her between the wall and his bulk. He wasn't taller than Marty, but he was much bigger, with a huge, thick chest and beefy arms.

For some reason, she suddenly thought of Bluto from the Popeye cartoons. Although Bluto seemed like a much nicer guy—even when he was pounding Popeye into a pile of mush.

She edged away from him, sliding along the wall, but he followed, slamming a hand on either side of her, caging her in.

She jumped.

He laughed, the sound cruel. He was close enough that she could feel his breath on her face and smell liquor.

"I need to get back inside. Nate will be looking for me."

"Mmm," he agreed, his eyes no longer cold, but now hot with lust. "If you were my woman, I'd watch you like a hawk. Especially with this little number on."

He lifted a hand from the wall to trace a finger down her collarbone, going lower toward the low dip of her neckline.

She grabbed his hand, pushing it away.

He laughed again. "Feisty. Do you fight Nathaniel, too?"

"Let me go," she said, trying to keep her voice calm.

"There's no reason for you to go. Nathaniel won't mind me sneaking a minute with you." Again he ran his finger up and down her collarbone as he talked. "We used to share women all the time. Hell, old Nathaniel has been with my own wife—but you know that. That he and Lynette used to screw everywhere, all the time."

Marty bit the inside of her lips as nausea and fear rose in her throat.

"But we've shared more women than just Lynette," he said wistfully, as if he were reflecting on some fond childhood memory rather than the repugnant behavior of a couple of jerks. "It used to be a game for us."

He leaned forward so his lips touched her ear. "But you know that, too. You were a game for us back then. But you could be a different game for us now. A friendly game—a nice, sharing game. Nathaniel gets a turn, and I get a turn. What do you say? I think you'll enjoy a real man for a change. Not some pansy in a suit, singing away while he could be screwing you nice and hard up against this wall."

A strangled sound escaped her and she shoved at his chest, but it was like trying to push against a tank. He easily captured her wrists and pinned them to the wall on either side of her head.

"There's no need to go. I'll only make it hurt in all the right places."

He smashed his mouth down on hers, the kiss painful and awful. She gagged and tried to turn her head away, but he had her pinned to the wall, immobile.

Suddenly his mouth was gone, and Marty slid down the wall, collapsing as his crushing weight disappeared.

Shock and anger tore through Nate as he saw Jared holding Marty, his mouth savaging hers.

Marty whimpered and tried to struggle away from Jared, but the hulking man held her clamped to the wall, leaving her floundering like a butterfly pinned to a mounting board.

Nate's fury exploded. He grabbed Jared's shoulder and spun him around, driving his fist into his face. Jared's head snapped back and he staggered a bit, but then he regained his balance and lunged forward.

A rush of air was forced from Nate as Jared's shoulder rammed into his chest. But Nate once again shoved him away and landed another vicious punch. This time, blood gushed from Jared's nose and he fell back backward, landing against the wall to the right of Marty.

Marty, who had been sitting in a shocked daze, practically crab crawled away from the downed man.

Nate rushed to her and knelt, pulling her half onto his lap, holding her close, stroking her hair.

Sam appeared and moved to stand over Jared.

"Are you okay?" Nate asked softly, touching her face.

Marty nodded. "Yes. Yes." But she was trembling and her skin was cold.

Lynette rushed to the group. "Jared. Oh God, Jared." She crouched next to him as he struggled into a sitting position. She searched through her purse, found a tissue, and pressed it to Jared's bloodied nose.

Jared snatched it away and held it in place himself, glaring at Nate and Marty.

"Oh, Jared," Lynette said despairingly. "What did you do?"

"I didn't do anything. That slut," he jerked his head in Marty's direction, "led me on."

"Bullshit," Nate ground out, and started rise to hit that bastard again. But Marty stopped him with just a touch to his hand.

"No. Please."

Nate sank back, pulling her tight to him.

Jared lurched to his feet, using Lynette to balance him. "I should press charges," he sneered at Nate.

"You?" Nate couldn't believe his audacity. The only one there who should have pressed charges was Marty. He tilted his head so he could see her face. "Do you want to press charges?"

"No," Lynette whispered pleadingly.

Marty looked at Nate, then to Sam. Finally her eyes reached Lynette.

Lynette looked awful, tears rolling down her pale cheeks.

The two women stared at each other for a few moments. Then Marty said, "I just want to go."

"Marty," Nate cautioned.

"Please."

Nate stared at her for a minute, then nodded. He rose and helped her to her feet.

"Hey, Marty," Jared called in a patronizing tone, "maybe I'll come by your place and we can finish what we started."

Nate spun back to face Jared. "Is that a threat?"

Jared shrugged and gave him an unconcerned smile. "I guess it depends. I'd call it a date."

Nate clenched his teeth, knowing Jared was just trying to provoke him. He'd seen Jared do it many times before, but this time he was on the receiving end.

"You are a real bastard," Nate said evenly. "Look what you are doing. To your wife. To your friends."

Jared sniffed and spit a gob of bloody phlegm on the floor, completely unaffected by Nate's words.

Nate stared at him for a moment, then said to Sam, "Take him down to the station—for disrupting the peace." He glanced at the spit on the glossy floor. "And littering."

He gently placed a hand on the small of Marty's back and led her toward the exit.

Chapter 19

Nate kept glancing over to Marty as he drove. She sat perfectly still, her arms crossed tight around her as if she was cold.

He bumped the heater up another notch.

After a moment, he asked, "Are you warm enough?"

She blinked at him, then nodded. "Yes."

She fell back into silence, and although he was concerned, he left her alone. They could talk more once he got her home.

But when he pulled into her driveway, she snapped out of her reverie. "I don't want to stay here."

"Jared was just bluffing," he assured her. "I've seen him do it dozens of times before."

She regarded him with an expression he couldn't read. "I don't want to stay here."

"Do you want to go to one of your sisters'?"

"No."

"Do you want me to stay here with you? I'll stay in one of the spare rooms," he added quickly. The last thing she needed was to think he was coming on to her.

She swallowed. "I—I want to stay at your place."

He frowned. "Why? No. I don't think that is a good idea."

She twisted in her seat to face him, her dark eyes beseeching. "I don't want to stay here because I don't want to walk into that house, the house I grew up in, the house that I always considered a safe place, and think about Jared. I can't explain it. It's like . . ." She struggled for the right words. "It's like when you get sick on your favorite food, and suddenly that favorite food never appeals to you again. I don't want my house associated with him."

Nate considered that. "I can see your point, although," he said with an awkward smile, "I'm not sure I want you associating my house with Jared, either."

"I won't. I just—need to be somewhere different."

He hesitated for a moment, then put his car into reverse and backed out of her driveway.

"I really should warn you, though. My house is a cabin. Only slightly nicer than a shack."

Marty didn't look like she believed him. Ah, well, she'd see for herself.

The road into Nate's house was narrow and winding. The snow banks were almost level with the car windows, and combined with bare, gray trees lining the road, created the illusion of traveling through a tunnel.

After one sharp turn, Marty could make out lights through the trees. He turned into a driveway that appeared to be a large round-turn, although it was hard to tell in the shadowy darkness.

Nate shut off the engine. "Well, here we are." His voice sounded reluctant.

She swallowed, feeling a little nervous herself. She

had wanted to be with Nate and to forget Jared. But now, as she peered out into the isolated blackness, she wasn't so sure this was a good idea.

Nate opened the car door and frigid, silent air filled the car. She took a deep breath and opened her own door.

Nate came around to her side of the car and held out a hand to her. "The path up to my house is a little slick, and in those heels, it's going to be downright treacherous," he explained, as if he didn't dare to touch her without permission. And she supposed he didn't.

She took his arm and they started up the slight incline to his front steps. The stairs led to a screened-in porch that ran the length of the front of the cabin.

Two wicker chairs, painted green, and a small table sat to the right of the front door and an old, wrought-iron daybed lined the wall to the right. The mattress was covered with a thick sheet of plastic to keep it from getting wet from the elements.

"I sometimes sleep out here when it's really humid in the summer," he told her, following her gaze.

She could picture him there, in nothing but shorts, sweat on his golden skin, listening to the crickets and the frogs.

He pushed open the door, using his shoulder because it stuck along the bottom of the frame.

She walked into a relatively large room. One side was set up as a living room. Three sofas of different colors and fabrics created a U around a large stone fireplace. On the other side of the room, there was an oval wooden table with four chairs; the chairs didn't match either.

But what struck her more than the mismatched furniture were all the books. Books piled up on a round coffee table in the center of the living area, and more on the floor. Row after row of them were lined up on makeshift shelves on either side of the fireplace.

"I don't have a television," he said again, following her gaze.

She nodded.

"Here." He gestured to one of the sofas. "Sit and I'll start a fire. You might want to keep your coat on until I get it going. My ancient furnace isn't the best."

"I think . . . I'd like to use your bathroom, if I may."

He smiled tenderly at her formalness. "Of course you may. This way."

He led her into the kitchen, a quaint little room with old-fashioned glass-paned cupboards, a deep porcelain sink, and wainscotting on the walls. The bathroom jutted off the side of the kitchen and appeared to have been added onto the cottage after the rest was built. The room was wallpapered with hunting dogs and ducks.

"Okay," he said, once he'd turned on the light for her. He cast a look around as if he didn't know exactly what he should do next. Finally, he smiled, concern still clear in his eyes. "If you need anything, just yell."

She nodded, and he left, pulling the door shut behind him.

She crossed over to the toilet, lowered the lid, and sat down, dropping her head into her hands.

She felt—icky. Not only because Jared had placed his vile hands and mouth all over her, but because he stole that wonderful, contented feeling she'd had with Nate. Then the brute had replaced all those delighted feelings with doubt and misgivings.

How *could* the man she'd danced with tonight, laughed with, ever have been friends with Jared Nye? Marty just couldn't wrap her mind around that.

Jared's words rang in her head. She was just a game. She had been back in high school, and she was now.

What if what Jared had hinted at was true—that she was still a game to Nate?

No, she told herself, she couldn't be. If she were just a bit of entertainment for Nate, he never would have attacked Jared like he had. And Nate had really beaten him up. He would have even kept going if Marty herself hadn't stopped him.

Still, maybe she shouldn't be here, not feeling so confused. But her only thought when he'd pulled into her driveway had been she didn't want to be in her safe place thinking about Jared Nye. Now, she wasn't sure she wanted to be here either.

She lifted her head and looked around. The bathroom wasn't luxurious, with only a small, stall-style shower and rough plank shelves on the wall, but it was tidy and smelled nice, like Nate's soap and shampoo.

She rose and stood in front of the pedestal sink, looking at herself in a medicine cabinet mirror affixed directly to the wall. Her lips were swollen and red. Her eyes were dry but bloodshot and puffy, like the tears were struggling to be released, and her hair stuck out all over her head, most of the jeweled clips gone or loose.

She certainly didn't look like the woman who left her house earlier tonight with the intention to wow Nate. She looked far from lovely.

She studied herself again as she pulled out the remaining hair clips. She looked deranged; she felt a little deranged.

She turned on the water, then reached for a towel. Instead her fingers connected with some of Nate's toiletries, which clattered onto the linoleum floor.

She quickly bent down to retrieve them but paused. They were prescription bottles. Three of them.

She hesitated, then picked up the first one. Vicodin. She assumed he had that for the pain in his knee after getting out of the hospital. The bottle was nearly full.

She read the second brown bottle. Ambien. A sleeping pill. She noticed a few of the pills were gone, but it, too, was over half full.

She picked up the last bottle. Imitrex. She recognized the name from television, but it took her a moment to recall what the medication was for. Migraines, she finally remembered. That bottle was nearly empty.

She wondered how often Nate had migraines. She never recalled him acting as if he had one in all the times they'd been together.

She checked the date on the label. The original fill date had been in August. She checked the other dates. They'd all been filled in August, probably upon his release from the hospital after his attack. Only the migraine medication had been refilled, though.

She stood and carefully placed all the bottles back.

Nate had been through hell. If anything could change a person, it seemed to her he'd experienced it. Suddenly she knew exactly what she wanted—and why she had insisted on coming here. She simply wanted to be with him and to get back that feeling of happiness from earlier in the night. To forget Jared Nye and his repugnant words altogether.

She glanced back at the brown prescription bottles lined up neatly on the shelf. Who would have done this to him? It was someone cruel, someone vicious.

Immediately Jared Nye popped into her mind. Nate didn't believe Jared would do that to him, but she wasn't so sure. She had seen hatred in Jared's eyes tonight, and she wasn't sure if it was directed at her or at Nate.

She shivered. She wouldn't think about it. She would stop thinking about who Nate had been and concentrate on who he was now.

Grabbing a towel, she returned to the sink. After splashing several handfuls of hot water on her face, she dried her tingling skin and looked in the mirror again.

Her lips still looked puffy, as did her eyes, but she felt better. Calmer.

She turned off the water and hung up the damp towel on a metal hook on the back of the bathroom door.

When she entered the living room again, Nate was crouched in front of the fireplace. He'd taken off his winter and suit coats. His tie also lay flung over the back of the blue velour sofa.

She watched as he added kindling to the burning newspapers on the grate. She was mesmerized by the movement of his muscles under the thin material of his white shirt and by the fine hairs visible on his arms, where he'd rolled back his shirtsleeves.

He stood to get some wood out of a box that looked a bit like an old treasure trunk to the left of the fireplace. On the way back, with two logs in his arms, he noticed her.

"Hey," he said softly. "How are you doing?" Worry darkened his eyes to an almost brown color.

"Okay," she told him. "Better."

"Good," he said, sounding ridiculously relieved, and she smiled slightly.

"I should have a good fire roaring here in just a few minutes." He hunkered back down, placing the logs on the hearth. He added more kindling.

Her eyes returned to those muscles bulging in his shoulders and along his sides.

He looked at her over his shoulder. "I realized while you were in the bathroom that we should have at least picked you up some clothes."

She nodded. "This dress isn't very practical for everyday wear."

"Well, if you want to go up in the loft, I put out some sweats you can wear. They'll be huge on you, but they will be warmer."

For the first time, Marty noticed the steep stairs that ran parallel against the back wall of the living room. They disappeared up into a loft, which had a white railing and overlooked the whole room.

How had she missed that? She must have been more dazed than she realized.

"Are you sure?" she asked, looking back at him before she started up the stairs.

He smiled, the grin slightly puzzled. "Of course, I'm sure. Why wouldn't I be?"

She supposed she felt a tad awkward about going into his room. It seemed private.

Carefully, she climbed up.

The loft wasn't huge, but cozy. There was a door at the top of the stairs that she assumed was a closet. She turned left to enter the loft proper. Two plain, although antique, dressers were nestled under the eaves opposite each other. Nate's bed, covered with a thick down comforter, was in the center of the room, pushed up against the far wall. The ceiling created an upside-down V, framing the bed. And a large arched window rose up behind the headboard.

She could picture the early-morning sun dancing over the warm comforter. And over Nate's bare skin.

She shook her head at her thoughts. She really was confused. So many emotions played through her. Maybe she wanted too many things. To get closer to Nate—but to just stay friends. To make love with him—but keep her heart uninvolved. To stay with him forever—but never commit.

Well, at least she wasn't asking for much.

She wandered over to the bed and ran her hand over the comforter. It was covered in soft, plain white cotton and would feel so nice against her skin.

She tested the mattress, also with her hand. Not too firm. A perfect place to snuggle down on a cold winter night.

"Did you find them?" Nate called up from downstairs, and she jumped, snatching her hand away. She looked around guiltily. She spotted the sweats on a wooden cane-back chair in the corner.

"Yes," she said, her voice jittery despite her attempt to sound composed.

"Good. Do you want coffee? Tea? A stiff drink?"

She smiled slightly, her nerves settling a bit. "Coffee would be good."

"Okay."

She could hear his uneven gait heading toward the kitchen. She, in turn, walked over to the chair to his clothes.

Shrugging out of her coat, she shivered, but this time it was the nip of the chilled air rather than her anxiety that created the reaction. She quickly tugged down the zipper on the side of her dress and wiggled out of it.

Without pausing to pick up the dress, she pulled on the gray sweatshirt which, despite her height, looked almost like a minidress on her.

She sat on the chair, unfastened the buckles on her

shoes, kicked them off, and then stood to peel off her hose. The gray pants were on her bare legs in a heartbeat, although they threatened to fall back down again because the waistband was so loose.

She rolled them up twice, which also shortened them enough for her feet to peek out at the bottom of the pant legs.

She swiftly shoved the shirt back down to keep the cold air from her belly.

"No wonder he has that thick comforter," she muttered to herself through chattering teeth.

She picked up her coat and dress and draped them over the chair. Then she balled up her hose and stuffed them into the toe of one of her shoes. She put the shoes under the chair.

By the time she finished that, the bulky material of the sweats had begun to warm her a bit. Except her feet, which were bare and freezing. Maybe he had a pair of socks she could wear, too.

She went to the edge of the loft and looked over the railing to see if Nate was back in the living room. He wasn't.

"Nate?" she called, but got no answer.

She turned back into the room, biting the inside of her lip as she debated whether to just go look in his bureaus for a pair of socks.

Her icy toes made up her mind for her. She opened the top drawer of the one closest to her.

Fortunately, she hit the jackpot. The drawer was filled with white athletic socks—apparently his sock of choice. She looked for the thickest pair she could find, and her fingers brushed against something nonsock-ish.

She moved her hand to reveal a letter, which had

been folded into thirds but now lay partly open, the flowery scrawl of very female writing clearly visible.

She immediately focused her attention back on the balled-up white socks, but reluctantly, returned her eyes to the letter.

What was she doing? First his medication, which was bad enough, but now his personal correspondence. Even considering reading the letter was deplorable.

She nudged one of the socks over the letter, grabbed a pair for herself, and then started to close the drawer. It was nearly shut when her hands by their own volition slid it back open again.

With two fingers, she poked the sock she'd just put over the letter out of the way. She looked guiltily over her shoulder, and then she tilted her head so she could read just a few of the words exposed. The words started midsentence.

> . . . *how lucky I am to have met you. I have looked forward to each of your visits and miss you horribly when you are gone. As you well understand, there is no one who truly comprehends the things we've experienced. The intensity—the life-altering changes. But every time I'm with you, I feel normal. And even though we have to meet in hotels and the back rooms of libraries, I feel at home.*

Marty reread the last line. Hotels and back rooms of libraries? What the heck? Hotels she got—but libraries?

Suddenly the loud crash of wood being dumped, presumably into the wood box, caused her to jump.

"Hey," Nate called. "Are you okay up there?"

"Yes." She cleared her throat because the single

word came out like a frog's croak. "Yes. I'm coming right down."

She brushed the socks back over the letter, even throwing in the pair she was going to put on, and carefully, so he wouldn't hear, pushed the drawer shut.

Taking a deep breath, she headed to the stairs. She wasn't going to think about the letter. She never should have read it in the first place. And in truth, it hadn't really told her much. Just that he'd had a life-altering experience—in the back of a library with this woman.

Jealousy pooled in her belly, but she quickly reprimanded herself. Like she wanted a life-altering experience in the back of a library, or anywhere else, with him.

Then she reached the bottom of the stairs and saw Nate lounging on the red-flowered sofa situated in front of the fireplace. His long legs were crossed on the coffee table.

He held a steaming cup of coffee against his broad chest and stared into the now-roaring fire. She could see the tendons in his neck and the slight smattering of hair at the base of his throat where the top two buttons of his shirt were undone. The flames cast him in gold.

Okay, who was she kidding? She so totally wanted a life-altering experience with this man just about anywhere he suggested, really.

"Hey," he said, his voice quiet, but it still caused her to jump.

Guilt will do that to you.

"I have your coffee." He gestured to another cup, sitting on the table. "I took the liberty of adding a little brandy to it. Just a touch—for your nerves."

It took her a moment to realize he was referring to

her nerves over Jared. Not the letter. Not her attraction to him.

"That sounds good. Thanks." She picked up the mug and joined him on the sofa, although she kept a little space between them. They both stared into the fire, sipping their coffees.

"I am so sorry this happened," Nate said, still looking into the fire. "I . . . I can't believe Jared went that far."

Marty sighed, feeling more drained than distressed now. "You shouldn't be sorry. He was drunk, and he is so jealous of you. I just think he lost his head for a moment." She took another sip of the sweet, creamy drink, then dipped a sidelong glance in his direction. "Not that I forgive him for his moment of craziness. He is *not* a nice person."

"No," he agreed. "He isn't."

She curled her legs up on the sofa, her bare toes nearly brushing Nate's leg.

They both were silent again, the only sound the crackling of the fire and a distant, faint tick of a clock.

Marty glanced around, locating the timepiece, an old alarm clock, on one of the makeshift shelves.

She smiled. "Look." She pointed. "It's New Year's."

Nate laughed. "Well, somehow, with all the events of tonight, we still managed not to miss it. Although it didn't go quite how I pictured."

"How did you picture it?"

"Well, I'd definitely planned to steal a kiss to ring in the new year," he admitted with an adorable little smile.

Her eyes strayed to his mouth. She remembered how wonderful those soft, sculpted lips felt against hers. A flash of longing shot through her.

"It's not too late," she whispered.

Chapter 20

Nate's heart hammered to a standstill at Marty's tentatively whispered words. Could she really mean it? After everything that happened tonight? Did she actually want him to touch her? To kiss her?

He shook his head. "Marty, I don't know if that is such a good idea."

Her dark eyes left his lips. "You don't want to now?"

A sharp, almost painful laugh escaped him. "Oh, I want to—God, I want to. But I think things have been confusing enough tonight. I don't want to make you any more uncomfortable or make things more complicated."

"Is a New Year's kiss complicated?" she asked, the question sounding almost rhetorical.

But he answered anyway. "Between us, I think so. I think what we have is very complicated."

Her chin dipped, whether in agreement or not, he wasn't sure.

But after a few moments she said with great practicality, "But since we're already complicated, I don't suppose a kiss would make it much worse."

He reached for her cup, gently pulling it out of her

hands. He set it on the table with his and turned to face her, taking her hands, heated from coffee, in his larger ones.

Even though he was dying to touch far more than her fingers, there was no way he was going to without knowing the ground rules. Without knowing where she wanted him to stop.

He couldn't risk her feeling pressured, or worse, forced. He would never allow anything between them to remind her of Jared and what happened earlier. She mistrusted men enough before tonight, and Nate had worked hard to gain her trust. He wouldn't destroy that by overstepping his bounds.

"Marty, I don't understand what you want from me," he said, his gaze probing, trying to see in her face what she was feeling.

She stared back, her expression unreadable.

Finally she said in a breathless voice so low he could barely hear her, "I want you to kiss me."

"Darling, I want to kiss you, too."

But he didn't move toward her, despite his burning need.

She looked into his eyes a moment longer and then slowly, she leaned forward and brushed her lips against his, a gentle testing of him.

Her lips were velvety soft. They clung to his with sweet yearning, begging him for something more. And God help him, he couldn't resist giving in to her.

His hands came up to hold the sides of her face, his fingers tangling in her mussed hair. And he kissed her like he'd been longing to do every time she was near.

His mouth sucked and savored. His teeth nipped that soft flesh, and his tongue licked that sugared velvet.

She tasted like sweet coffee and heady brandy. She tasted like heaven, and he couldn't tear his mouth away.

He pulled her closer, practically dragging her into his lap, his mouth hungry and demanding.

Her hands knotted in the material of his shirt, and a smothered whimper hummed against his greedy mouth.

A whimper—like he'd heard her make when Jared had been kissing her.

That single sound was as effective and as immediate to his desire as a bucket of icy lake water over his head.

He jerked away, roughly pushing her back to the other side of the couch.

She blinked at him, confusion clouding her heavy-lidded dark eyes.

But his eyes kept staring at her full lips, reddened and puffy, first from Jared's attack and now from his own assault.

He'd done exactly what he'd told himself again and again that he wouldn't do.

"Nate . . ." The uncertainty, the tremble to her voice tore at him. "I—"

"I'm sorry," he interrupted. "I think—I think we should get some rest. This has been a taxing night. Why don't you go on up and sleep in my bed. I'll stay here on the couch."

She hesitated as though she wanted to argue. She probably decided she'd be safer at home.

And just when he was about to offer to take her back there, she said, unconvinced, "Are you sure?"

"Absolutely. Go on up. I'll stay right here."

She gave him one last uncertain look, then she stood. "Good night, then."

He watched as she slowly climbed the stairs. Once she disappeared, he swiped a hand over his eyes, then pinched the bridge of his nose. He cursed quietly to himself.

What the hell had he done? One kiss and he was all over her. He was a pig.

Marty stared at the ceiling, the thick comforter pulled up to her chin. But even with the heavy bedding over her she felt chilled.

What had just happened?

The situation didn't make any sense at all. In fact, Nate didn't make any sense either.

He'd said that he didn't understand what she wanted from him.

But she didn't understand what he wanted either.

One minute he'd been kissing her as though he couldn't get enough of her. And the next, he was shoving her away as if she repulsed him.

Frustration didn't begin to cover what she was feeling. That man downstairs was toying with her!

She sat up and thumped the pillow, fluffing it up, and then collapsed back against it. She crossed her arms over her chest.

That wasn't exactly fair. After all, she had basically told him if he didn't keep their relationship platonic, she'd leave. Which was what he was trying to do—and she was making that pretty hard for him, what with her low-cut dress and telling him that she wanted him to kiss her.

She released a long breath. Imagine his dismay if she told him what else she'd like him to do. It had to be something about being in his bed, because her wants were becoming increasingly naughty.

She flopped onto her side and faced the wall.

She was really beginning to regret this friendship idea. Because now, it appeared that she wouldn't be able to get naked with him without verbally recanting the plan. Which meant, essentially, she was agreeing to a relationship. Which would be the kiss of death before they even got started.

She groaned, flipped to her back, and pulled the covers over her face.

And there was the letter, which she didn't really know anything about. It could have been written to him ten years ago. But it could have been written to him yesterday. In which case, should she be thinking about recanting on a friendship pact with a guy who was giving some other woman life-altering experiences in the back rooms of libraries?

Again a wave of jealousy flooded her veins and pooled in her belly. And jealousy meant she was invested in him.

She growled, the sound hushed by the heavy layers of bedding over her face.

When had this gotten so difficult?

She lowered the covers and frowned at the ceiling. Actually, Nate was right; their relationship had always been complicated.

So what could she do to satisfy the intense need that had now managed to flush out the jealousy, and get her one-track mind, and body, right back to how she was going to get Nate naked?

She'd never been the type to be so sex obsessed. But she was now.

She rolled onto her other side and gazed toward the open space that overlooked the living room. The orangey light of the fire danced on the ceiling.

Orange was a sensual color.

She groaned quietly, flopping onto her back. Damned one-track mind.

This wretched attraction! She kicked the covers to straighten them out. The smooth cotton settled back over her bare legs like a breathy, whispering touch.

She pictured Nate touching her that way.

She made another noise in the back of her throat. This was torture!

She sighed and scrunched her eyes tightly closed, determined to sleep. But the pitch black of her tightly closed lids proved to be the perfect backdrop to picture Nate, flashes of him like pictures in a viewfinder. Thick, disheveled hair. Amber eyes. A lopsided, sexy smile. His black suit displaying his wonderfully broad shoulders. His white dress shirt fitted to his torso. The top buttons undone, golden brown whorls of hair on his muscular chest.

"Ahh," she moaned through gritted teeth.

Desire coursed through her, begging for satisfaction. Her hand moved downward, over the sweatshirt, toward the waistband of . . .

"Marty?"

Her eyes popped open, and she bolted upright to see Nate's shadowy form at the top of the staircase. The orange firelight illuminated one side of his face, showing the tufts of mussed hair, the cut of his jawline, the sculpted curve of half his lips, one concerned eye.

"Yes?"

"I just wanted to make sure you are all right. I could hear you tossing and turning. It sounded like you were having a nightmare."

"Umm." Nightmare, no. Alarmingly torturous fantasies, yes. "I can't sleep."

"Are you thinking about Jared?"

"No." She took a deep breath. She was going to go for it. Otherwise she was going to spontaneously combust from wanting him. "I was thinking about you."

He remained absolutely still.

"Do you want to know what I was thinking?"

He nodded, an almost imperceptible tip of his head.

"I was thinking that I desperately want to make love with you. Now. Tonight. In this bed."

A hitched breath escaped him, but still he didn't move.

"Do you want that too?" she asked, unable to keep the fear out of her voice—fear he would say no.

"Yes."

A relieved sigh tripped over her lips. Boldly, she lifted up the cover in invitation.

This time there was no stoicism in him, no hesitation. He strode toward her, his limp barely noticeable, and paused at the edge of the bed.

Even with only the faint, flickering light of the fire downstairs, Marty could see the blaze of hunger in his eyes, shimmering and intense.

He reached out and brushed his fingertips down the inside of her leg, starting at her knee and trailing slowly over the curve of her calf to her ankle.

Her fantasy about the cool graze of the sheets being like his touch was so far off. His touch wasn't cool, it was burning hot and electric. Little shock waves started at the place where he touched her and shot through her whole body.

Then those thrilling fingers moved back up her leg, past her knee, to her sensitive inner thigh.

She gasped, and his hand stopped and was gone.

She looked up at him beseechingly. "Please don't stop."

"I won't. But I need to know one thing." He studied

her, his eyes intent, but now not just filled with need but with purpose. "Is this just one night?"

The electricity that had been curling merrily through her stopped dead like a fuse had just been blown.

"Will you stop if I tell you it's only one night?"

"No."

Relief, almost as intense as her attraction, washed over her, leaving her weak.

"But—"

Her eyes locked with his as she waited, afraid of what he might say. Afraid he might stop, even though he said he wouldn't.

His hand returned to her leg, his thumb rubbing the inside of her thigh, dangerously close to the crotch of her panties.

"I do reserve the right to try my damnedest to make you change your mind." His lips curved in a sexy and cocky little grin.

His thumb continued to stroke her electrified flesh, but she managed to murmur, "Give it your best shot, big boy."

Chapter 21

Nate always liked a good challenge. And he had the feeling he was going to like this particular challenge a whole lot.

Marty gazed up at him, the covers still held out from her body, and a sassy smile quirked one side of her lush mouth.

He brushed his thumb against the edge of her panties, nearly touching her feminine core. The smile faded to a look of unadulterated need.

Again, his thumb stroked, this time closer. So close he could feel the damp heat radiating from her, the spring of her curls through the lacy material.

She was hot—for him. His penis spiked against the fly of his trousers.

Another sweep of his thumb. Then another. Each time bringing him just a little closer to that scorching heat.

Then he removed his hand from her petal-soft flesh.

If he was only getting one night, he sure as hell wasn't rushing. In fact, this could take hours.

She bit the inside of her bottom lip and looked as if she wanted to protest at his hand leaving her. But when he moved his fingers to his own shirt, her disappointed look changed to anticipation.

He undid each button until the shirt fell open, then he moved to the button of his pants. He unfastened them and let them slip down his legs to the floor. He shrugged off the shirt, letting it join the pants.

He stood before her in nothing but a pair of plain white boxers.

Her wide eyes roamed over him, dark and hungry.

He reacted immediately, his penis hardening even more, almost painfully, tenting out the loose cotton of his underwear.

Her eyes dropped to that spot. She licked her lips, then met his eyes again. Did she have any idea how sexy she was?

"I think it's your turn, darling," he said, not making a move toward the mattress or her.

She hesitated just for a fraction of a second. Slowly, she peeled his sweatshirt up over her head.

His breath sputtered in his lungs, then stalled, leaving him breathless. No photograph, no designer ad did Marty Stepp justice. She was ravishing.

Her skin was milky pale, but the waning firelight made her glow a pearlescent gold. Her breasts might have been considered a little on the smallish side, but they were absolutely perfect—round, pert orbs with puckered, rosy gold nipples.

Her torso was long and curvy, nipping in at the waist, flaring out at her hips.

His penis and fingers twitched, both parts of his body wanting to touch her.

"My God, Marty, you are so gorgeous."

She smiled, although there was a hint of uncertainty there. How could she possibly doubt her beauty? But he knew she did. And he also knew she wouldn't after tonight. She would never, never doubt he thought she was gorgeous.

"I have to touch you," she whispered, her eyes locked on his chest. "You look just as I imagined."

He smiled at that admission. "You pictured me like this?"

She shook her head and gave his boxers a pointed look. "No, I pictured you nude."

He smiled. "That's a pretty naughty thought for the lady who made me promise to be just friends."

"That lady was a fool." She rose up on her knees, and with almost a look of worship in her eyes, pressed her hands to his chest.

He breathed in sharply as her long, elegant fingers moved over him, stroking down over his chest to his stomach. Then they massaged back up. She leaned forward and kissed his neck, where his collarbone met at the base of his throat.

His hands came out and caught her sides, pulling her against him. Her pebbled nipples teased his chest and her belly grazed his.

He leaned down and captured her mouth, his teeth gently tugging at her full bottom lip, his tongue searching for hers.

She moaned and opened for him, their tongues touching, fleeting sweeps of heat and passion.

Her hands clutched him around the neck and her fingers tangled in his hair. He slid his hands down her sides, savoring the silkiness of her skin. He cupped her lace-covered buttocks, bringing her full against him. Their skin melded just as their mouths did, almost becoming one. Almost. They still had those small scraps of material between them that stopped them from becoming truly one.

He slid his hands up her back until he reached her shoulders, then he gently pushed her back against the mattress, his lips never leaving hers.

He shifted his weight so he was only half on her and one of his hands was free to explore her. He lightly trailed his fingers down her side.

She wiggled, laughing into his mouth. Her laughter felt as wonderful against his lips as it sounded to his ears.

"Ticklish?"

She smiled up at him, her eyes hazed with desire. "Very."

"Good to know."

Before she could respond, if she had even been going to, he dipped his head and flicked his tongue over one of her beaded nipples.

She gasped and arched against him. He licked again, this time swirling his tongue around the distended bud.

She moaned.

He smiled against her breast. What wonderful noises would she make when he did the same thing—only lower?

He gave her responsive little nipple a quick kiss and decided to find out. He pressed nibbling kisses down her ribs to the center of her stomach. His tongue delved into her shallow belly button.

She wiggled again. So he did it a second time, receiving the same reaction.

"Evil," she murmured, and he got the feeling that in this instance "evil" was a *not* bad thing.

His lips traveled past her navel, kissing first one of

Kathy Love

her hipbones then the other, which subtly showed the way toward the delights waiting farther down.

His attention did go there and to the lacy panties still hiding her from him. They appeared to be white or maybe pale pink and made completely of lace.

He leaned in and kissed the hem of them, hugged low on her belly.

She squirmed, but this time he didn't think it was because it tickled.

His lips brushed the edge at the top of her thigh.

She trembled.

He waited a second until she quieted, then ran the tip of his tongue directly up the center of the lace.

She arched up against him with a sharp, little cry, then she rose up on her elbows to look at him. Her eyelids were heavy and her lips parted. But despite the obvious passion in her expression, she also looked embarrassed.

"Nate, you don't—don't have to do that," she said, as if she thought what he was doing was some sort of punishment.

Keeping eye contact, he shifted himself so he was kneeling on the floor. He hooked his fingers over the edge of her panties and tugged them down. He dropped them onto the pile of his clothes.

She stiffened slightly as he then pulled her toward him until her legs were positioned on his shoulders and she was opened wide for him.

Gently he touched her, tracing a finger down her spread sex.

She gasped, but her eyes stayed focused on his face.

He smiled at her. "So beautiful." He stroked her again, this time finding the tiny nubbin begging for his touch.

"Nate," she breathed. "Oh."

His grin widened as he circled and stroked, watching

the myriad of reactions cross her face. Embarrassment faded to enjoyment, which quickly turned to rapture.

With his thumbs, he spread her wider and then placed his mouth where his hand had been, and finally he tasted her, delving his tongue against her, around her. Her essence was sweet, like honey mixed with crisp mountain rain.

Marty froze, and she scooted backward away from him.

He let her move away, although he kept his hands on her thighs.

"Marty? What is it? Don't you like what I'm doing?"

She gave him a pained look. "I—yes. But I . . ." She closed her eyes for a moment, obviously mortified. Finally she blurted out, "I can't relax with you down there. I'm not used to that."

She had to be kidding. What sane man wouldn't want to be right where he was?

He rose up slightly, resting his cheek on her knee. "Marty, I *want* to do this. I *want* to taste you. You wouldn't deprive me of this pleasure when I might only get this one night, would you?"

"We can do other stuff."

He grinned, surprised that the woman who had propositioned him *and* who had also traveled the world as a supermodel, no less, was so sexually shy. The opportunities must have been there for a lot crazier sex than this.

"We are going to do other stuff, darling," he promised and pressed a kiss to her knee. "I plan to do everything I've been fantasizing about since you returned to Millbrook."

"You fantasized about me?"

He widened his eyes and then chuckled. "You silly

woman. I haven't been able to think about anything but you since you nearly brained me with that album."

She still looked dubious, but her eyes glanced down her body to where he'd been. He could see embarrassment war with her desire.

"Okay," she finally whispered.

He smiled with great satisfaction, then kissed the inside of her thigh. The muscles in her legs were tense as he moved back to her. And she jumped when he touched his fingers to her center, so he moved slowly, allowing her passion to overcome her nerves.

The pad of his finger made brief contact with her pebbled clitoris, then slipped away only to return. Little by little, the muscles in her long legs relaxed and her knees fell open, offering him better access.

With his fingers still stroking her, he leaned in, and like Indiana Jones trading the bag of sand for the jewel, he replaced his finger with his tongue.

Marty still felt the transition and stiffened, but he kept up the gently insistent pressure. His tongue circled and flicked.

Gradually, her breaths came in gasping little huffs and the tautness melted as she began to squirm. Her hips rose, pressing her closer to his mouth, demanding more pressure or less.

He sucked or licked, following her lead.

She began to writhe, her hips bucking, her knees clamping to his shoulders. Suddenly her muscles seized up again, but this time it wasn't with anxiety, but rather with an orgasm that tightened her body like a taut bow.

"Nate!" she cried, jerking up against him, and he felt her whole body spasm. She fell back on the mattress, her back arched, her arms out to her sides.

Nate had never seen anything so arousing, so beautiful. He placed a kiss to her damp sex and then slid up her body, needing to touch all that lovely skin splayed out across his bed.

Her breath was still coming in short, harsh puffs, and her eyes were glazed over with the afterglow of her climax.

He touched her hair, brushing the wild strands from her cheeks.

"Was that okay?" he asked.

She focused on his face, her hazy eyes widening. "That was amazing." She reached up and brushed her fingers over his lips with reverence. "Absolutely amazing."

He smiled against her fingertips, then pressed kisses to each one. He leaned down and kissed her mouth.

She responded by wrapping her arms around his neck and pulling him down onto her. Her skin was hot and soft and wonderful. She slid her hands over his shoulders and down his back, slipping them inside his boxers to cup his buttocks, to draw him closer.

His erection pressed into her belly, and he groaned. She moaned in response and rocked against his hardness. He continued their kiss, trying to get his hunger under control, but the kiss was only driving him madder. His tongue slipping into her mouth only reminded him of other places he wanted to slip into.

"I . . . want . . . you . . . inside . . . me," she told him in between their hungry kisses, as though she'd been reading his mind.

Her words frayed his self-control. "Mmm, I want that too," he muttered roughly.

God, did he want that. Her skin, her taste, her reaction was driving him wild. He couldn't remember ever feeling this desperate for a woman, this out of control.

He moved away from her to kick off his boxers and reach into the nightstand at the side of the bed. He grabbed a condom from a box there, then he fell back on her.

She rose out of her haze for a moment at the sight of the silver packet. And he feared for a moment the condom somehow had snapped her to her senses and made her doubt what they were doing.

Instead, she took it from him and tore the foil open with her teeth, which he found oddly thrilling.

She positioned herself closer to him and lifted the condom to the head of his penis. She stopped.

"When I called you big boy, I really had no idea," she said in her sassy way, but he thought he saw a bit of alarm in her eyes.

He placed his hands over both of hers, and together they rolled on the condom. He loved the feeling of her fingers moving under his hands and down the length of him. It was highly erotic, but he was starting to think anything this woman did to him would drive him over the edge.

Once the condom was on, his mouth found hers and he pushed her back down on the mattress, covering her with his full weight.

She seemed to exult in his weight as her arms wrapped around him, holding him tight. Her knees came up to cradle him.

Their kiss grew more heated, more consuming. Marty's hands stroked up and down his back, her nails scraping lightly over his oversensitized flesh.

"Nate," she begged, her hips wiggling against him. His penis pulsed, nestling between the damp folds at the juncture of her legs.

He had wanted this to last. But he couldn't survive not being inside her for one more moment. He was too hungry for her tight warmth and she was so tempting, lying open under him.

With more force than he'd intended, he entered, sliding into her glorious, hot tightness.

A broken gasp echoed in his ear, and he stilled.

"Are you okay?"

She nodded quickly. "You feel so big, so heavy."

"Does it hurt?"

"No," she said with a wondrous smile. "You feel incredible."

He pumped his hips, slowly pulling himself out and sliding back in.

Her mouth fell open and her eyes shut. "Yes," she breathed. "Yes."

And that was it. Nate couldn't have stopped moving, couldn't have stopped making love to this woman, even if his long-lost mother and all her alien friends suddenly showed up at the foot of the bed.

Marty yawned and stretched her legs, loving the smoothness of the sheet on her bare skin. But more than that, she loved the feeling of the warm, naked man beside her, his chest pressed to hers, his arm around her waist with his broad palm and long fingers splayed across her back.

She raised her head, barely able to see Nate in the darkness. The fire in the living room had died down, leaving the room shadowy and nearly black.

She jumped slightly when he said in a voice that was wide awake, "Hi there."

"I thought you were asleep," she whispered, her own voice raspy from sleep.

"I dozed," he told her, the hand on her back stroking up and down her spine. A delicious shiver ran through her.

"How could you not sleep after that? I think I fell unconscious."

He chuckled. "I think you did, too. And men get the bad rap."

She stretched again. "Well, if most men are making love like that, then it's hardly a surprise."

"That good, huh?" She could hear the smugness in his voice.

"Nate," she said in all honesty, "you make love like a house on fire."

Nate was quiet for a moment, his hand stilled on her back. Then a rich, rough burst of laughter escaped him. "I sincerely hope that was a compliment."

She kissed his chest. "That was definitely a compliment." She laid her head against the tickly hair of his chest. She listened to the steady beat of his heart. She'd never felt this wonderful, this satisfied.

His hand continued to caress her back.

"So Arturo wasn't too great in the sack, huh?" The question startled her. But she could also hear the odd combination of satisfaction and insecurity in his tone.

She debated whether she really wanted to talk about it. Finally she sighed and admitted, "I never got in the sack with Arturo."

She felt Nate's head lift off the pillow. "How long did you date him?"

"Two years."

Nate was silent for a moment. "How did he never make love to you? What? Was he gay or something?"

Mary knew the question was asked jokingly. Too bad her reply wasn't.

"Yes."

Chapter 22

Nate's hand stopped tracing the column of Marty's spine. She had dated a gay man for two years?

"Didn't you know?"

She was quiet, and he thought his question had probably offended her, but in the dark, he couldn't see her face to know for sure.

"For the first year, no. I didn't," she said, then laughed, the sound full of self-derision. "He was my first real boyfriend, and I just thought we were taking things slow. By the second year, well, I still didn't guess he was gay, but I got a pretty clear picture that he wasn't attracted to me. The third year, we weren't really together—other than to make public appearances, things like that—but I still thought maybe I could become what he wanted. But of course I couldn't."

She laughed again, old pain sharpening the sound.

Nate tightened his hold on her. He hated the idea that this idiot had led her to believe she was the one with the problem in the relationship.

"You did all you could," he told her. "You simply didn't have the right equipment."

She rubbed her cheek against his chest; he loved the softness of her skin.

"I know." She didn't sound like she truly believed it.

"Did he date you because he was trying to deny who he really was?"

Marty paused, her cheek still pressed to a spot right over his heart. "Maybe. I think he thought giving off the impression of being straight certainly couldn't hurt his career. Women love him."

"How did you meet?" Nate wasn't sure why he felt like he needed to know every detail—but he did. He wanted to know everything about her.

"We worked together several times, and we got along really well. One thing just led to another, and we became a couple. I don't think he specifically planned anything. It just happened."

"Were you already gaining notice in the industry?"

She nodded, another brush of velvety skin. "And I helped him get a lot of jobs. Big jobs. Calvin Klein. Dolce and Gabbana. Versace. But his goal had always been to break into acting."

"And he has."

"Yes."

"So he took advantage of the help you could offer," Nate stated flatly.

"Yes."

"Did he break things off when he got into acting?"

"I left him."

He moved his hand from her back to her hair, caressing the wayward locks.

"Did you love him?"

She shrugged. "I thought I did. I did love him as a friend. We have run into each other a few times since, and we are okay. But I did feel used—played for a fool, I guess."

He moved his hands to catch her sides, drawing her fully onto him and sliding her up his body. He sank his fingers into the mussed hair on the back of her head and pulled her down to him, kissing her passionately.

"Well, this is your night to use me," he informed her. "So have at it."

She laughed, the sound genuine.

His heart swelled that he had been able to please her, make her happy, when she was pained by ghosts.

She cupped his face and pressed another long, breath-stealing kiss to his mouth. Then one of her hands snaked down between them to find his arousal, already surging against her.

She stroked him. "It would be a shame to waste all this glorious naked maleness."

"Absolutely," he agreed, and bit back a euphoric sigh as her long, talented fingers encircled him and moved again.

The next time Marty woke, the room was filled with gray winter light. It was impossible to tell the time. It could be 7 A.M. or it could be noon. She rose up slightly and looked for a clock.

She couldn't find one, so she fell back on the pillows, deciding to believe it was still early.

She curled onto her side and looked at Nate. He was asleep, one of his arms flung over his head, all the sinewy muscles visible and gorgeous. His other hand was on his belly, which was bared. In fact, only one little corner of the comforter was draped over his waist, and the rest of him was magnificently nude.

The cold certainly didn't bother him, but then again, sleeping beside him was like sleeping next to a furnace. He was hot—in many ways.

She studied his face, realizing this was the first time she'd ever seen him absolutely at rest. Nate, even when he was quiet and peaceful, never gave the impression of being still. Something about him was too dynamic. Too vital.

She was glad he was asleep. He needed it. He never complained, but she knew his insomnia really aggravated him.

Plus, she got a chance to admire him as long as she liked, she thought with a selfish little smile.

And he did look wonderful. His disheveled hair framed his face, and his sinfully long, burnt gold lashes fanned out beneath his closed lids. His mouth was so luscious, with a distinctly sculpted top lip and a softer, fuller bottom lip. And then there were all those lovely, lean muscles still prominent under his skin even in complete relaxation.

He was gorgeous. By far the most gorgeous man she'd ever seen.

Her smile widened. And definitely the most talented. She had no idea that making love could be like that. Not a clue. Despite what most people would think, her jet-setting life as a model wasn't spent in the fast lane, but rather mostly in the breakdown lane. She'd only had two lovers—three now. And they hadn't been anything like Nate. He was unbelievable. Amazing. Earth shattering.

She started to brush a lock of his hair from his cheek, but caught herself. She didn't want to disturb him. Instead she nestled her head into her pillow and simply enjoyed the sight of him and the satisfaction still humming through her limbs.

She had no idea how long she stayed like that, occasionally drifting into a pleasant, relaxed state somewhere between sleep and wakefulness. But eventually, nature called and she didn't think she could ignore it any longer.

Carefully, she shoved back the covers and slid her legs over her side of the bed. She glanced back at him to make sure he was still sleeping, then she stood.

To her relief, the bed made no noise. She crossed her arms over her chest, shivering at the cold air prickling over her skin. She tiptoed around the bed and found Nate's sweatshirt. She tugged it over her head and glanced at him once more.

He was in the same position he'd been in when she first woke up.

She smiled again. It was a very nice pose—the stuff of female fantasies. But instead of allowing her to admire the sight, her rather insistent bladder shouted for her attention again, and she crept to the stairs.

The steps only squeaked twice on the way down, but once she hit the wood floor, she raced to the bathroom.

She sighed with relief once she got there, as did her poor, overextended bladder.

She flushed the toilet, praying that the noise wouldn't wake Nate. It likely wouldn't, she decided. The old furnace in the living room had rattled to life and it was blowing air noisily. She went to the sink to wash her hands. Her reflection in the mirror caught her attention. The woman who peered back at her this morning didn't look anything like the one who'd been there last night.

Last night she looked disheveled and distraught. This morning she looked tousled and very well tumbled. She definitely liked this woman much, much better.

She grinned foolishly at herself, but then jumped when Nate's voice bellowed through the cabin.

"Marty!"

But before she could even throw open the door and rush out to see what was wrong, the bathroom door flew open and Nate stormed in.

A look of overwhelmed relief crossed his face as he saw her. Then the relief dissolved to embarrassment.

"Sorry," he said, grimacing slightly. "I thought you just took off."

She smiled, actually flattered by his complete panic. "In what? My dress and high heels? Or in this?" She glanced down at the sweatshirt. "I don't even have on underwear."

His eyes immediately darted to the juncture of her thighs, only covered by a few inches of material. Desire was clear on his face—and on his body.

"But then again, you aren't wearing any underwear either." She eyed his erection with amused and desirous interest.

If Nate was embarrassed about standing in front of her fully nude and aroused, it didn't show on his face.

Then again, he had no reason to be embarrassed. He was a god.

He prowled toward her, looking very powerful rather than vulnerable in his nudity.

He tugged her against him and kissed her, hungry and forceful.

Instead of being startled by the possession in his touch, she reveled in it. She couldn't help herself; it felt wonderful to have him want her so fiercely.

His hands slid down her back to find her bare bottom, his hands hot against her cool flesh.

He lifted his head. "You're freezing."

"Not with you touching me." She leaned back in to continue their kiss, but instead, he caught her hand and led her to the shower. He turned on the water, the spray thundering against the walls of the stall.

He reached for the hem of the sweatshirt and peeled it over her head, tossing it aside.

His eyes roamed over her. Then he reached out to touch one of her breasts, the distended nipple greedily prodding his hand. He gently squeezed it, and surges of aching need shot through her, centering between her thighs.

She arched into his touch. He squeezed again, and she gasped.

"Let's continue this someplace warmer," he murmured, and reached down to give the painfully hardened nipple a quick lick.

Before she'd recovered from that sizzling caress, he lifted her into the shower, steamy water sluicing over her stimulated skin like dozens of fiery little tongues lapping down her body.

She gasped again.

He followed her in, his large frame boxing her between the shower wall and his chest.

"Damn, this shower is small for two."

She wrapped her arms around his torso, resting her head against his shoulder. "No, it's just right."

They stood together, letting the water and their desire warm them.

Marty kneaded the muscles of his back as he stroked hers, every shared touch stoking the fire building in her.

Nate released her and picked up the bar of soap. He rubbed the bar between his hands, placed it back in the holder, then began to massage slippery bubbles over her skin.

She leaned back against the shower wall, her eyes closed, her breathing hitched. Her whole body concentrated on his hands massaging over her skin.

"You have the prettiest breasts," he said, his voice huskier than usual.

"Small," she said, opening her eyes to look up at him.

"Perfect," he stressed and worked the suds over them, shaping his palms to their roundness. His fingers teased her nipples.

She moaned, arching against him.

His hands moved from her breasts, sliding down her ribs to spread more foam across her belly. Then one hand slipped between her thighs, a slick finger sliding inside her, teasing her there as he had her breasts.

He leaned forward and captured one of her nipples, gently running his teeth over it.

She bit back a sharp, thrilled cry.

His mouth sucked and nipped while his finger swirled and dipped deep inside her, only to glide back out and swirl some more.

The combination of sensations pounded through her, overwhelmed her until abruptly, waves of release were washing over her like the gushing water over her flesh.

"Nate," she cried out, and he seized her cry of climax in his mouth, kissing her senseless.

She leaned heavily against the wall, eyes closed, as Nate kissed her face and her throat.

"How do you do that?" she mumbled weakly.

She felt him smile against her shoulder. "Do what?"

"Make me respond so easily."

"Hmm." He considered the question between kisses. "I guess you are just mad about me."

She opened her eyes, but he wasn't looking at her. He continued to spread nibbling little bites over her shoulder.

Was she mad about him? Oh God, yes. Her heart

swelled in her chest. She was *so* mad about him. Crazy mad. For a moment the idea scared her, but she pushed it aside.

She reached for the soap, which was back in the dish. "My turn."

She soaped up her hands and began massaging his chest. Her hands slid lower to the hard flatness of his belly, and her fingers brushed over the raised ridges on his side. For the first time she noticed the pink puckered scars on his right side. Three of them, unevenly slashed up his rib cage.

She had seen the scars on his knee; how had she missed these?

It had been dark last night, and this morning his right side had been away from her. She leaned down, gently running her fingers over the marks.

"My God, Nate," she gasped, gaping up at him. They were dreadful, brutal scars.

He glanced at them. "From the attack. The doc isn't sure about what caused those either."

Marty's heart wrenched, and her stomach roiled. How had he lived through such violence? Thank God he had lived.

She rose up and kissed him with all the gratefulness, all the emotion inside her, needing to hold him.

He returned her touch with just as much fervor.

Her mouth left his and kissed down his body in a frenzied combination of hunger and exaltation, until she was kneeling in front of him. Her knees were between his spread feet.

She kissed the taut muscles beneath his belly button, then she brushed her lips against the head of his penis.

All the muscles in Nate's body seemed to tense.

She pressed her mouth against him again, this time using her tongue to lick over and around him.

A shuddering breath escaped him.

"Do you like that?" she asked.

"Yes."

She smiled, feeling powerful. She took him farther into her mouth, using her hand to fondle him as well.

"Marty," he growled, his fingers knotting into her hair.

She continued to lick and stroke him with her lips and tongue and fingers.

And she quickly proved that she had the same effect on Nate as he had on her.

Chapter 23

Marty smiled as she came down from upstairs in her borrowed sweats—both from the residual effects of her lovely shower with Nate and from the sound of him singing along with a song on the radio. The beginnings of a fire crackled in the fireplace. Being here, at Nate's cabin, just felt good—right.

She walked into the kitchen to find him in only a pair of jeans, working at the counter.

He really was impervious to the cold, which was nice. It certainly led to lots of lovely views of that well-built body.

"Hey," he said when he saw her. The look on his face was an odd combination of sheepishness and happiness. "I think I may have bad news."

She frowned and waited for him to continue.

"Look outside."

She wandered over to the sink and peered out the window above it. Snow fell in thick, heavy clumps, and from the look of the ground and Nate's car, it had been falling that way for hours.

"Wow, there has to be almost a foot out there. How did we not notice it earlier?"

She immediately realized the answer to that question and felt her cheeks warm.

He wiggled his eyebrows lecherously in response, but said seriously, "I don't think I can get the car out the camp road, but if you really want to leave I can call someone. Maybe Tommy Leavitt or Derek Nye . . ." He realized his mistake at mentioning a Nye, even if it wasn't the one who'd attacked her. "Well, someone might be able to get you out."

She shook her head, probably a bit too quickly, too eagerly. "That isn't necessary."

"Well, then, it looks like you're stuck here for a little longer." He looked pleased.

A ridiculously happy feeling swirled in her belly. "Well, if I am, I guess I am."

"So does that mean I have another night to convince you that we should make this fling thing more long term?"

Another swell of happiness skittered through her insides. But she sighed and attempted to look blasé about the idea. "I suppose."

Who was she kidding? She was already convinced. She never wanted this to end.

She glanced back out the window, noticing for the first time the great expanse of flat snow out past Nate's car.

"Are you right on the water?"

"Yep." He continued to work at the counter, getting out a cutting board and a knife. "I actually have fifty acres, all of it water accessible."

"Wow. I didn't know that. What a beautiful view."

"Even better in the summer," he told her, then he gestured to the vegetables on the counter. "Hungry?"

She nodded. "Starving."

"Well, I am making my specialty."

She leaned on the counter, watching him chop up mushrooms and green peppers. "What is it?"

"Eggs," he said with a lopsided smile.

She laughed. "Can I help?"

"Nah, go relax. I'll do this and bring the plates in by the fire."

She hesitated, but the lure of the warm fire was too much to be ignored. She padded into the living room and settled on the red-flowered sofa. The fire was now blazing cheerfully, and the heat felt wonderful.

She glanced around. She liked this cabin. Sure, it didn't have all the conveniences of a typical home, and it was a little chilly, but the place had character.

Nate came in, carrying a large mug of coffee. The rich scent mingled with the wood smoke.

"Here, to help warm you up." He handed her the cup, then headed back into the kitchen.

She took a sip of the coffee, then sighed. *Delicious coffee brought to you by a hunky, half-naked man as you lounge in front of a toasty fire. Who the hell needs a microwave?*

She took another sip of the creamed and sugared liquid. The pile of books on the coffee table caught her attention. She set down her mug and reached for the one on top.

A Death Less Ordinary.

She frowned at the title. Was it a mystery novel? She flipped the book over and read the back-cover blurb.

It was a book about near-death experiences, she realized. Did Nate believe in this sort of thing? She recalled those vivid scars on his side, on his face. Did he have a reason to believe it?

She opened the front cover and read a bit about a woman's soul leaving her body, only connected to her physical being by a silver thread. That didn't seem like something that would interest Nate. She set it aside and reached for another book.

Helping Children in Trouble.

Now, this book she could see him reading, what with his interest and concern for Peter and Frederick Knowles. She placed that on top of the near-death book.

She picked up another one.

Your Dream Job: Starting Your Own Business and Making It Work.

She looked up from the book as Nate entered with a plate in each hand. His gait faltered slightly as he looked at her, but she couldn't tell if it was a reaction to her or a pain in his knee.

"Are you okay?"

He nodded. "What have you got there?"

She held up the business book. "I was just reading about starting my own business."

His posture seemed to relax, but she couldn't be sure. "Fun reading, eh?"

She set it on the table and accepted the plate he offered. "You have a very eclectic taste in books."

He shrugged. "I'll read anything. I'm the type who reads the back of the cereal boxes when I'm eating breakfast."

She smiled, easily able to picture that. "Mmm," she sighed as she took a bite of the eggs. "These are good."

"This is quite different than our first breakfast together," he said before taking a bite of his eggs.

"Well, if I'd known you were such a sex machine, I might have been a bit nicer."

He laughed. "I guess I should have told you that right off the bat."

She smiled, then leaned forward to kiss him, just a brief, sweet kiss.

They parted and resumed eating their eggs. Contentment encompassed them like the heat from the fire.

"So, are you planning to start your own business?" Marty asked, reaching for her coffee mug.

He nodded, but swallowed his food before he answered. "I'm actually thinking of starting a summer camp for kids—an Outward Bound–type thing. I really want to help kids who might be on the wrong path in life."

She was impressed. "I see a theme here." She lifted up the book about helping troubled kids. She put that aside and held up the near-death experience book, giving it an askance look. "Although I don't see how this one ties in."

He shifted against the couch cushions. "Well, I told you, I read everything."

"I think a summer camp sounds like a wonderful idea. You are so good with kids; you'd be great at it."

"I'd really enjoy it."

"So, how does one go about starting a summer camp?" She took another bite of eggs.

He sighed. "First you need a lot of money—which I'm working on right now. Then I'm hoping to approach Mason about helping me get all the appropriate building and zoning permits. And I also plan to ask Chase to help me with the actual building of the camp."

Again, Marty was impressed. "So you are really planning to go through with this?"

He nodded. "Yeah. Although I haven't told anyone yet. I need to get things in order before I say anything. I don't want to get the station in an uproar about me leaving before I have to. But I need to do something different with my life, and this is just the thing."

Marty pictured it: sun, water, campfire song, and s'mores. Running a summer camp did sound like just the thing. It sounded wonderful—working with kids, making a difference in their lives. She could be very happy living like that.

"So, I don't suppose you'd like to give up your glamorous life as a model to become a camp counselor," he asked as though he could read her mind—or maybe it had been the dreamy look on her face that gave her away.

"Mosquito bites, poison ivy and all," he added with a slight smile.

"Are you trying to tempt me or dissuade me?"

He placed his plate on the table and slid closer to her, taking her empty dish and putting it near his. He turned back to her, the amber of his eyes vivid. "I am always trying to tempt you."

He lowered his head, his lips molding to hers in an unhurried, awe-inspiring kiss.

Coming home to this man and these lips every day was well worth a serious case of poison ivy with mosquito bites on top.

She looped her arms around his neck and continued to taste him. Oh, *so* worth it.

Nate watched Marty as she pursed her lips and debated over the cards in her hand. She rearranged a few of them, then quirked her mouth again.

Despite the fact that they had gone back up to bed

after breakfast and spent most of the afternoon making love, his body still reacted to the twist of those full lips. He was insatiable when it came to this woman.

And he was falling—hard.

"Do you plan to go any time soon?" he asked more gruffly than he'd intended. His frustration was with his wayward body, not her.

She frowned at him. "Okay, Mr. Impatient." She considered her cards again. "Do you have a four?"

"Go fish."

She huffed and drew from the deck set between them on the floor. "You rushed me," she muttered.

He smiled smugly. "Do you have a queen?"

She rolled her eyes and tossed the card at him.

"I never knew I was so good at this game."

Marty nudged his legs, which were stretched out across the rug, with her toes.

"Do you have an eight?" she asked with a suddenly sweet smile.

"Go fish."

She grumbled something under her breath and picked a card from the pile.

"Do you have an ace?"

She gave him a dirty look and handed it to him.

He slapped the cards down. "I win again!"

Marty pitched her cards down. "You cheat."

He gave her a wide-eyed, wounded look. "I did not cheat."

She shifted from her cross-legged position to stretch out on her back and stared up at the ceiling. "I've heard that before."

He frowned, propped his head on his elbow, and studied her profile. Was there more to that statement than just a reference to their game of cards?

"Who have you heard that from before?" he asked softly.

She turned her head to look at him. Something flickered in her cocoa brown eyes. "It's just a figure of speech." She then smiled, but it was her forced little half smile.

She turned back to stare at the ceiling.

He continued to watch her. He didn't know if he should push the issue any further, but he did get the definite feeling there was more to this. Maybe someone other than Arturo had hurt her badly too.

"Did someone cheat on you, Marty?"

She didn't look at him. She didn't answer.

He immediately felt guilty for prying. "Listen, I'm sorry. If you don't—"

"His name was Rod," she said, cutting him off. "He had quite the habit of cheating and lying."

Nate remained quiet.

"At last count, he was up to seven—seven women who he cheated on me with. There may have been more, but those are the ones I know about."

His gut twisted. What kind of asshole would cheat on her? What woman could this guy possibly want more than Marty?

Nate gritted his teeth, imagining her pain at each of those discoveries.

"But when I walked in on him this last time with a model nearly half my age, I decided that I couldn't do it anymore. And I just left."

Nate felt pride loosen the anger tightening his stomach. She'd gotten up her nerve and walked.

"That night of the nor'easter, actually," she added with a humorless laugh.

Instantly, his insides screwed tight again. *The nor'easter.*

He pictured her at the gas station that first night he'd seen her again, the snow falling as heavily as it did today. He recalled her erratic driving. Had she been crying? Had her mind been on Rod?

"So you were with Rod right up until you left New York?"

"Yes," she said, her voice heavy with self-derision.

He had hoped her answer would be different.

That was only a few weeks ago. Less than a month ago Marty had been involved with another man.

"How long were you together?"

She still didn't look in his direction. "About a year and half or so."

A year and half. That was a long time, especially compared to what she'd been willing to offer him. She'd give this jerk a year and half, and Nate wouldn't have even gotten twenty-four hours if it hadn't been for the snow.

Twenty-four hours. Long enough for an affair. Long enough to soothe her wounded ego. Long enough to get back at Rod. And long enough for Nate to imagine they could have something more.

"But you did tell him it was over, right?" He had to know.

She shook her head. "I didn't say anything. Just left."

He levered himself up. "I need to get some wood. The fire's dying down."

He buttoned up his flannel shirt as he strode to the door. Then he shoved on his boots, not bothering to tie them, not bothering with a coat.

The cold air felt good on his skin, an icy slap to the face. The snow stung where it landed on his bare skin like Marty's admission stung his heart.

She couldn't be over this guy. How could she be—a year and half versus, what? Maybe four weeks total? And Rod didn't even know it was over. Maybe it wasn't really over. Maybe Marty would go back to him tomorrow.

He trudged through the heavy, wet snow toward the woodshed.

Here he was, believing they could actually fall in love—hell, he was already in love, and she was trying to recover from a crappy relationship. She was having a rebound fling.

Using more strength than necessary, he yanked open the squeaky old door and stomped to the woodpile. He started to lift one of the logs, then stopped, bracing his hands on the uneven stack of wood, hanging his head.

Was this how it felt? All those times he'd slept with women just to satisfy his own needs? Without any thought of their feelings—or their hearts?

He released a weary sigh. He supposed this ache in his chest was nothing less than he deserved.

Marty waited on the porch, the cold piercing through the thick terry cloth of Nate's socks to her feet and the cold air seeping through his oversized clothes.

She could see his footprints where he'd gone down the steps, but after that they disappeared into the dark night.

He hadn't been gone long, but he'd left so abruptly she was worried. Had something about Rod upset him? Or worse, had she done something to upset him?

Relief rushed through her limbs as she made out his

shadow coming around the corner of the cabin, his arms piled high with wood.

"Nate," she said, holding the screen door open for him, "are you okay?"

"Sure," he said, not looking at her, heading toward the inside door.

She caught his arm. "Nate, what did I do?"

He frowned at her, giving her a puzzled look. "You didn't do anything." He glanced at her hand as if to say, *let me go*, but she didn't.

"Are you upset by Rod?"

"No."

She could tell that was a lie. "Why? Why would he upset you?"

"Well, I don't like that he hurt you."

"But why do I get the feeling that *I* somehow hurt you?"

He turned back to look at her. "You need to get inside; it's too cold out here."

She started to resist but realized he was right, and he didn't have on a coat on either.

But once inside, she asked him again. "Nate, what did I do?"

He dropped the logs into the wood box, the loud clatter making her cringe.

He picked up two pieces, then kneeled down in front of the fireplace, moving the screen to one side of the hearth. He took the poker and stirred up the coals. They sparked orange in the dark evening light.

"I think maybe I should try to call Tommy or someone to see if they can get in the road. You don't want to get stuck here another night." He still didn't look at her.

"Or is it that *you* don't want me stuck here another night?"

He prodded the coals again. "I think it's for the best."

"Why?" What had happened so quickly to change everything between them?

He threw the logs onto the grate. A few embers flew into the air, glowed brightly, then extinguished. He put the screen back.

He stood and brushed off his jeans. Finally, he looked at her, his eyes glowing like the sparks.

"I'm not comfortable being your rebound affair."

She stared at him. "What?"

"I . . ." He stopped and that muscle in his cheek jumped. "I thought maybe we could eventually have something real. After you realized we have more than sexual attraction. After you realized I was serious about you."

He glanced at the floor, then back to her, the glow in his eyes extinguished. "But I can't handle having this thing with you when there is a possibility that you might suddenly decide you've forgiven Rod and go running back to him."

She had no idea how her heart could soar and plummet at the same time, but it did. "Why would I forgive Rod?"

"He cheated six times before this last one, and you stayed with him," he pointed out, although there was no censure in his voice—he was just stating a fact. "How do I know you won't go back now?"

"Because I don't want to go back to him," she said adamantly. "I don't love him. I don't think I ever did. If anything, Rod was my rebound from Arturo. But by the time I realized that, it had become really difficult for me to walk away from him. He'd managed to become really involved in my career." She paused. "I *let* him get really involved in my career. He is a relatively well-known photographer, but he started acting as my manager—that way he could finagle us into magazines and fashion shows as a team. So, to leave, I had to decide if I was willing to leave my career too."

"And have you decided?" he asked her cautiously.

"Well, I did have this really great guy offer me a job as a camp counselor." She stepped toward him.

"And are you going to take him up on the offer?" He remained in front of the fire, which crackled and popped back to life.

"I guess that depends." She stepped forward again, stopping right in front of him.

"On what?"

"Well, this great guy sort of made it sound like he wants a relationship, too."

Nate nodded slowly. "Uh-huh."

"So do both offers still stand?"

He stared down at her for a moment, then he pulled her against him. "Oh yeah."

Chapter 24

"Hi, Brandi, it's Marty. Is Diana in?" Marty asked into the receiver of her cell phone.

There was a pause. "Diana has been trying to reach you for days."

Unlike the last time Marty had called, there wasn't concern in the receptionist's voice but reproach.

"I know," Marty said apologetically. She could hardly be offended by Brandi's tone. She knew the receptionist was probably getting the brunt of Diana's irritation since she couldn't take it out on Marty directly.

"I'll put you through," Brandi said, already sounding a bit mollified.

The phone had barely clicked on hold when Diana's voice demanded, "What the hell is going on with you? I've been trying to reach you for days."

"Brandi told me."

"Great. So now why don't you tell me where you are?"

"I'm still in Maine."

"Okay," Diana said slowly, taking a deep breath. Marty was willing to bet she was counting in her head, trying to calm down before she spoke again. "When are you coming back?"

It was Marty's turn to take a deep breath. "Diana . . . The thing is—"

"Wait!" Diana barked, then her voice calmed. "Wait. I don't like how this sounds. So, let's start this again."

Marty took another deep breath, then blurted out, "I'm retiring from modeling."

"No," Diana said, and not as a response of shock but as a definitive *this is not an option.*

"Diana, I'm not happy."

"That's because of Rod. Now that he's out of the picture, you can start enjoying your career again. He is out of the picture, right?"

"Yes."

"Well, then, things are just going to get better and better."

That much was true, Marty thought. Especially since New Year's Eve, things *had* just gotten better and better. Even now, thinking of Nate made her insides feel all warm and tingly. The thoughts of Nate strengthened her courage.

"Diana, I'm staying in Maine."

"No," the agent said. This time the single word sounded distressed.

"It's what I want, Di. I'm not trying to make things difficult for you. I just can't go back to modeling. I don't want that life anymore."

Diana sighed. "Okay. But we do have a huge show coming up. Vera Wang's spring collection. And you have been requested as the headlining model."

Marty knew if she really wanted to be a model, if she really loved the business, the attention of such a prestigious designing house would have thrilled her to the bone. It didn't. And that as much as anything made her realize she was making the right choice.

"Diana, they will be happy with Nina Carr or Kim Lu." Both of the models she named were currently hot and several years younger than Marty—always a plus in the fashion biz.

"They want you."

"I have to decline. Diana, I really do appreciate all that you have done for me. Let me know what the situation is about getting out of my contract."

"Are you really happier?" Diana asked quietly.

"Very happy."

Her agent and friend sighed. "Then I'm happy for you. Keep in touch, okay?"

"I will. Thank you, Di."

"Okay." Diana's no-nonsense voice returned. "I better see if I can get Nina or Kim on the line."

"Bye," Marty said quietly.

"Bye, girl."

Marty disconnected her phone and waited for the second thoughts and the sadness to hit her. They didn't. She felt this great sense of freedom, and she felt like she was definitely making the right choice.

Just like she felt she had made the right choice about Nate. It had been only three days since New Year's Day and their decision to make this thing between them real. But they had been the best three days of Marty's whole life. She couldn't imagine feel crazier about a man.

She still hesitated to use the "L" word, because in her experience, as soon as she decided she felt that, things went to hell in a handbasket. Or in her case, hell in a Prada purse.

She looked at the teapot clock in her kitchen. It was four o'clock. Nate would be off duty in two hours, and she could tell him what she'd done. That she was here to stay.

Nate puttered around the kitchen, chopping veggies, trying to understand how the heck one prepared tofu, when there was a rap on his cabin door and then Marty came dashing in.

"Hey," he greeted her, both laughing and breathless as she ran directly into his arms, practically bowling him over. "Where were you? I called your house and your cell, but I didn't get an answer. I thought I was supposed to pick you up."

She kissed him before she answered. "I was busy," she said mysteriously. "Come with me."

She grabbed his hand and led him to the porch.

"What am I looking at?" He squinted into the black night.

Suddenly a vehicle in his driveway beeped and illuminated.

Nate frowned and tried to see what exactly it was. "That looks like an SUV."

Marty laughed merrily and dangled some keys in the air. "My Jag really wasn't very practical for these Maine winters. And especially this camp road."

He stared at her for a minute, then looked back at the car. "You bought a new car?"

"A Highlander."

He continued gaping at the vehicle. Slowly, the interior lights faded off.

"Does this mean you quit modeling?" he finally asked.

She nodded.

His heart rapped madly against his rib cage, but he

tried to keep his thoughts focused on Marty. "Are you okay with this?"

"I am more than okay," she said with one of her wide, heart-stopping smiles. "I am ready to start doing arts and crafts and archery."

Nate whooped, hugged her around the waist, and spun her around. They were both laughing, and then they were both kissing.

After several seconds, he broke the kiss and gazed down at her. "You won't regret this."

"I know." She smiled, her eyes shining with trust. The fact that trust was directed at him was astounding. It was humbling.

"Although," she added, "I think I might regret the SUV."

"Why?"

"No more getting snowed in for days."

"Oh, I'm pretty sure we can come up with other excuses," he assured her with a lascivious grin, then found her lips again.

Marty pushed the food around her plate, trying to arrange the pile so it appeared like she ate more than she did. Nate was an amazing lover, but an amazing cook he was not.

He returned to the dining-room table with a new bottle of wine.

She immediately forced a bite of the mushy, salty stir-fry into her mouth. She smiled, trying to keep the expression from appearing pained.

Nate sat down and refilled her glass. "You are going to have to drink a lot more of this if you hope to eat any more of that."

She immediately looked relieved. "It's not too bad."

He pushed his plate away. "You're right. It's extremely bad. I have no idea how to prepare tofu. I think I definitely need to invest in a recipe book."

She glanced at his library of books. "You don't have one in among all of those?"

He shook his head. "Well, vegetarianism is still a new thing for me. Hopefully, I'll get better."

"You told me your attack triggered your decision to be a vegetarian. How so?"

For whatever reason, her question seemed to catch him off guard. He set down his wine glass and picked up his fork, toying with his own food. "Um, I don't really know," he said. "I just decided I needed to make some major changes in my life."

She thought about that. "I would imagine a lot of people have the feeling that they need to take better care of themselves following an experience like that."

Nate immediately nodded. "Yes."

She watched him for a moment. He set down his fork and took a sip of his wine. Nothing about his movements was out of the ordinary, but she got the weird feeling he was uncomfortable. Was it talking about the effects of the attack or was it the attack itself that made him seem a little uneasy?

She knew she should probably just let it go, but she couldn't. "Have you found any suspects in your case?"

He glanced up from his wine. "No."

"And you don't remember anything?"

His eyes got a distant look as he considered her question. "No. Nothing definitive. I remember some disjointed images like shadowy flashes on a movie screen, but no faces and nothing I can really even understand."

She debated over whether she should mention Jared Nye again. She just couldn't shake the idea that he might be involved. That man was so filled with hatred for Nate.

She took a sip of her wine. Then after swallowing the lightly fruity liquid, she decided to go for it. "Have you thought any more about Jared? That he might be involved?"

Instead of immediately rejecting the idea like she thought he would, he nodded. "Yeah. Since I had his prints on my desk from New Year's Eve, I decided what the hell, and ran them against the prints that were taken from the crime scene here."

"And?"

"There wasn't a match." He shook his head. "I will admit, after what he did to you, I do think maybe Jared is capable of other things."

"Was it only Lynette that caused your falling-out?" Marty had a hard time believing the anger she saw in Jared was only based around his wife and her supposed crush on Nate.

"That was definitely the beginning of the end of our friendship. But in retrospect, I think Jared has been getting worse over the years. He never outgrew bullying people." He shook his head. "And for whatever reason, since he's been married to Lynette, he just seems angrier."

Marty thought about that. "He said that you—you used to share women."

"What?" He gaped at her. "No," he said. "Shared women? No."

He fell silent for a few moments, then he tilted his head as his eyes widened with realization. "Jared did have a tendency to date women after I'd dated them. But we didn't share. And even though he constantly accused me of flirting with Lynette, he was always the one to come on to my dates. Although never like what he did to you."

"He wants what you have." Marty had no doubt about that.

Nate nodded. "Yeah, I guess that is true, although I never really realized it. But he has always been competitive with me."

"Maybe Jared really does love Lynette, and it's killing him that you were with her first."

Nate shook his head. "He sure has a funny way of showing love."

"He has had a funny way of showing friendship, too," she pointed out.

"True enough. After the attack, I couldn't understand how I'd ever been friends with him." He took a drink of his wine. "Jared might have started treating me like shit because of Lynette, but he's always treated plenty of people worse than me, and I used to think that was all right. I overlooked it. I was so callous."

She reached across the table and caught his hand, squeezing his fingers. "You aren't callous anymore."

He shrugged nonchalantly, but she could see pain and regret in his eyes.

"That attack was the best thing that ever happened to me," he said, his eyes focused on their hands. "If I were still the guy I was before, you wouldn't be sitting here with me."

She squeezed his fingers again and said teasingly, "You're right. I'd have hightailed it back to New York faster than you could have asked me if my boobs were real."

He winced. "Did I really ask you that?"

She sighed. "Something close to it."

"Why are you here?" He gave her a worried look like maybe she had lost her mind.

She laughed. "Because you have changed. I guess God, or whatever higher power there is, really does work in mysterious ways."

He lifted her knuckles to his lips and brushed a kiss across the back of them. Then he looked deep into her eyes. "You have no idea."

"You have to tell him," Derek said to Jared.

Jared stopped watching the football game to glare at him. "If you're going to start that crap again, you can just leave now."

Derek turned back to the television, but he didn't see the game. Instead, the events of that late June night flashed in front of his eyes. Visions far more violent than the most aggressive football sack.

They'd all been out that night—Jared, Lynette, Josie, himself, and Nathaniel. The night had been a typical one in that Jared began picking a fight with Nate, which he did often. Nathaniel left, again the usual outcome. But after that, the night became like none that Derek had ever experienced or ever wanted to again.

He took a long swig of his beer, then looked over at his brother.

Jared even looked different these days. Harder. Meaner.

When Jared had married Lynette, Derek had hoped a steady female in his older brother's life would mellow him. Derek believed that Lynette really loved Jared. But the marriage seemed to have the opposite effect. It ate at Jared that Lynette had once loved Nate—even though that was over ten years ago.

"Jared, what is going on?" Derek asked quietly, trying to keep his voice soothing, nonconfrontational. "Are you and Lynette having problems?"

"No. Christ, you should start working for the police department. They are all full of questions and all full of moral righteousness, too. You'd fit right in." Jared polished off the rest of his beer and reached for another bottle he had waiting on the coffee table.

They both stared at the television, although occasionally Derek would cast his brother sidelong glances.

Derek had once idolized his older brother. He'd admired how tough Jared was and how he could get people to back down—to run scared. And given how rough their childhood had been, those were important qualities. They were necessary for survival. All three of them had grown up being bounced between their alcoholic mother and her wide array of abusive boyfriends and a county-run foster shelter. Jared had been the only constant in Derek's life, and the big brother had always protected his little brother.

But somewhere along the way, Jared's defenses for survival had simply become a part of him. He was hard and angry—and brutal. He'd become this sort of wild animal that no one could reach or tame.

Jared was filled with a greediness that a childhood of going without had turned into a fundamental part of his personality. Josie was the same way. They both wanted and wanted, and they never could get enough.

That was what drove Jared that June night. And Nathaniel happened to be the one who had what Jared wanted. And even though what Jared had done wouldn't have gotten him what he wanted, the greed mixed with his feral personality made him unstoppable.

Derek took another gulp of his beer, then closed his

eyes. That was what he kept telling himself, anyway—that he couldn't have stopped Jared.

He looked at his brother. But he could stop it from happening again.

Jared took a sip of his beer, then cursed at the television as if the football team could hear him.

Derek looked around at Jared's basement rec room. A big-screen television, a dartboard, two recliners, and a worn sofa and beat-up coffee table. Two brothers drinking beer and watching the Sunday game. It was a perfectly normal scene. Except the Nyes weren't normal.

He needed to tell Nathaniel.

He needed to tell her. Nate stopped tapping his pen on his desk and looked at the clock. He was supposed to meet Marty for dinner at the Parched Dolphin right after work. That gave him exactly thirty minutes to find the right words.

"Marty, I died and came back." He shook his head.

"Marty, I saw the light." She'd think he was a loon. Of course, no matter how he phrased it, she was going to think he was a loon. That was the very reason he hadn't told anyone except the other survivors at the near-death meetings he'd attended in Portland.

He never, never intended to tell anyone, but for some reason he felt like Marty had to know.

Maybe it was because she had shared so many of her own painful experiences with him, revealing her feelings about herself and men. Or maybe it was because she'd given up her career to be with him. Or maybe it was because he loved her and wanted her to truly understand him.

But whatever the reason, he had to tell her. He *would* tell her—tonight.

Chapter 25

Marty was amazed how her heart could soar in her chest just by simply seeing Nate.

He walked into the restaurant, spotting her in a booth in the corner.

"Hi," he said, leaning down to give her a kiss. She sank her fingers into his silky hair and held him against her lips for a moment longer than might have been proper in a public place. She didn't care—she needed to touch him.

Once the kiss ended and he'd taken a seat across from her, he grinned. "That was a very nice greeting."

"I've been thinking about doing that all day," she admitted.

"Have you?"

"Uh-huh. And other stuff."

She had expected to see a wicked gleam in his eyes at her naughty little innuendo, but instead he only nodded.

"Are you all right?" she asked.

"Yes. Yes." He opened the menu that the waitress had already brought to the table. "Just a tiring day."

She nodded, but couldn't help feeling like there was more that he wasn't saying.

"Well, Ellie and Abby are still all in a dither that I'm staying. I think it's going to take a while for it to sink in."

Nate nodded, but again she got the distinct feeling he was distracted. She was positive when he asked, "Do you believe in supernatural-type things?"

She frowned. "I don't know. Maybe. Give me a for instance."

"Past lives?"

"Like you used to be Henry VIII and I used to be Cleopatra?"

He gave her an offended scowl. "You think I was Henry VIII?"

"It was just an example," she assured him. "Hmm, I guess I might believe it. I'd like to believe it. That we keep going on after we're done with this life."

He nodded, seeming to file that away. "How about near-death experiences?"

"Oh, like that book you have?"

"Yeah."

"Is that what is inspiring this conversation?"

"In part."

"Does that book talk about things like seeing a bright white light? And angels?"

"Yeah, I guess some people see angels." Something about the way he said that caught her attention.

"Do you believe it?"

Before he could answer her, Sam strolled up to their table. "Hey, kids, imagine meeting you here."

"Hi, Sam," Marty greeted him, genuinely pleased to see him.

Nate looked pleased too, but Marty felt like it was something more akin to relief in his eyes.

"I was just stopping by to grab a quick meal before my shift," Sam explained.

"Oh, well, join us," Nate said, and again, Marty felt like Nate was grateful for Sam's interruption.

"You don't mind?" Sam asked her.

"Not at all." And she didn't, but she still wondered why Nate was acting so strange.

"So, Nate tells me that you and he are going to start a summer camp." Sam looked a little puzzled by the idea.

"Yes," Marty said. "We are both interested in making a difference in kids' lives."

The conversation turned to that topic for much of the meal. And by the end of the meal, as Nate continued to talk animatedly about the camp, Marty started to think she'd only imagined his strange behavior earlier.

The three of them left the restaurant together. Sam said his good nights and headed to work.

"Sorry that ended up being a kind of rushed dinner," Nate apologized as he walked her to her car.

"I don't mind. It was exciting to tell Sam about the camp. *And* it just means I get the chance to get you in bed sooner."

He grinned, an eager look on his face. "I do like the sound of that." He tugged her against him and kissed her long and hard. "See you at home," he murmured against her tingling lips.

She *loved* the sound of that.

Josie followed Nate and Marty out of the Parched Dolphin. She watched them until they got into their cars and left the parking lot. Then she fished through her purse for her cell phone.

"Jared, you aren't going to believe what I just heard.

Nate and Miss Model are going to build a summer camp for troubled kids on that land."

She held the phone away from her ear until Jared stopped swearing.

"I agree," she said smoothly. "So what are we going to do to make sure she doesn't stick around to invest in that little venture?"

Josie listened and then smiled. "Yes, I do believe that will work."

Marty padded through Nate's kitchen toward the living room. The worn floorboards chilled her pink, waterlogged toes, but Nate's thick terry cloth robe kept the rest of her shower-warmed body cozy.

"Hey, I thought you were going to join me," she called into the shadowy room, the only light the flickering orange from the fireplace.

She peered at each of the sofas, expecting to find him there. He wasn't.

She wandered farther into the room and finally spotted him lying on the floor in front of the fire. He'd brought down the pillows and thick comforter from his bed and had a bottle of wine waiting, open, on the coffee table with two glasses already full.

Nate was sprawled on his back, his long, jean-clad legs crossed at the ankle and his hands folded behind his head. His face was turned toward the fire, and Marty couldn't see his features, only mussed hair. All the yummy bare skin of his chest and arms.

"Hey, you," she said softly.

No answer.

"Nate?"

A long breath, not quite a snore, greeted her.

She suppressed a little laugh. It seemed that they had found the remedy for Nate's insomnia. Sex—and lots of it.

They'd barely made it inside the cabin after the restaurant before they were ripping at each other's clothes and making love on the brown vinyl couch, which happened to be closest to the front door. Afterward, while the sex had been fantastic, they'd decided the cold vinyl got two thumbs down.

So as she'd showered, he had set up a much more romantic and comfortable place. So comfy that he'd fallen asleep.

Ah, well, she could hardly blame him. Even with his newly discovered sleep aid, he still only slept about five or so hours a night.

She crept over to the red-flowered sofa and curled up with one of the glasses of wine. It was tempting to curl up against Nate's lovely bare chest, but she didn't have the heart to wake him. He looked so peaceful.

So she sipped her wine and watched the flames dance in the stone fireplace. She was surprised she didn't feel more tired, but she didn't. Her body felt mellow from their wild lovemaking, but her mind was abuzz. Excitement over the summer camp and about her new relationship zipped around in her head and zoomed through her whole body.

She was so happy. This was everything she wanted: a wonderful guy, a career she could really be proud of, and a full heart. It was a dream.

She had no idea how long she'd sat there reflecting on her good fortune when Nate stirred, stretching his long limbs.

"Hey." He squinted up at her. "Did I fall asleep?"

"Yup."

"Man," he grumbled. "You are wearing me out."

She smiled smugly.

"Come here," he said, crooking a finger at her. He slid over on the comforter to make room for her.

She set down her glass and joined him. They spooned together, her head on his arm. His other arm looped around her waist, and he rested his head on a pillow so she could feel his breath against her cheek.

They watched the fire.

He moved his fingers, the slight movement barely perceptible over the thick material of his robe, yet she could feel it like he was touching her bare flesh directly.

She snuggled her back tighter against him.

His hand continued to move, unhurried touches. And when his stroking fingers found the opening in the robe and brushed over the skin of her belly, she closed her eyes and breathed in a shaky sigh. His hands were bliss.

He continued to caress her, the pace leisurely—maddening. Over her belly. Up to the underside her breasts. Then back down.

He didn't touch her breasts or between her thighs, but the arousal he was creating was just as powerful.

He slid his hand up her side, nudging the robe away from her so her naked front was exposed. The heat from the fire and the yearning from his touch made her bared skin sizzle.

"Nate," she whispered and started to squirm around to face him.

He caught her tight around the waist, holding her in place. "Shh, just let me touch you like this."

"But—" she started to argue, then his hand stroked down her belly again, and he gently bit her bared shoulder.

She gasped.

His hands swept lightly over her. His mouth continued to nip and suck the skin of her shoulder and her neck.

It was absolute torture. Her breasts ached for his attention. Between her thighs she throbbed. And he caressed everywhere else.

Finally, when she thought she would scream from unbearable need, he nudged her upright so her back was still toward him and she faced the hot fire.

He slipped the robe off her and kissed the nape of her neck. Electric currents shot through her and she shivered. He kissed down her spine, and more electrical surges zoomed through her, all centering on those areas he had yet to touch.

"You are driving me crazy," she murmured, letting her head fall back against his shoulder.

"That is the plan," he said, then pressed a kiss to the side of her neck. Even the tickle of his hair was too much for her oversensitized skin to take.

She gasped, the sound harsh and desperate.

"Nate, please. Please touch me," she begged.

"Where? Here?" His slid his hands slowly around her to cup her breasts.

"God, yes."

She felt him smile against her neck.

"You're enjoying this, aren't you?" she said petulantly.

"Oh yeah," he said, and plucked both her nipples at the same time.

She moaned, arching into his hands, her head falling against his shoulder again.

His hands stayed at her breasts, teasing, tweaking, fondling. The heat, his hands, the nibbling of his mouth on her neck—it was too much. Too wonderful. Fire pooled between her thighs, lapping at her, nudging her over the edge.

Then one of his hands drifted down her belly and delved between her legs, only a fleeting touch designed to drive her insane. It was working. She was on fire.

"Nate, please, please, I need you inside me." Her begging sounded almost hysterical. She didn't care. She needed him.

He shifted her around so she was on her back, spread out before him on the comforter.

He looked at her, his eyes as hot as his caresses, burning over her.

She reached up for him, but he moved away. Slowly, he unbuttoned his jeans, then he stood and pushed them down.

He had a physique that any male model would kill for, his muscles rippled under his golden skin. His huge erection jutted up against his flat, hard stomach.

He returned to her side and brushed his fingers down the outside of her leg closest to him.

"Please, Nate," she pleaded, reaching for him again.

He smiled, an arrogant little twist of his lips that she would most definitely make him pay for—after.

He shifted so he was positioned between her legs, and she had to fight from bucking her hips toward him.

He leaned forward and stretched over her to get something.

In her haze of desire, she realized it was a condom. Good thing someone was thinking. She wouldn't have given it a single thought.

She watched as he rolled the latex down over his whole girth and then he positioned himself to enter her.

She whimpered with anticipation. But if she expected the frenzied joining that they had earlier in the evening, it wasn't happening.

He penetrated her slowly, inch by deliberate inch.

Then he slid back out of her with the same calculated slowness.

The whole time he stared into her eyes, watching the expressions on her face.

Marty had never experienced anything like it. She and Nate truly were one. She was his and he was hers.

And slowly, and relentlessly, he rocked her to the most powerful, most soul-shattering orgasm she'd ever experienced.

Nate followed into paradise, never once taking his eyes from hers.

And as they both drifted back to earth, Nate kissed her sweetly, lovingly.

Then he lifted his head and said with great seriousness, "I have to tell you something."

Marty's heart froze in her chest, and suddenly she was terrified. Part of her wanted to simply say no. That she didn't want to hear it. Not if it was something that could change what had just happened between them.

She wanted to stay just as she was, joined with him forever.

But that couldn't happen. So she stared up at him, and in a quiet, steady voice, she asked, "What?"

Chapter 26

Nate looked into Marty's dark eyes and saw fear there. He didn't want that, not after what they'd just shared.

He rolled them so they were on their sides, facing each other. Gently, he brushed a lock of hair from her face, wishing he could brush away her worried expression as easily. Wishing he didn't have to tell her this. But he did.

"You know that after the attack, I was in a coma."

She frowned. This obviously wasn't how she thought the conversation was going to begin. She nodded.

"Well, while I was in that coma, I died."

She looked stricken. "You did?"

He nodded, then took a deep breath. "And while I was dead, I—" How did he say this without sounding like a complete lunatic? "I crossed over to the other side."

Her gaze roamed over his face, then her eyes locked back with his.

He could see she was confused, and he wished he could just stop or pretend it was a joke, but he couldn't. He needed her to understand this, to understand him.

More than anyone, he needed her know what happened to him.

"You may have heard about the experience," he continued. "And a lot of it was like that. I left my physical body and could see myself in the hospital bed below. I did travel toward a bright light. But in the bright light, I didn't see angels or God or anything like that. I saw my life. You know that phrase 'seeing your life flash before your eyes'? Well, it was like that. Rapid-fire images that played out from my birth to that moment—my death."

She opened her mouth as though she was going to say something, but then she closed it again, urging him with her eyes to continue.

"But even though the images were so fast, I felt every event like it was just happening." He shook his head, still overwhelmed by the memory of it. "In just minutes, I was aware of every action in my life."

"But you don't remember things now," Marty said, puzzlement clear in her eyes. "You didn't remember the dance. Right?"

"You're right, I didn't, and I can't say I actually remember 'seeing' it in the light. But when Sam told me about what happened, all the emotions of it came flooding back. I didn't remember it as much as I felt it. All your pain, all your humiliation. That's what happened in the light. I didn't just see my life. I felt it. I experienced the emotions of everyone I ever came in contact with. Everyone I ever helped. Everyone I ever hurt."

He took a deep breath and released it shakily. "And I quickly learned I hurt far more people than I ever helped."

"No—" Marty started, but he shook his head to stop her.

"You don't have to try to comfort me. I did hurt

people, you included. But the amazing thing about this experience is that I got to come back—and I get the chance to change things. To change myself."

"Kind of like Ebenezer Scrooge," Marty said.

He chuckled. "Yeah, I guess a lot like that." Then he quickly grew solemn again. "Marty, I know this sounds crazy. And I can't expect you to believe me, but—but I hope you do."

She lifted her fingers to his face and stroked his cheek. "I have to believe you, because I've seen first-hand how much you've changed. I could see it the first night back in Millbrook. And believe me, I was trying very, very hard to see the old Nate."

He smiled slightly. "Why?"

"Because I was scared to be so attracted to someone I really thought I should hate."

"You should have hated me," he informed her.

"Well, new Nate made that pretty hard for me."

He leaned in and kissed her lightly. "Thank God."

"Mm-hmm," she agreed as she pressed another kiss to his mouth.

Nate caught her waist and pulled her tighter to him, amazed by her. He'd hoped she would understand after digesting the whole idea for a while. But he never expected her to accept it so easily. God, he loved this woman.

"So have you told your family about your experience?" she asked, nestling her head under his chin.

He laughed. "No," he said. "My brother and father are having a difficult enough time with the vegetarianism. A near-death experience would throw them over the deep end."

"You might be surprised."

"Yeah—no."

She laughed, then kissed his chest.

"So you don't think I'm crazy?"

"For giving up meat? Hell, yes, I do. I'd go crazy without a burger every now and then."

He pinched her butt, and she squealed. "You know what I mean," he said.

She lifted her head, her eyes serious. "No. I don't think you're crazy. I think you had the most amazing experience a person could have. An intense, life-altering experience."

Suddenly her eyes widened like an inspiration just came to her. "Have you ever told *anyone* about this?"

"Yes. Believe it or not, there is a near-death support group in Portland. I attended a few of their meetings, just because I had to see if anyone else had experienced this."

"Does the group meet in hotels and libraries?"

He nodded, perplexed by her line of questions.

She laughed, but then seemed to realize he wasn't in on the joke. She gave him a sheepish smile. "I—I read a little section of a letter I found in your sock drawer that appeared to be from a woman who shared this same life-altering event. I assumed it was an old girlfriend and she was talking about sex." She cringed guiltily.

He stared at her for a moment, then burst into laughter. He rolled over onto his back, still laughing.

"I don't think I'm understanding what is so funny." She sounded both baffled and irritated by his reaction.

He breathed in deeply to calm his amusement. "That letter was from Ruth Cowell, a seventy-eight-year-old woman. She crossed over while she was having surgery to get a pacemaker. And I think she'd be quite appalled that you thought I had sex with her."

"Oh."

Nate hugged Marty against him. "It's flattering that you thought sex with me was life altering, though."

"Yeah, well, I came up with that theory before I actually had sex with you."

He raised his head from the pillow to look at her. "So what do you think now?"

"I still think it's life altering." She slid up his chest to kiss him.

God, he loved this woman.

Marty finished giving the moving company her information and hung up the old avocado phone. She didn't have a lot of stuff, but what she did have was sitting in storage in New York. She'd put it there when she'd moved into a place with Rod. Rod had been very particular about his home, and none of her stuff would have fit.

She could still hear his voice. "It's all about aesthetics. And my furniture and art has been carefully chosen to create the most pleasing visual effect."

Marty rolled her eyes just remembering it. Rod would have a conniption at Nate's mismatched sofas and dining-room set.

She chuckled to herself. Suddenly Rod just seemed like a distant memory. Her mind was too full of Nate.

She supposed some people would have doubted what Nate had told her—or at the very least doubted his sanity. But to her, it was the perfect, most sensible explanation for what she knew about him. She knew something monumental had to have happened to change him so much.

She wouldn't say that she'd ever really given credence to things like near-death experiences—or anything mystical, really. But she'd always liked the idea there was more out there. Something bigger than herself.

But most of all, she liked the idea that a person could get a second chance. She hadn't gone through what Nate had, but she still felt like she was getting a second chance.

There was a knock on the front door.

She frowned. Who could it be? Nate was at work—as was all her family.

As she walked down the front hallway, she could make out a shadowy form through one of the side windows framing the door.

She flipped the lock and tugged the door open.

"Josie." Marty had to be gaping at the woman, but Josie Nye was the last person she expected to see at her door. Or at least in the bottom five.

Josie's red hair was brushed back from her face as if she'd been running her fingers through it, and her lips were pinched into a troubled frown. "I'm sorry to bother you," she said, "but I really need to talk to you." She looked over her shoulder as if she expected someone to be watching her. "May I please come in?"

Marty didn't know which part of the sentence caught her attention, the "please" or the desperate tone of her voice, but she nodded, opening the door wider to allow her inside.

As soon as Josie was in the foyer, she turned back to Marty. "It was really hard to come here."

Marty nodded, although she didn't know exactly why. Why was Josie here? They had never been friends. In fact, Marty had probably only spoken to Josie two or three times in her life.

"I need to talk to you about Jared—"

Marty shook her head. "I just want to forget the other night."

"I know," Josie agreed, "I know. What Jared did was awful—unforgivable." She took a deep breath. "But that is just the tip of the iceberg as far as what's going on here."

Marty frowned. What iceberg? Was Josie going to tell her that Jared had attacked Nate? Was she coming to Marty for help? The redhead certainly looked nervous enough to be considering turning in her brother.

"This is so hard for me to tell you. So hard for me to say about my own brother."

Josie was going to tell her about the attack. Marty nodded, silently urging her to continue.

"The attack was Nate's idea."

She stared at her, the words taking several seconds to sink in. "What?" Was Josie crazy?

"Nate came up with the idea. That Jared attack you. So he could play the hero. So you would turn to him. Trust him."

"What?" Marty shook her head, confused, stunned. "Why?"

"They need money. And they came up with this idea that if Nate could win you over, gain your trust, they could get your money."

Again, Marty shook her head. "Nate never asked me for money."

"He's asked you to join him in his summer camp, hasn't he?"

The realization that Josie knew about the camp was as jarring as if she'd slapped Marty. Nate had specifically asked her not to mention the summer camp to anyone because he was waiting to tell everyone until he got funding—just in case he didn't. With the exception of Sam, who was also sworn to secrecy, Marty was the only other person who knew.

Marty wrapped her arms around herself, a cold chill running down her spine. Finally she said defensively, "I don't think that is any of your business."

"I know he has, because that's the plan. To ask you to work with him. Has he asked you for money yet? That's the next part of the plan."

"No." Her insides froze. "No, he hasn't."

"He will."

Marty suddenly remembered Nate telling her that it took a lot of money to get a summer camp started—and that he was working on getting it. But he didn't say how. Was she what he was working on? Was that his plan all along?

"It's true," Josie insisted, drawing Marty's attention back to her. Her eyes were filled with remorse. "Although he's not going to build a summer camp. That was just another thing the two of them came up to win you over. The new Nate with his giving soul, caring for kids and animals. They sat around my kitchen table laughing about the idea."

Even though Marty shouldn't have been able to picture that, not from the Nate she knew, she could. The two men sitting, drinking beer, planning how to con stupid Marty Stepp out of some money.

"Nate needs money to keep his property, period," Josie said. "He can't make the land taxes, and there is a lien on the property. But if he can pay the taxes off, he can turn around and sell the property to a developer from Massachusetts and make a fortune."

Marty considered that. Land on the water was worth a lot. "But why is Jared helping him?"

That seemed to give Josie pause. But she continued,

her voice still upset. "Jared owns the property behind Nate's. The developer wants both lots."

Marty stared at a point on the floor, trying to comprehend all this. "Why are you telling me this?"

"Because—because I can't stand back and let them do this to you again. I remember high school. I remember what they did."

Marty shook her head. "I don't believe you." But even as she said it, she knew there was a small seed of belief inside her, and it was growing.

"I'm telling you the truth," Josie insisted. Her eyes were filled with desperate regret. "I'm taking a huge risk to be here. Jared has a terrible temper. He is going to kill me."

If this story were true, Marty knew Josie was indeed taking a huge gamble to be here. Why? Josie had no reason to care about her.

"I just don't understand why you would endanger so much for me."

Josie bit her lip. "I've been used by Nathaniel too. I had just divorced my husband, and I started seeing Nathaniel. We dated quite a while, and I thought things were going great. But when I didn't get quite as large a divorce settlement as I was expecting, he dumped me. Turned out he was far more interested in my money than me." She looked close to tears. "I can't just watch another woman get used. This needs to stop."

Used. That word resonated in Marty as much as anything Josie had said yet. Marty's mind shifted to the times Arturo had kissed her passionately—always for the waiting camera. Only for cameras. And the times Rod had told her he loved her and had sworn she was the only one he'd ever loved. Oh, and he got her another photo shoot, and guess who the photographer was? Then the phone would ring and it would be a strange girl asking for Rod Mitchell.

"He is using you." A voice echoed alongside her thoughts like the haunting background music of a suspense movie.

Marty stared into Josie's face, but all she could see were flashes of men's faces. A teenage Nate. Arturo. Rod. And finally Nate as he'd looked last night, telling her his fantastic story of white lights and empathy.

"I'm sorry."

Marty blinked, Josie's face returning.

"I had to tell you," Josie said and headed back to the front door. "I couldn't let him set you up again."

She nodded absently, her mind awhirl. She didn't say a word as she watched Josie leave. She stood there for several seconds staring at the closed door, trying to sift through her confused thoughts.

Only one thought kept jumping to the forefront of her mind. *Men use you. For their careers, for fame, for money. Not one man has ever wanted you for yourself.*

She hugged herself tighter. *Maybe it's because there isn't anything inside me worth wanting.* Maybe a face and smile were really all she had to offer.

She stumbled down the hall back to the kitchen. She was such a fool. She—she had to go. She couldn't stay here one more minute.

Chapter 27

Nate paced his cabin, going to the living-room window for the hundredth time.

Where the hell could Marty be? He'd called her cell—she had it turned off. He'd called her house—no answer. She'd told him that morning that she had some errands to do like arranging to have her stuff shipped from New York. But she said she'd be back here before he got off work.

He checked his wristwatch. It was after nine. He'd been off work since six. Where could she be?

He checked the camp road again for headlights. Then he went to the kitchen. He picked up the phone and dialed Ellie's number.

"Hello," Ellie's friendly voice greeted him on the third ring.

"Hi, Ellie. It's Nate."

"Nate, how are you?"

"Marty wouldn't happen to be there, would she?"

"No. Why?"

Nate's chest constricted. He had this weird feeling that something wasn't right. "She was supposed to meet me a couple of hours ago, but I haven't heard from her."

"I can go over to Grammy's house and see if she's there," Ellie said. She sounded concerned, too.

"I don't want to bother you. I'll go over. I'll call you as soon as I hear from her."

Ellie hesitated, but then agreed. "I'll call Abby, too."

"Thanks."

He hung up the phone and immediately reached for his coat.

On the drive over to Marty's place, he couldn't shake the sensation that something was wrong. He hoped he was just being silly. That she was over at Abby's. Or she fell asleep and didn't hear his calls. Or she was shopping. Anything as long as it meant she was okay.

When he got to her house, he saw the windows were dark and the driveway was empty. He parked and got out anyway.

She definitely wasn't here, but for some reason, he felt as if he should check inside the house.

Using the key Ellie had given him, he unlocked the back door and stepped inside. He groped along the wall for the light switch and flipped it on.

The kitchen was empty. No sign that Marty had been here today—or ever. The dishes were done and put away. Even the dish drainer was gone from the counter.

His chest tightened again.

He strode through the house, turning on lights as he went. There was no sign of her anywhere.

But when he reached her bedroom, the apprehensiveness that had been twisting inside him with each step made it nearly impossible for him to breathe.

There was no sign of her in the room. The bed was

made. Her luggage was gone. He noticed that even the Quiet Riot album was back in a box on the floor as if it had never left the other albums in the last fifteen years.

She was gone, Nate knew it as surely as he knew his own name.

The telephone was ringing when Nate got back to his cabin. He rushed to the kitchen, still praying that he was wrong and he'd answer it to hear Marty's voice on the end of the line.

It wasn't. It was Ellie.

"Nate." No hi or hello—that was a bad sign.

"Have you heard from her?" he asked, hopeful.

"Not directly. When I called Abby, she realized she had a message on her answering machine from her. Marty must have left it this afternoon."

Ellie sounded upset. Nate waited, holding his breath deep in his chest.

"Nate, it says that she's decided to go back to New York. That she wants to keep modeling."

Nate closed his eyes, then rested his head against the frame of the kitchen door.

"Nate? Are you there?"

"Yes."

"Are you okay?"

"Yeah." He straightened up. "Yeah, I'm okay."

"If she calls, I'll tell her she needs to call you."

"That would be great. Thanks, Ellie."

But as he hung up the phone, he knew that call was never going to come.

***

"Man, what are you doing here so early? You should have stayed in bed; you look like shit," Sam said when Nate walked into the station.

"You know, I've never understood the point of telling someone that they look like shit. Presumably if a person looks like shit, then they feel like shit, too. How is that supposed to improve the situation?"

Sam frowned, attempting to follow Nate's logic. It was obviously a stretch. "You haven't been sleeping, have you?"

"I've been sleeping fine."

Sam followed him into his office, much to Nate's dismay.

"Have you heard from her?" Sam asked.

Nate shrugged off his coat, hung it on the back of his chair, and sat at his desk. "No."

"Have you called her?"

"I don't have any way to reach her, except her cell, and she's had it turned off since she left."

"She owes you an explanation," Sam said, as if saying it would somehow make it happen.

Nate nodded, although in his many sleepless hours, he'd come up with the most probable explanations himself. And he wasn't going to share those with his baby brother.

"You know," he said, looking through his case files, "you know what I actually need an explanation about? What happened to Lloyd Reed's car. Why don't you get to work on that."

Sam looked as though he was going to argue, but then he nodded and left.

Nate was relieved when the door shut behind him.

It had been five days since Marty left. He hadn't

heard a word from her, and if Ellie and Abby had, they weren't sharing. He knew Marty would tell them not to.

Part of Nate was angry, but mostly, he was hurt. As far as he could figure, she'd left for one of two possible reasons. One, she decided she did want to go back to Rod and her far more glamorous life in New York. Or, and this was the one that hurt him the most, she thought he was a lunatic.

If she'd left to be with Rod, well, there was nothing he could do about that. But if she left about the near-death thing—he should have just kept that to himself. How could anyone really understand something so bizarre?

Sure, she seemed like she had believed him and had accepted it. But maybe, once she got by herself and could really think about it, she decided he was crazy.

Let's face it, there were plenty of times over the past six months when I wondered about my mental health, too.

Still, he felt like she owed him some sort of explanation. The hell of all this was wondering what she was thinking about him and the things they'd shared.

Who was he kidding? The whole thing was hell.

He rubbed a hand over his face and noticed the stubble on his cheeks and chin. He'd forgotten to shave. He couldn't forget a single moment with Marty, but he'd forgotten to shave.

He laughed to himself, the sound hollow and miserable.

Nate was so lost in his own despondent thoughts that he almost missed the soft rap at his office door.

But he did hear it and glanced at the door, expecting to see Sam back to hound him. Instead it was Derek Nye.

Nate waved at him, gesturing for him to come in.

Derek didn't react immediately, glancing back at the front of the station, then shifting his weight from one foot to the other. Finally he took a visibly deep breath and turned the doorknob.

"Hey," he said, his deep voice as unsure as his actions had seemed.

Nate frowned. "Hey. What's going on, Derek?"

Derek had never been as aggressive and domineering as the rest of the Nye family, but Nate had never seen his old friend actually appear timorous. Nate didn't know apprehensiveness was a part of any Nye. But there was no denying Derek looked very worried and very uneasy.

"What's up?" Nate asked again when Derek didn't answer his first question.

Derek wandered over to the metal-framed chair across the desk from Nate. He looked like he was going to sit, but then he moved to stand behind it.

"I—" Derek stopped and gripped the back of the chair.

Nate frowned, but waited.

Derek dipped his head for a moment, apparently studying the back of his hands. Finally, he looked at Nate, meeting his eyes directly.

"I have some things you need to know."

"Okay."

Derek took another deep breath. Whatever he needed to tell Nate was obviously bad.

"Josie was the reason that Marty left town."

Nate hadn't expected that. "What?"

"Josie told her that you were using her for money to save your property."

"That isn't true."

Derek gave him a "no duh" sort of look. "I know that. But Josie and Jared came up with this insane idea that if you stayed with Marty you would never sell your property. My brother and sister are sure that if you didn't have Marty's income you would one day sell it for the cash you could get. But if you were already wealthy via Marty, you wouldn't ever need to sell."

"What?" This was insane. "Why would they decide that?"

Derek shrugged, obviously confused by the reasoning, too. "They are greedy—and I guess they couldn't believe you would pass up the opportunity to make a bundle by selling the land. They see that land as easy money—for both you and them."

Nate shook his head, totally befuddled. "But I already *did* pass up selling it."

Derek nodded, again looking down at his hands on the back of the chair.

Nate noticed that his knuckles were white from clutching so hard.

"That isn't the whole story, is it?" Fear suddenly gripped Nate. "Is Marty okay? Jared didn't do anything to her?"

Derek's head shot up. "No," he said quickly. "No. Jared didn't do anything to *her*."

Relief flooded Nate and he relaxed against the back of his chair. But gradually the way Derek had responded registered in his head. The emphasis of the sentence was on *her*—as if he had done something to someone else. A wary premonition filled him.

"He didn't hurt her, but who did Jared hurt?"

Derek's head was down again, and this time when he lifted his eyes to meet Nate's stare, there was terrible pain in their depths.

"I tried to stop him. I—I know that sounds so lame, so friggin' weak. But I did." Derek's voice trembled. "He was furious and drunk, and I couldn't make him listen. I told him if he went to your place he'd do something stupid. He told me to mind my own fuckin' business, and he headed to your cabin.

"I followed, but by the time I got there, he was already inside. He'd already gone up to your bedroom and knocked you unconscious with a whiskey bottle."

Nate shook his head. It was hard to hear. Hard to imagine that a man whom he'd once considered a friend had done that to him.

And now that Derek had started the story, it was like he couldn't stop. He had to tell it all, even though it was obviously upsetting him.

"He dragged you out of bed, and he began kicking you." Derek's voice cracked. "He kicked and kicked and I kept on trying to get him away from you. But I couldn't, he was so angry, so crazed. I—I finally did. But by then, I thought it was too late. I thought you were dead."

Nate stared at him, shaken, but in truth not as traumatized as Derek. His arms shook even though he still held the chair, and his face was contorted in pain and shame.

"Why? Why did Jared do it?"

Derek sighed, trying to steady himself. "Over the land. He did it because when you decided not to sell to that developer, Jared lost the chance to sell, too."

"But I talked to him about it. I told him I didn't want to let the land go because it had been in my family. He said he understood. He didn't even seem particularly upset."

Derek nodded. "He was." Then he laughed humorlessly.

"Obviously he was. He saw it as having the short end of the stick again. You had the actual land that was worth something—the waterfront lot. He had the crap behind it. You had Lynette's love first, and Jared got the Lynette who still pined for you. He feels cheated. Deprived of things that should be his."

Nate considered that explanation and realized that was true. Jared had always felt cheated. That was why he struck out at people—and why he hated Nate so much.

Nate sighed and studied Derek for a moment. "This had to be hell for you."

Derek nodded, his eyes not meeting Nate's again. "I do love Jared—he's my brother. But I couldn't let him get away with this. I couldn't live with that."

"Thanks for telling me."

Derek waited, and when Nate didn't say anything more, he gaped at Nate. "That's it? That's all you are going to do, thank me? I waited six months before I got the balls to tell you. Don't thank me."

Nate shook his head. "I don't know what else to do."

Derek's features hardened. "You need to arrest him, and me. You need to make sure Jared never hurts another person again."

Nate stared at Derek, impressed—impressed at his sense of morality, when he knew that the Nyes had never had many examples of that in their lives to follow. He hesitated just a moment longer, then reached for the phone. He punched in the numbers to Sam's phone.

"Hey, Sam, I need you to go down to the docks and arrest Jared Nye." There was a moment of silence. "On the charge of aggravated assault on a police officer."

Derek released a breath as Nate returned his phone to the cradle. "It's done."

Nate nodded.

"You have to arrest me too," Derek said.

"We can just let this go, Derek. You did the right thing—that's enough for me."

"No. I didn't do enough. I didn't stop Jared. You nearly died. I didn't do enough."

Nate wanted to argue further, but he could tell it would be pointless. Derek felt the need to be punished, maybe as much for arranging his brother's arrest as for his own involvement in the crime. Derek loved his brother. This had to be hell.

Nate stood. "I'll handle your arrest. But I want you to know right now, I'm going to try to get you the lightest sentence possible."

Derek nodded, but Nate knew he wasn't worried about the ruling. He had already condemned himself to a life sentence of guilt and hurt when he turned in Jared.

"You did the right thing," Nate told him.

"I know," Derek said resolutely. "I know."

After Derek was booked, Nate left the station, deciding he really needed a day off. He had no desire to be there when Jared was booked, and frankly, he had too much on his mind to be an effective cop today.

He did feel mild relief to know for certain who had attacked him. But oddly, other than his sympathy for Derek, he didn't really feel much else. At least not in relation to the assault, because in a strange way, Jared had done him a huge service with that attack. Jared had made him a better person. He couldn't regret the attack, because without it, he'd still be a selfish, coldhearted ass.

Nate pulled into his driveway and headed into his

chilly, dark cabin. Somehow, the small rooms felt huge and empty now.

But for all the anger he didn't feel over his own attack, he *did* feel furious over what the Nyes had done to Marty. They'd hurt her. They'd made her doubt him—doubt him enough to run.

He wandered around the cabin, restless, angry. His robe, which Marty had been wearing that last morning she'd been here, was still draped over the back of a kitchen chair. He picked it up and smelled the thick terry cloth. Her scent wasn't there, but he could imagine it, wildflowers and citrus.

Maybe he should have felt some irritation with Marty, too, for not trusting him. But he couldn't. He knew Marty had only given him her trust tenuously, and what Josie had told her fed right into all Marty's fears of men.

Josie had told her that Nate was using her. That was Marty's biggest fear. Being used—and never loved for who she was rather than what she could offer.

Suddenly her story about the old man in Ecuador popped into his head. How she didn't want to finish telling him the story because it revealed too much about her. About her feelings that no one ever saw past her face, never saw the beauty inside her.

It must have been so much easier for her to believe that he was just like every other guy. And then she'd employed the same tactic she always did—run and put distance between herself and the one who had hurt her.

Nate carefully placed the robe on the back of the chair again. He started into the kitchen when he suddenly realized what he had to do.

He opened a kitchen drawer and pulled out the

phone book. After flipping to the right section, he dialed the number to the Millbrook Public Library.

Ellie answered.

"Hi, Ellie. It's Nate. I know Marty has probably told you not to tell me anything about her whereabouts. But I really need to talk to her. I love her."

Ellie was silent for a minute. Then she said with resignation, "Darn it. She's going to be mad at me, but I'm a sucker for romance."

He heard her shuffling things around on her desk. "Here it is." She read him the number.

"Where is that?"

"Midtown Manhattan."

"Thanks, Ellie," he said, excited. "You won't regret this."

"Please just tell her what you told me," Ellie said.

"Oh, I will."

Nate hung up the phone and looked at his watch. Just after nine o'clock. If he left now, he could be in New York by six—maybe even earlier if he sped.

He quickly headed upstairs to change out of his uniform and pack a few clothes.

"Marty?" Diana called sharply.

Marty blinked and turned away from the window that looked out over Manhattan. It was gorgeous view, an exciting view. It was the view she'd spent her youth imagining. But now, she'd been imagining pine trees and snow and icicles hanging from the gray, bare branches of alders and birches.

"I asked if you had a problem with the fact that Arturo will be in this Vera Wang show too," Diana said.

Marty shook her head. Would it really matter if she did

care? The show was tonight. Not much could be done about it now. But she didn't care. She didn't care at all.

"You know, you really don't look well," Diana said, moving from where she'd been perched on a chair in the sitting area of the hotel room to join Marty by the window. "You look exhausted."

Marty forced a smile. She was exhausted. "Not used to all the noise of the city, I guess."

Diana raised an eyebrow at that. "You've lived in New York for years, and you were back home for a month. Now the noise bothers you?"

"It's easy to get used to a peaceful life."

Diana didn't say anything for a moment, instead staring out at the city. "You don't want to be here, do you?"

Marty closed her eyes briefly. Her eyes burned; they had since she got back to the city. She kept blaming it on the smog, but it wasn't.

It was tears constantly right there, waiting to be released. But she wouldn't allow the tears to come. If she did, she feared she'd never stop crying. And who needed to be crying for the rest of her life? Suffering with the scratchiness was the only option.

As far as Diana's question, no, she didn't want to be in New York. She had a feeling that was why Diana kept checking in on her every day—to make sure Marty didn't run.

Marty realized she was sort of getting known for that—running.

Certainly Nate knew it. She'd left him without giving him even a second to defend himself. She'd berated herself a hundred times for doing that. For believing Josie Nye, when everything Nate had done from the moment Marty returned to Millbrook was designed to prove he was trustworthy. Not because he wanted her money or he wanted anything from her but trust.

And in the end, she hadn't been able to give it to him.

That wasn't Nate's fault. That was a flaw within herself, a deep, horrible disfigurement far worse than any of Nate's scars. Nate's scars had healed and continued to fade. Marty's, no matter how much she thought she'd healed, were still open and raw.

It had been so easy for Josie to convince her of Nate's awful plans, because Marty wanted to believe it. It was so much easier to believe that Nate would use her and to hurt, rather than to give herself up to love and trust. She was a scared, pathetic woman.

She sniffed. "No. I do want to be here," Marty said firmly, as much for herself as for Diana. She had to want to be here—she didn't have anyplace else to go. This was her life. She'd chosen as soon as she got in her car and drove away, the Welcome to Millbrook, Maine, sign in her rearview mirror.

"Okay," Diana said, although she didn't look like she believed her any more than Marty believed herself. Her agent glanced at her thin, diamond-studded Rolex. "All right, I need to go, it's already a little before five now. You need to be at the Plaza by six at the latest. The show starts at eight."

Marty nodded. "I'll be there."

Diana stared at her for a moment, then strode over to the bed to get her coat. "I'll arrange for a car to be waiting for you at a quarter before six. Take a hot shower. That will make you feel better."

"I will," Marty said, but she knew the only thing that could possibly make her feel better was being back in Nate's arms. But she couldn't go back. He wouldn't forgive her for believing Josie, for running.

Chapter 28

Nate walked into the hotel lobby, a swanky place with glossy hardwood floors, thick oriental carpets and glittering chandeliers. Hotel patrons dressed in fancy clothes and suits milled around the lobby. This was definitely a long way from a rundown cabin on a lake. He looked down at his own worn jeans and thick tan barn coat. Maybe Marty had left because she wanted this lifestyle back.

He debated just simply turning around and heading back out the revolving door. No. He wasn't going to leave here without letting Marty know exactly how he felt about her.

He walked up to the check-in desk and long wooden counter with several clerks working behind it at computers. He waited as one of the clerks finished with a lady in a large hat with feathers sticking out of it.

Finally, he stepped up to the clerk, offering her a wide smile. Her eyes roamed over his outfit, but when she looked back at his face, he didn't see the disdain he expected. Instead, the woman smiled almost coyly. "Can I help you?"

Good, he thought. Maybe if she liked him, for whatever reason, she'd be more willing to help. He had a feeling that it wasn't general practice to give strange men off the street the room numbers of famous models.

"Yes," he smiled wider. "I do need some help. I'm here to see one of your guests, Marty Stepp. But I can't remember her hotel number."

But before the woman could answer him, a female voice behind him said, "So you are the real reason Marty is moping around and generally looking like she lost her best friend."

Nate spun around to see a woman with glossy, dark hair cut into a sleek bob, sharp, angular features, and shrewd blue eyes.

Her eyes widened slightly. "Or maybe her best lover." Her eyes roamed over him.

Nate frowned. He was starting to feel like maybe he was a novelty to the women of Manhattan. But he didn't care what he was, as long as he got to Marty. He offered the woman his hand. "Hi. I'm Nate Peck. Do you know Marty Stepp?"

She accepted his hand, shaking it with a very firm grip of her own. This woman was all business.

"I'm Diana Henley. Marty's agent."

Great. What a stroke of luck. "Are you on your way up to see her?"

"Just leaving, actually, She's getting ready for a big fashion show tonight." She checked her watch. "Which we are all going to be late for at this rate." She stepped up to the woman at the counter and requested that a limo be waiting for Marty at a quarter to six. Diana finished up with the clerk and started toward the exit at a brisk pace.

Nate watched her. Well, he might not get Diana's

help, but at least he had learned that Marty would be down to the lobby before six. He'd just sit and wait.

"Nate!"

He turned to see Diana at the doors. She waved for him impatiently. "Are you coming?" She checked her watch again.

He paused for a split second, then he strode after her. Diana was definitely no-nonsense. As he followed her through the revolving doors, he had the weirdest sensation he was following the white rabbit down the rabbit hole.

We're late. We're late. For a very important date.

Rabbit holes and abrupt, harried agents were the very least he'd face to see Marty.

Marty sat in the stylist's chair while Luis, the renowned stylist, put the finishing touches on her make-up.

"There," he said, flipping back his own long, black locks. "You look lovely. A waif with big sad eyes and those pouty kissable lips."

Marty snorted at that. "I'm not sure that description is lovely. But I know you did the best you could with what you had to work with."

"Oh please." Luis rolled his eyes dramatically. "You are wonderful to work with. A true beauty. Every man in the place will be torn between wanting to protect you and wanting to take you home and make love to you all night."

Marty started to deny his compliments again when a male voice cut her off. "Well, almost every man. But I always was a fool."

Marty looked past Luis to see Arturo reflected in the mirror.

He smiled warmly, his pale blue eyes standing out against his dark hair and olive skin. He was already made up and in his first outfit of the evening, a tailored suit with a thin purple tie. He looked great.

She smiled slightly. "Not a fool. Just not the man for me."

"But maybe the man for me?" Luis pointed out, openly admiring Arturo.

Arturo smiled politely but didn't flirt back. Luis was too flamboyant for Arturo. Arturo preferred muscular, masculine boys. Just like Marty did. Funny, she could almost find their similar taste in men humorous now.

"You're done, love," Luis told her again, and dashed off to handle a mascara emergency with one of the other models.

Marty stood up from the chair and turned to look at Arturo. "You do look great."

Arturo smiled, tilting his head in a way that made him look very boyish. "You look sad."

She started to say she was fine, but then, as if her mouth was working independent of her brain, she said, "I am sad."

He moved closer to her. "What is it?"

"I just screwed up the best thing in my whole life."

"Please, tell me you aren't referring to Rod Mitchell," Arturo said, not hiding his dislike.

If she'd gotten that reaction from one ex-boyfriend about another, she would have thought it was jealousy. In this case, it was just genuine dislike.

"No." She smiled slightly. "Not Rod."

"Good. So who is this guy?"

"A man from my hometown in Maine. The chief of police."

Arturo looked impressed. "I love a man in uniform."

Marty smiled. Once that would have upset her, but now, it actually seemed surreal that she'd ever dated Arturo.

"So what happened?"

"I didn't trust him and I ran. I'm such a fool."

Arturo gave her a scolding look. "We are all fools when it comes to love. But you've realized that you made a mistake. So go back to him and apologize."

"I can't."

"Sure you can. You're just scared. Marty, I am the king of scared. Why do you think I spent so much time hiding behind you? I was terrified for people to find out I was gay. But eventually I realized that I was miserable—and that really isn't an insult to you, because if I could have fallen romantically in love with any woman, it would have been you."

"Thank you," Marty said sincerely.

"You're welcome. But I was miserable pretending I wasn't gay. So I finally decided I might as well stop hiding. Being honest and admitting the truth couldn't be any worse than denying who I was. And now I'm happier than I've ever been in my life."

She digested that for a moment. "But my problem isn't like yours. I already blew this relationship."

He shook his head. "No. You said you ran. You don't know if you've blown it or not. You're just scared to expose yourself, just in case he won't forgive you. Or if he does forgive, that he'll hurt you later on down the road. It *is* the same thing. You are already miserable without him—why not risk it all and go see if you can make it work? The worst thing that can happen is that he won't forgive you, and you're no worse off than you are now."

She stared at him for a moment, then smiled. "When did you get so wise?"

"Well, I do play a doctor on television."

Marty stepped forward and looped her arms around his neck. "Thanks."

He squeezed her tight. "Go for it, girl."

She nodded against his shoulder, then let him go.

"You better go get your first outfit on. This party is about to get started."

She agreed and headed in the direction of her clothing rack, where all her outfit changes for the night waited along with one of Vera Wang's assistants, who would help Marty change in rapid succession in and out of the clothes.

As the woman helped her dress, Marty thought about what Arturo said. She was miserable. She should just risk it and go back and apologize. Grovel if she had to. Nothing could be worse than not seeing him, not telling him that she'd made a big mistake. And she could trust him. She could heal.

She glanced over at Arturo talking with one of the other male models. No, not just talking, definitely flirting.

She smiled fondly as she watched him. Who knew, maybe her wounds were already healing.

She sighed and smoothed her hands over the modish dress of black and pink. The assistant, Elsa, held out a pair of white go-go boots. Even Vera Wang was falling into the retro craze.

She reached down and tugged the tops of the boots up over her calves, then straightened just as the deafeningly loud music announced the show's commencement.

Nancy Sinatra's voice announced with attitude that these boots were made for walking.

Very appropriate, Marty thought as she was positioned in the line of models for her turn to head down the catwalk. She was going to walk too. But instead of walking away, she was walking straight back to Nate and telling him she was madly in love with him.

Nate sat in a seat at the front of the stage, completely amazed. Music blared and wave after wave of models strutted down the stage in outfits that were truly amazing. It was a bit like watching a carnival. A carnival during the sixties.

He glanced around him. The audience also looked like they were part of the carnival. The fashions he'd seen briefly in the hotel were just a warm-up for what he was seeing here. Many people were dressed elegantly—then there were the others with feathers and huge glittering jewels and bows. Big bows.

He glanced down at his own suit, a tuxedo, which the very efficient Diana had materialized for him. He supposed he couldn't really comment about the bows, as he was wearing one. He pretended to scratch his neck and then tried to loosen the collar subtly, so Diana—who sat beside him—wouldn't notice.

He looked back up at the stage, and there was Marty, strolling directly toward him. Her short hair was parted on the side and slicked down, pin curls glued to her cheeks.

She looked fantastic in the pink and black dress she wore. Marty looked every bit the mod girl. If she had been around in the sixties, poor old Twiggy would have been looking for a new job.

He couldn't tear his eyes from her as she reached the end of the catwalk. Turned. Posed with her hand on her hip, her lovely shoulder jutting out sexily. Then turned again and headed back down the runway.

He actually rose up in his seat a bit, trying to see her as long as he could until she disappeared backstage.

Diana touched his leg. "Don't worry. She'll be back."

He settled back into his chair, even though he really just wanted to climb up the stairs at the front of the stage and follow her into the back.

But he didn't. He waited patiently for her every return. She was so captivating up there. So . . . stunning, with poise and grace and confidence. Even though he was dying to talk to her, he quickly got lost in the show. In the appeal of the woman Marty was onstage.

"This is the final walk," Diana told him as women and men came out as couples dressed in wedding clothes, still in very retro styles. The Turtles' "Happy Together" reverberated around them.

This time the models came to the end of the runway, then parted into lines of women and men like an actual wedding party.

Finally, Marty appeared, and Nate's breathing stopped. She was dressed in a wedding dress. The white material was sheer, nearly see through, with simple, form-fitting lines that showed all her lovely, long curves. She looked absolutely breathtaking.

She met a man in the middle of the stage, and they walked down together.

Nate frowned with jealousy as he noticed that Marty kept smiling at the man beside her. And the man smiled too. They looked fond of each other in a way that didn't seem like part of the show.

They reached the end of the runway and stopped. The designer, a woman Nate didn't know, joined Marty and the smiling guy. The designer looked very pleased with both of her headlining models.

People in the audience began to stand and applaud wildly.

The designer moved from between Marty and the smiley male model to speak with each of the other models. As soon as she did, smiley guy had his arms linked back with Marty's, and they were grinning at each other again.

Then the lights came up, and the models, now able to see the audience, began to wave.

Nate stood too.

He had just risen to his full height when Marty, who had also been waving at the audience, stopped absolutely still.

Nate's eyes locked with hers. And they stared at each other.

Then her companion leaned his head near hers, obviously concerned about her.

She glanced at him, but then turned her gaze directly back to Nate. She said something that Nate couldn't make out.

Then to Nate's complete shock, the man at her side tugged her arm and led her down the stage steps. They weaved their way through the audience, heading directly toward him.

Nate started out of his row too, squeezing past people to get to the aisle. To get to Marty.

Just as he wedged past the last person, a large woman in lots of pink marabou, Marty appeared right in front of him.

"Hi," he said like a complete idiot.

"Hi," she said, not seeming to notice he was a complete idiot.

She looked so wonderful, for a moment, he couldn't do anything but look at her. God, he'd missed her. God, he wanted to touch her.

"Nate—" she started.

But he raised a hand to stop her. "Before you say anything, please just hear me out."

She nodded slightly, but he couldn't read her expression.

"I know you have a hard time with trust," he told her. "And I know that when you get hurt, your first instinct is to run. But I also realized something else."

"What?" she asked, worry now clear in her eyes.

"No one has ever followed you when you did run. But I'm going to follow, and I'm going to keep following until you realize that you can trust me. I'm not going to let you run away from something that could be so great. That is so great. Marty, I love you."

Marty stared at him until her dark eyes began to glitter and tears rolled down her cheeks.

He stepped forward and caught her hands. "Darling, don't cry. Please."

She released a sound that was halfway between a laugh and a sob. "I was going to come back."

"You were?" He ran his hand up her arms, unable to stop touching her.

She nodded. "I realized that I ran because I was scared you would hurt me one day. But by running, I was hurting anyway. So I had nothing to lose by going back and begging you to forgive me."

"You wouldn't have had to beg. I love you. I want us to spend our lives together."

Marty flung herself against him, clinging to him as

if she thought he might suddenly disappear. "Oh, Nate, I love you so much."

His heart thundered in his chest, and he kissed her hair, her neck, until he found her lips. He had no idea how long they stood, locked together. But eventually someone tapped Nate's shoulder.

He tore his lips from Marty's to see the male model who had brought Marty to him.

"I just wanted to point out that I'm the one who actually brought her to her senses," he said.

Marty shook her head, giving the guy an indulgent smile. "Yes, he did. Nate, this is Arturo."

Nate smiled; suddenly all competition he'd felt with the other man evaporated. He held out his hand. "Well, then, I owe you a lot of thanks."

"Just be the guy for her that I couldn't be," he said sincerely.

Nate nodded. That was not going to be a problem.

After giving Marty a tight hug, Arturo left to offer them privacy. As much privacy as they could have in a room full of people.

"You were amazing up there," Nate murmured into her ear as he held her tight again.

"Thank you. But you know what I'm really amazing at?" she said.

He grinned against her neck. "Why, yes, I do."

She tweaked a lock of his hair.

"What are you amazing at?" he asked contritely.

"I'm an amazing camp counselor."

"So I guess that means this is your last show," Diana said from behind them. They parted to look at her.

Marty nodded. "I'm sorry, Diana."

Diana shrugged. "As soon as I heard him ask for you at the hotel, I knew he was the reason you wanted to stay in Maine." She eyed him. "And who could blame you."

Nate smiled at the compliment, then said to Marty, "Diana got me here. Got me the tux."

Marty's gaze roamed over him. "You look good in a tux."

"You look good in a wedding dress."

"Okay, if you two are talking weddings, I know you are a lost cause. I'll call you in a few days." Diana waved and headed off to find some of the other models she represented.

"Thanks, Diana!" Marty called after her.

Diana waggled her fingers without looking back at them.

"So I guess I'm unemployed," Marty said to Nate.

"No, I have a position for you," he assured her. "In fact, I have several positions for you."

"Letch."

"That's not what I meant," he scolded. "I was talking business partner, best friend, lover, hopefully wife."

"Oh," she said, then kissed him.

"So who's the letch now?" he asked against her lips.

"Me," Marty agreed readily.

Nate laughed, his whole body humming with happiness and love. "Did I mention that I love you?"

"I love you too." And Marty kissed him soundly.

Epilogue

"Hey, guys," Marty shouted over the hammering as she squinted up at the roof of the huge log cabin.

The pounding stopped immediately and three heads popped up over the peak, looking down at her.

"Please tell me it's time for dinner," Chase called down. "I'm starving."

"Me too," Mason agreed.

Marty nodded. "Ellie just finished grilling the chicken. So get down here."

"All right," Mason said happily and started down the ladder at the side of the building.

Marty laughed at Mason's eagerness. With Ellie as a wife, and all her fantastic cooking, it was amazing Mason wasn't huge.

But as he jumped off the third rung from the bottom and all his hard muscles rippled, Marty decided he wasn't in danger of getting chubby any time soon.

Chase followed, all his muscles flexing as he climbed down.

Marty shook her head. Hanging out around the work site was never too hard on the eyes.

"Nate is just tacking down the last couple of shingles," Chase said as he and Mason approached her.

As if on cue, the hammering started again.

"That's it? Just a few more?"

Chase nodded, turning to admire the large structure. "Yep, the dining cabin is done."

Marty grinned. "Wow, that is great."

"Are you coming?" Mason asked as the two men started down the pine needle–covered path to the lake.

She shook her head. "Nah, I'm going to wait for Nate."

They nodded and headed down to their wives and children and the lure of food.

Marty gazed back at the log structure. It was beautiful. The three men had done an amazing job. They had all done an amazing job. Marty had spent her fair share of the summer swinging a hammer too.

She climbed the long, wide steps that led up onto the porch. Then she wandered inside into a large, open room, her footsteps echoing off the high-beamed ceilings.

Huge arched windows that practically made up the whole wall at either end of the room added lots of light to the warm, white pine interior, and a massive stone fireplace took up almost another entire wall.

Eventually the empty room would be filled with long, rectangular tables and bench seats. The dining room was big enough to seat 150 people easily. That would include a hundred children, twenty counselors, four healthcare staff, six kitchen staff, ten program directors, and Nate and herself. Not quite 150, but close—and they had room to keep growing.

It would probably take one more summer to get the camp fully ready to open. But they were actually ahead of schedule. This summer they'd finished all the sleeping cabins, the rec hall, and now the dining cabin.

She spun around in the center of the room, amazed at all they had achieved. Not only with the summer camp, but in their personal lives, too.

Abby and Chase had a little boy, Christopher, only four months old. And they would be going to Prague in November so Abby could give a lecture at a scientific conference on her research.

Emily turned two in July, and Ellie was expecting again in February. Ellie was busy creating a literacy program for the schools in the area, and Mason had raised enough money to add more improvements to the waterfront and now Main Street.

And Marty and Nate were getting married in a week.

Marty's heart fluttered, and she spun a little faster, feeling light and giddy.

"It looks great, doesn't it?" Nate's voice caused her to stumble to a dizzy stop.

She spotted him leaning against the wall near the door. He looked absolutely gorgeous, with a thin sheen of sweat on his bare chest and shoulders and his jeans slung low on his hips.

"It looks fantastic." She beamed proudly at him.

He pushed away from the wall and joined her in the center of the room.

"I talked to Derek earlier today," he told her. "He wants to come help after he gets out of Bangor Correctional."

Marty nodded. "I think that's a good idea. He really wants to make things up to you."

"He did as soon as he told me about what Josie and Jared did to make you leave."

She shook her head. "No, he did when he told you it was Jared that attacked you."

Nate shrugged. "Well, Jared is paying now."

Marty nodded, although she didn't think fifteen years was nearly enough. But Nate was satisfied.

Nate turned to admire the room, obviously not interested in talking about Jared Nye any longer. Nor was she.

"So, are you glad you decided to do this?" he asked, as he pulled her against his damp chest.

She kissed him, tasting salt and hard work on his skin. "I can't imagine ever doing anything else."

"Or being with anyone else?"

"No one else," she agreed. But then she frowned. "Although I do think we should put off our wedding."

Nate stared into her eyes, worry darkening them. "Why?"

"Because I'm going to get calamine lotion all over my wedding dress," she said, scratching a patch of poison ivy on her shoulder.

"I'm not letting you back out over a small case of poison ivy," he informed her.

"Small case! I'm covered from head to toe! That's the last time I help clear brush."

He grinned. "I warned you way back last winter of the risks of running a summer camp."

"So you did." She kissed him again, their lips lingering, caressing. "But I even have it on my face," she said, pointing to a spot on her forehead. "I look like a leper."

He stepped back from her and studied the pink-covered patches on her legs and arms, then finally the spot on her forehead. He tugged her against him again. "I think you look great."

He pressed another kiss to her mouth, then lifted his head to gaze in her eyes. "So beautiful."

Marty smiled as a warm, wonderful feeling tingled through her body. Finally she truly believed that someone saw the real Marty Stepp. And she finally knew who the real Marty Stepp was too. She was a summer-camp owner, a retired model, an unusually tall woman, and the member of a happy, growing family. And she was madly in love with the most extraordinary man in the world.

She was also hungry.

"Let's go eat," she said, linking her fingers with his. "Don't worry; I think there is a tofu pup or two down there for the crazy vegetarian."

Nate chuckled, and they headed down to the beach to eat dinner with their family.

Don't miss this excerpt from Kathy Love's
FANGS FOR THE MEMORIES,
coming in September 2005 from Brava.

"So are you saying that you don't really want me?"

She didn't speak for a moment, keeping her attention focused on her feet. "I do want you."

Rhys caught her wrist to pull her to a halt. He turned her to face him. "Why do you say it as though you think you should be ashamed?"

Her wide eyes met his, and he did see shame there. "Rhys, how you feel right now, it's not real. It's—it's like we are both living in a fantasy world, and eventually reality is going to return. And I'm afraid of how you will feel when that happens."

He frowned, confused and also a little upset. How could she think this was fantasy?

"No," he said, shaking his head, "this is real. Now is real, and all the things I feel for you are very real."

She looked down at the cup of tea that she'd barely drunk since they left the coffee shop. She fiddled with the edge of the plastic lid.

"You don't know me," she said slowly. "Not really. And maybe—maybe once you do you won't want . . . you might decide I'm not what you want."

"You've said that to me before, after we made love. That I don't know you. And I suppose that is true—that we haven't had long together, to get to know everything about each other—but what I do know, I want."

Her eyes stared into his, almost pleading. "But you may not later, and I don't know if I can risk that."

"It isn't possible for me to stop wanting you. I've waited a long time to feel this way. It will never leave my system. You will never leave it."

She continued to stare up at him, the shame had disappeared but now it was exchanged with longing. She still didn't believe him, but she wanted to.

And she would.

He pulled her against him, his mouth finding hers. He intended for the kiss to be persuasive, a sweet lulling caress that would calm her doubts.

But as soon as he tasted the velvety texture of her lips, clinging hungrily to his, all thoughts of coaxing were gone.

He wanted her.

Need tore through his veins, urging him to deepen the kiss. She responded, opening to him, giving him access to the sweet moisture of her mouth.

Sweet moisture.

He groaned as her tongue touched his, a fleeting brush. A tiny taste.

Just a tiny taste.

He nipped at her bottom lip, the flesh fragile and sensitive. His teeth sank just a little harder into the pillowy softness. Pink and warm and so, so sweet.

Jane gasped, and Rhys immediately released her.

He stared down at her, his chest heaving, as he realized that his hunger for her had so easily spun out of control. By a mere kiss.

"I'm sorry," he breathed.

She shook her head, looking as dazed as he felt. "No, it was . . ." The tip of her tongue touched her lower lip, making it glisten in the lamplight. Red and shiny.

His stare locked there for several seconds before his

stunned mind registerd what he was looking at: she was bleeding.

"Jane," he said, alarm chilling the desire in his limbs. "Shit." He reached for her, his fingers nudging her chin up to get a better look at what he'd done.

Jane frowned. "What?"

"Your lip is bleeding. I must have bitten you."

She brought her hand up to touch her mouth. Her fingers looked very pale, small and elegant, brushing over the reddened skin.

She frowned down at her fingertips, then showed them to him with a reassuring smile. "Barely a nick."

He stared at the faint crimson smear on her fore and index fingers. Revulsion filled him. How had he lost control like that? He'd never intended to hurt her. Never.

"I'm fine," she told him. "Please stop looking at me like you've mortally injured me. I didn't even notice until you pointed it out."

"But you gasped."

She smiled again, this time sheepishly. Her cheeks reddened to nearly the same color as her lips. "Only because—because I was feeling . . . overcome."

He peered into her green eyes, the darkness of the night and the shadows of the trees surrounding them couldn't dull the vividness of their color.

But even though she gave him another encouraging smile, he couldn't let go the irritation he felt with himself.

"Maybe we should go back."

She hesitated, and for a moment he thought that she was going to say something, but then she simply nodded, falling into step beside him.

***

On their quiet walk back to the club, Jane's mind raced. She felt confused, scared, and exhilarated all at once. But Rhys had that effect on her, a way of making her feel more than she ever knew she could. He made her feel more alive. More aroused. More beautiful.

And that kiss. She released a shaky breath. That kiss had been like being tossed, head first, into a sea of unadulterated passion.

When he had tasted her, nipped her . . . She'd felt his desire throughout her entire body. She had felt him inside her as surely as she had when they had made love.

How could she feel all of that from just a kiss?

Granted, Rhys really knew how to kiss. Even now, her toes curled in her scuffed oxfords.

But her rational mind reminded her that she needed to try and remain distanced from him. She needed to remember that they didn't really know each other. That she needed to wait.

But her heart told her that, between his wonderful smile and his gorgeous eyes, she was already lost. She was already crazy about him and no amount of repeated warnings and logical reminders could keep her from this man.

The boom of bass brought her out of her reverie. She was surprised to see that they were back at the club.

Now a long line of eccentric looking patrons waited to get inside. Rhys didn't even look at them. He, too, seemed lost in his own thoughts, and from the serious look on his face, they didn't seem to be particularly nice ones.

They headed down the alley and he knocked hard on the steel door. After a few moments she heard the series of locks click, and Mick opened the door. He stood back to let them enter. The fluorescent light reflecting off his bald head was the only hint of animation on the huge man's features.

Rhys nodded his thanks at the man, but didn't speak either. He led her to the elevator.

As before, he held the gate and waited for her to enter. She did and stood in the center of the elevator.

He dropped the grate and pushed the button marked with a *4.*

Jane turned slightly, so she could look at him—his lean, muscled body and his beautiful face.

She remembered what she'd thought about him when she'd first seen him, sitting on that bar stool next to her. He was a heartbreaker.

He still could be, her head warned her. *And it could be your heart that he breaks.*

He suddenly turned his head. His eyes were like pools of molten amber; they locked with hers, pulling her into their heat.

It's too late, her heart told her. *You are already in too deep.*

"I want to sleep with you tonight," she said, and her heart gave a triumphant punch in the air.

By Best-selling Author
Fern Michaels

Weekend Warriors	0-8217-7589-8	$6.99US/$9.99CAN
Listen to Your Heart	0-8217-7463-8	$6.99US/$9.99CAN
The Future Scrolls	0-8217-7586-3	$6.99US/$9.99CAN
About Face	0-8217-7020-9	$7.99US/$10.99CAN
Kentucky Sunrise	0-8217-7462-X	$7.99US/$10.99CAN
Kentucky Rich	0-8217-7234-1	$7.99US/$10.99CAN
Kentucky Heat	0-8217-7368-2	$7.99US/$10.99CAN
Plain Jane	0-8217-6927-8	$7.99US/$10.99CAN
Wish List	0-8217-7363-1	$7.50US/$10.50CAN
Yesterday	0-8217-6785-2	$7.50US/$10.50CAN
The Guest List	0-8217-6657-0	$7.50US/$10.50CAN
Finders Keepers	0-8217-7364-X	$7.50US/$10.50CAN
Annie's Rainbow	0-8217-7366-6	$7.50US/$10.50CAN
Dear Emily	0-8217-7316-X	$7.50US/$10.50CAN
Sara's Song	0-8217-7480-8	$7.50US/$10.50CAN
Celebration	0-8217-7434-4	$7.50US/$10.50CAN
Vegas Heat	0-8217-7207-4	$7.50US/$10.50CAN
Vegas Rich	0-8217-7206-6	$7.50US/$10.50CAN
Vegas Sunrise	0-8217-7208-2	$7.50US/$10.50CAN
What You Wish For	0-8217-6828-X	$7.99US/$10.99CAN
Charming Lily	0-8217-7019-5	$7.99US/$10.99CAN

Available Wherever Books Are Sold!

Put a Little Romance in Your Life With
Melanie George

__**Devil May Care**
0-8217-7008-X $5.99US/$7.99CAN

__**Handsome Devil**
0-8217-7009-8 $5.99US/$7.99CAN

__**Devil's Due**
0-8217-7010-1 $5.99US/$7.99CAN

__**The Mating Game**
0-8217-7120-5 $5.99US/$7.99CAN

Available Wherever Books Are Sold!

Visit our website at **www.kensingtonbooks.com**.